TARNISHED REPUTATION

Raines's furious cry was stifled as his lips crushed hers in a hard kiss. Never had she been kissed this way before and instead of feeling repulsed, she found her nerves tingling with a sensation quite new to her. He abruptly broke away and held her from him, studying her expression.

Color rose to her cheeks. She averted her eyes, but not before sensing that he was as shaken by the kiss as she.

"Well Miss Scott," he said with a mocking smile. "Was I a satisfactory substitute for James?"

Raines moved skillfully from within his grasp, her face burning with shame. "Lord Kemp, I'm afraid I must resign!"

"Resign? Was my kiss so terrible?" he teased. "Perhaps I should try again."

He chuckled as she backed hastily away from him.

"I may be in your employ, but I have no intention of selling my virtue as well," she said with as much dignity as she could muster.

He stared at her in wonder. "Good lord, I believe you are serious about leaving."

"I cannot continue working for an employer who — who is bent on seducing me!"

Kemp seemed struck by her words.

"Well, we certainly can't have that," he said gravely. "There is nothing for it but that I shall have to marry you."

THE BEST OF REGENCY ROMANCES

AN IMPROPER COMPANION   (2691, $3.95)
by Karla Hocker
At the closing of Miss Venable's Seminary for Young
Ladies school, mistress Kate Elliott welcomed the invitation to be Liza Ashcroft's chaperone for the Season at
Bath. Little did she know that Miss Ashcroft's father, the
handsome widower Damien Ashcroft would also enter her
life. And not as a passive bystander or dutiful dad.

WAGER ON LOVE   (2693, $2.95)
by Prudence Martin
Only a rogue like Nicholas Ruxart would choose a bride on
the basis of a careless wager. And only a rakehell like Nicholas would then fall in love with his betrothed's grey-eyed
sister! The cynical viscount had always thought one blushing miss would suit as well as another, but the unattainable
Jane Sommers soon proved him wrong.

LOVE AND FOLLY   (2715, $3.95)
by Sheila Simonson
To the dismay of her more sensible twin Margaret, Lady
Jean proceeded to fall hopelessly in love with the silver-
tongued, seditious poet, Owen Davies—and catapult her
entire family into social ruin . . . Margaret was used to
gentlemen falling in love with vivacious Jean rather than
with her—even the handsome Johnny Dyott whom she secretly adored. And when Jean's foolishness led her into the
arms of the notorious Owen Davies, Margaret knew she
could count on Dyott to avert scandal. What she didn't
know, however was that her sweet sensibility was exerting a
charm all its own.

Touch of Venus

BY PATRICIA LAYE

ZEBRA BOOKS
KENSINGTON PUBLISHING CORP.

ZEBRA BOOKS

are published by

Kensington Publishing Corp.
475 Park Avenue South
New York, NY 10016

Second printing: October, 1990

Printed in the United States of America

For my parents who always knew I had a dream. For my father who didn't live to see me make it and for my mother who did.

Chapter 1

The bright sun touched the English countryside in a playful manner, darting back and forth behind wisps of clouds, then reappearing to kiss the lambs with its warm fall rays. The beauty of the morning was lost on Raines Scott as she walked across the moor toward her Uncle Percival's manor, head bent, deep in thought. She had left the castle early because she knew the topic of discussion taking place inside concerned her future. Her uncle, who was a dear man when you did not cross him, was trying to decide what to do with this troublesome, strongwilled niece who had recently been dropped on his doorstep by the untimely death of her father.

Raines knew that according to the custom of 1816 she was faced with only two choices: marry an older, perhaps widowed man, who was willing to agree to a union with a penniless young lady of good family; or, accept a position considered respectable by the standards of her time, then face a life of service and spinsterhood. As the girl thought of her two choices a frown crossed her pretty brow and she carelessly swept a blond curl away from her pink cheek. Suddenly she stopped in midstride, the distant glaze left her periwinkle eyes and a soft, throaty laugh escaped her. She had reached a decision on her future. Gathering her blue skirt up so she would not trip on it, she ran back toward the manor. She would tell her aunt and uncle that she had decided her own future and would not settle for anything else.

Running like a boy, her slender limbs propelled her forward until, out of breath, she reached the castle. Putting her hand to her chest, she gasped for breath as she paused before mounting the steps slowly.

"Lor, Miss Raines! Your uncle is put out with you for being on the moor so long and unescorted in the bargain," scolded Nettie, the middle-aged servant, who greeted her at the door, holding it open for her to enter. "And running like a common village chit!"

Ignoring the reprimand, Raines asked, "Where is Uncle Percival now?" She stopped to catch her breath and straighten her gown, handing her pelisse to the maid, who still frowned disapprovingly. Raines did not want to delay the conversation with her guardian, because she knew there was a good possibility she might lose her nerve.

"He's in the drawing room with your Aunt Thea." Nettie leaned closer and whispered in a conspiratorial tone, "They's been having a regular row betwixt themselves this fine morning. The master's a kind hearted man, but the mistress can be a bit cold at times. If you'll forgive me for saying such."

"Nettie, we must not judge poor Aunt Thea too harshly. She is overwrought at having an unwanted, and very poor relation dumped on her threshold at

8

this most inopportune time. She has married off her own three daughters, although Papa always said he bet it cost Uncle Percival a pretty shilling to accomplish that feat, and now she finds herself saddled with me. 'Tis enough to upset the good woman."

"Humph! If you ask me, she's a mite closefisted to boot. I ain't an educated woman, but seems to me that your papa is described as more reckless with money than I ever witnessed him to be." The servant shook her head as she surveyed their surroundings. "How come your uncle inherits the manor and all the farm land, while your poor sweet father, God rest his soul, got naught?"

The young girl sighed deeply, before she answered, "I don't understand all about wills and estates. But Papa always said it had something to do with Uncle Percival being the eldest and everything falling to the first born, or something like that." Raines touched the woman's arm affectionately. "Truly, Nettie, we must be appreciative to Uncle Percival for taking us in. He did make all the funeral arrangements and close the flat for us, and pay all those horrible collectors who began pounding on our door the moment poor Papa took ill. Now we simply must be grateful for all my aunt and uncle have done for us."

"What's to become of us now? I can't stay on in this household where it's been made clear my services aren't wanted, yet I can't leave you alone. Lor, 'tis too much for an old woman to have . . ."

Raines interrupted. "Enough of this nonsense! Nettie, I have made up my mind what I plan to do and 'tis settled." She stood and marched to the door. "I am going in and tell Uncle Percival what my

9

plans are."

She heard Nettie gasp, but she did not pause to give the servant time to talk her out of the plan. Her small kidskin shoes skimmed daintily over the cobblestone floor as she hurried toward the drawing room. Tapping lightly on the strong oak door, she waited until her uncle's booming voice ordered her to enter.

Drawing herself up to her full height of five feet five, she held her head erect and walked into the room. A fire glowed in the hearth, cutting the chill only slightly. There were few pieces of furniture in this huge library with its dark paneling and draped windows. Again, as she had so often before, she thought of how differently she would have decorated the room, had it been her home. It was so cold and austere, almost like the man and woman she now faced.

Upon seeing who their visitor was, her aunt scolded, "You have been out on the moor, young lady. Don't you realize the dew will ruin your new shoes?"

"I have a lot on my mind this morning, Aunt Thea, and I simply had to go out and walk to think and clear my head."

"And did you succeed in clearing it?" the woman asked, in a voice tinged with sarcasm. It was evident that she wasn't fond of this willful niece.

"Thea, don't be too harsh with the child. I can understand her worry. She still misses her father very much and we must be patient with her," spoke the man, in a deep voice. He smiled at Raines adding, "Come close to the fire, my dear. Your aunt and I have just been discussing your future this morning. 'Tis good that you decided to pay us the honor of your presence. I . . . I have been meaning to discuss with

10

you a proposition which has been put before me by a certain Mr. Winston Rockhill."

Raines accepted the chair which her aunt motioned for her to be seated in, because her knees trembled uncontrollably. She was more frightened than the day her father had first taken ill, and she had learned that he would not recover. "Do . . . do you mean the widower who has been to visit you? Whatever interest could I have in his affairs?" she asked, trying to keep the tremor out of her voice, because she had a strong idea where this conversation was leading.

"You know the poor man has been left with five young children to raise, since his beloved wife of fifteen years died from childbirth fever after the last little tyke was born. He has been without a wife these long years since." He turned to his wife and asked, "How long has it been, dear?"

"Three years, love. And a finer gentleman doesn't exist than Mr. Rockhill. He has borne this burden like a true gentleman. Why, many men would have gone instantly to the tarts at the Golden Quail . . ."

"Hush, my dear, such talk isn't for the delicate ears of young Raines."

"I'm sorry, Percival! I was only trying to make a point as to Mr. Rockhill's sterling character," replied his wife, in a bit of a miff. She did not enjoy being criticized in front of this arrogant niece.

"St . . . still I do not see how this concerns me," Raines stammered, growing more sure each moment what would be next.

Her uncle looked nervous, and even a bit embarrassed as he cleared his throat and looked to his wife for support. However, Thea, still pouting for being

11

corrected, sat mute. At last, seeing that he would get no help from her, Percival said, "The good man has inquired as to offering you a proposal of marriage."

"Never!" cried Raines, forgetting her manners. "I will never wed a man I don't love!" Jumping to her feet, she strode to the fire, and nervously warmed her hands in an effort to wipe away the chill which filled her. She felt trapped and more alarmed than she had ever been in her life. If only Papa . . . No, she had to stop thinking about him, since he could not help her. Now she must learn to fend for herself and fend she would! Raines faced them with clenched fists. "I will not marry him!"

"Nonsense, girl," scolded her aunt. "That is silly headed talk about love. You can learn to love a man who can support you, and who, I'm sure, will be kind to you." When she saw this was not swaying the young girl, Thea said in a somber tone, "After all, dear, you are a young lady without funds to be independent . . ."

"Now, Raines, we would never turn brother Roger's child out in the cold. Pray don't misunderstand us."

That is exactly the way I understand it, thought Raines forlornly. She knew that she had to get out of this house and quickly, if she was to live any type of life, other than being a drudge to an odious man with five children.

"I have a plan," said Raines, relieved at last to be able to say aloud that which she had been forming in her mind since her stroll on the moor. Standing straight she announced, "I have thought this matter over clearly and it is my intention to get a position and support myself."

"A position! I can't believe my ears. No Scott woman has ever hired out for wages in the history of the family," cried Thea, who looked horrified at the suggestion. She looked to her husband for support. "Percival, you must put a stop to this abominable talk. Why the child isn't qualified to do any sort of work and to be a mere servant . . ."

"No, I'm not talking about serving as a maid. I . . . I plan to seek a post as . . . as . . ." Raines groped for some type of job, since all morning she had tried to think of something she might be qualified to do, "an . . . an interpreter or a lady's secretary." She brightened as she thought of this. "Yes, I'm certain I can find a position of this sort. You must remember that Papa taught me Greek and French, and I speak fluent German. Uncle Percival, please say that you will at least give me a chance to find such a position, before you close your mind to the idea. I simply can't tolerate the thought of marrying a man who is truly most repulsive to me." Raines shuddered as she thought of the habit Mr. Rockhill had of sniffing his snuff whenever he became nervous.

"Well, I did tell Mr. Rockhill that you were still in mourning, and it would be some time before I approached you with his proposal. I will give you two weeks to find this job you think you are qualified to do. After that, you must agree to marry this kind gentleman who will look after you like one of his own children, and who offers you a comfortable home. Is that a bargain? Two weeks to find an honorable position and if you fail, then you will agree to marry Mr. Rockhill?"

Raines gulped and felt faint. Two weeks was not

13

long, yet it had indeed been easier to gain than she had anticipated. "It is a bargain. Now, Uncle Percival, I must go and tell Nettie to pack our belongings for we must be off to London today, if I am to succeed at my plan."

"I will tell Wescott to bring the carriage around after the noon meal, if you are indeed prepared to go through with this ridiculous notion."

Raines walked briskly over to her uncle and patted him on the arm. "Thank you, Uncle. Don't look so perturbed about this. I will succeed."

"Where will you stay while in London?" asked Thea, speaking for the first time, and letting her disapproval show in her face and voice.

"Nettie and I can take rooms at The Boar's Head. Mrs. Hutchins owns the inn, and Papa and I have stayed there often when he went to London to attend meetings. It is a very respectable place, Aunt Thea, and the lodgings will be reasonable."

"You know, my dear, that we have a full staff here at Rosewood and can't afford to keep Nettie on indefinitely. Of course, I'm sure Mr. Rockhill will consent to you taking your personal maid with you when you take up residence there." Thea picked up her embroidery hoop and began working dainty stitches.

"I have a little money left over from gifts which Papa gave me on special occasions like my birthday and Christmas. I have enough saved to pay my expenses in London and Nettie's wages for a few weeks."

"That won't be necessary, my dear niece," said her uncle. "I plan to meet your expenses as long as you

14

are under my roof. Put away your little nest egg and stop this foolishness about finances." He glared at his wife, who immediately frowned and looked back down at her needle.

"That is most generous of you, Uncle. Now, if you will excuse me, I have a lot to do before one o'clock, and I wish to be in London before night." Raines left the room and rushed to find Nettie. She could not get out of this house and away from cold, inhospitable Aunt Thea fast enough.

Finding Nettie in her room folding linens, Raines said laughingly, "Nettie! Quick! Pack all our belongings! We're off to London after luncheon!"

"Whatever has come over you, Miss Raines? London? What kind of talk is that?" The woman continued folding the quilt, while she stared at the young girl as though she were mad.

"I haven't time to explain everything right now. Just do as I say! We're off to London and I can't get out of this despicable place fast enough. It has got to be better in the city. I just know everything will work out. Now hurry, woman! Get our belongings in the valise, or I'll leave you behind with the curmudgeon and his skinflint of a wife. When the carriage pulls up out front I'll be gone, so if you plan to ride along, please begin packing." Raines giggled excitedly and danced around the room.

The elderly woman looked at her ward, shaking her head. "Lor, but I do believe you've been in the madeira and 'tis but early morn yet."

But when the coach pulled away from the manor

15

both women were in it, and both gave a sigh of relief to be away, even though they had no idea what lay ahead for them in London.

"I'll never go back, Nettie! You can't make me, and neither can Uncle Percival. I hate that place with its cold people and my silly, simpering aunt who looks down her nose at me because my papa was warm and kindhearted and didn't manage his money as well as they thought he should. I know what it is like to be the poor relation, and I have no intention of ever being poor again!"

" 'Tis a fine speech for you to make with not a pound to yer name," scolded Nettie, but her voice sounded sad, rather than reprimanding.

Raines patted her hand and smiled. "Don't fret, Nettie. I'm going to London to take control of my life and change it I shall. Just you wait and see. I have two weeks to come up with some strategy and come up with it I shall!"

"Lor have mercy on our souls, Miss Raines! Two weeks!" gasped the older woman.

"Two weeks until a new life," replied Raines, looking out the window to prevent Nettie seeing the worried twitch of her brow.

The sunny weather of the morning had turned into the typical English afternoon in October with its rainy, wind-chilled mist. Yet not even the wind blowing off the crags from the North Sea could dampen Raines's spirits. The farther they traveled from Rosewood Manor, the higher her spirits lifted. She had one remarkable quality and it was the ability not to dwell on the past or wallow in self-pity. No matter how low her father's finances dropped at times, and even for a gentleman of good family there had been times the larder stood almost bare, even then, Raines had managed to find something bright and promising about life.

It was this optimistic outlook on life which now gave her the strength to go alone, attractive, twenty years of age, into the perils of London town.

"Nettie, I love London," Raines said, leaning over and looking out the window of the carriage. "We are on the outskirts of town and already I feel bolstered."

"Just ye be careful that you don't fall prey to none of them that's wicked. London town is full of the likes of them that preys on pretty young ladies."

"Hush, Nettie! You sound almost like Aunt Thea," scolded the girl, leaning back and smiling a mischievous grin.

"Do you have rooms saved for us at the Boar's Head?" asked Nettie who still was not convinced that this trip was a good idea, although she had no alternate plan for her mistress.

"No, but Mrs. Hutchins will make room for us. She never turned Papa and me away when we came to town, and we came on many a trip."

"Miss Raines, forgive me if I'm speaking out of turn, but what exactly are your plans?"

"Uncle Percival has agreed to give me two weeks in London to secure a position suitable for a lady of my upbringing. I have agreed to bow to his wishes and marry the widower Rockhill if I should fail."

"Humph! I thought that old buck was sniffing around the place too often not to be up to something," retorted Nettie with a frown.

"Mr. Rockhill may be a gentleman of the finest

17

sort, but I have no intention of marrying a man I do not love. Now, Nettie, let's not dwell on that another minute. When we get to the inn, I'll send out for the *Times* and begin reading the want columns this very night. I feel positive that something will turn up to save me from marriage."

"And what about me? Miss Raines, do you want me to begin inquiring as to a position somewheres? I just don't think I can stand to leave you alone. I probably could find a house where they wouldn't mind you sharing my room."

Raines threw her arms around the older woman. "Bless you, Nettie! That won't be necessary. Trust me. I promise to find a position where an additional servant is needed also. It shouldn't be too difficult to find joint employment." Raines prayed that her voice carried more conviction than she felt at this moment. However, Papa had always told her that she had a level head, and now was the time to use it.

Chapter 2

Raines arrived in London filled with a spirit of confidence, but as the days wore on and the prospects of employment grew slimmer, even she began to have serious doubts.

With only two days left until her uncle was scheduled to send the carriage for her, she scanned the newspaper once again, searching for some redeeming position. Over the past two weeks she had applied for several jobs as governess only to be passed over for an older or less attractive woman. It had not registered on her that her beauty might be a handicap, until the last post had been filled by a drab, nearsighted woman dressed in a dowdy gray outfit. Raines knew she would have made a better tutor than this woman, but the countess, who had interviewed her, had made the remark that she had no intention of hiring another young woman of any appearance, because in the past it had led to burdensome problems.

Scanning the *Times* for the second time, Raines started to hurl the paper to the floor in dejection when an advertisement, which she had barely noticed the

19

first time, caught her eye.

The notice read:

NEEDED: Gentleman schooled in assessing
and cataloguing of coinage. Must be agreeable to
travel and relocate. Salary pending. Contact
Lord Kemp, 19 Malborough Street-Kensington
Court betwixt the hours of 8 a.m. and 11 a.m.
Only qualified persons need apply.

Raines studied the advertisement, a pout crossing
her pursed lips. What could the job entail? Suddenly
she hurled down the newspaper and turned to Nettie,
who had been sitting quietly mending one of her best
gowns which Raines had hooked and torn on a nail in
the Boar's Head.

"Nettie, is there a secondhand clothing store in the
area?"

"Why, yes, ma'am. I believe we passed one on the
other side of Knightsbridge." She looked up from her
stitching. "You ain't thinking of working in one of
them awful places, are ye?"

Raines laughed, rushing to pull her cloak from the
peg behind the door. "No, but I want to go shopping
there. Come on, Nettie, or the store will be closed for
the night. We don't want dark to catch us unescorted
on the streets of London."

The two women marched out into the late afternoon
air which was a sharp contrast to the warmth of the
hearth in the inn. Pulling her cloak tighter, Raines set
the pace down the street, and Nettie scurried along
trying to keep up with her. The maid did not question
the young girl, but she did stare at Raines in an

odd way.

The brisk walk began to revive Raines and as the blood flowed more quickly, her spirits soared once more. She was going to get the position in the morning and of that she was positive. If it took being dowdy to get employed, then she would be just that.

At the clothing store Raines checked the garments in the window before going inside. "Yes, this place should have what I'm looking for," she stated. So raising her chin, she opened the door and marched inside.

The clerk glanced up, unable to suppress his surprise at seeing a lady accompanied by her maid enter his store. He rushed over to be of service. "My lady, what can I do to serve you?"

Faltering for the first time, Raines glanced around her. The place smelled of moth balls, musty garments, and the coal from a poorly banked stove. "I . . . I have need for a dark colored gown of good material but which has seen better times, and a . . . a cloak and hat to match. Have you any such items which might fit a person of my size?"

The man was completely shocked and didn't hide the expression from Raines. "Pray not for you, madam," he began.

" 'Tis of no importance who the items are for," snapped Raines, "just answer if you have anything in my size."

He walked over to a motley looking stack of rags and began thumbing through them. "It so happens that the Duchess of Pentral discarded some items which might be just what you are looking for, if . . . if the lady is near your build," he stammered.

Nervously the clerk pulled a black wool gown with matching cape from the bottom of the pile and held it up for Raines's inspection. The garment was of good cloth, but showed a slight fraying around the wrists. Raines studied the garments carefully, then satisfied that they would serve her purpose, she instructed the man to wrap them for her. Nettie had watched in silence, her disapproval evident in the frown on her face.

The following morning Raines dressed quickly in the black morning dress and stepped back to observe her reflection. The black color was becoming to her fair complexion and the dress, even though out of style and showing wear, still did not make her appear frumpy enough. Quickly Raines swept her hair away from her shoulders and into a chignon in the back. Next she set the small clutch hat with its pathetically molting feathers on her head and studied her reflection once more. Suddenly she laughed at the person she saw in the mirror. Indeed she had succeeded in converting herself into a homely looking spinster of the most oddish taste.

Nettie had watched in silence. Finally, she said, making a clucking sound, "Lor, Miss Raines, you don't look like the lovely young lady you be. Why, I'll bet you don't have a relative that could look this plain, lessen it was one of them Scott cousins."

Throwing back her head and laughing, Raines eyes twinkled with mischief. "Shame on you, Nettie," she scolded, teasingly. Then sobering, she added, " 'Tis my intention to look frail, but of good family, in mourning, yet sadly in need of immediate employment." Stepping away from the mirror, she reached for her purse. "Come along, Nettie, I'm off to be interviewed by Lord Kemp, himself."

The two walked briskly down the street and it amused Raines to see that for the first time gentlemen did not smile or even seem to notice her appearance. She had succeeded in making herself plain. The feat of passing gallants unnoticed was true proof of her achievement.

At 19 Kensington Court she instructed Nettie to wait by the entrance post, while she climbed the steps and struck the brass knocker.

Abruptly the door was opened by a manservant who eyed her suspiciously. Recognizing her for a lady of good birth, if impoverished, he bowed and said, "If you have come concerning the notice in the paper, Lord Kemp is only interviewing gentlemen for the position."

Raines heart lurched and her throat tightened. She knew she had to think fast or her chance would be lost, for the butler was beginning to close the door. "I have come on urgent business and wish to speak with Lord Kemp," she said, stepping into the hall. "Please advise his lordship that Miss Raines Scott is here to speak with him on an important matter."

Surprised at the curtness of her order, yet accustomed to obeying those of higher rank, the butler inquired, "What shall I tell Lord Kemp your business is, Miss?"

Without a bobble, Raines snapped, " 'Tis a matter to be discussed only with his lordship, so please, do as you are told. I haven't all day to stand around and waste time chattering with inept servants."

A slight flush rose in his cheeks as he bowed and

turned to leave. Raines clutched her purse tightly to stop her hands from trembling. What would Lord Kemp say when he learned that she had indeed come for an interview? Being logical, she decided that the worst he could do was throw her out of his establishment, and since she was not likely to ever cross his path again, that could be of little importance to her. But there was no way to get the job if she did not gain an audience with him.

In a moment the servant was back, and she could tell from his expression that his master had been perplexed about whom she might be. "If you will follow me, Lord Kemp has agreed to give you five minutes, although he claims not to be familiar with your name," said the man, with renewed haughtiness.

Without comment she followed him into a large library where a man sat at a desk shuffling papers. His head was bent and he did not look up until the butler announced her presence.

The moment the man raised his head a look of irritation crossed his face. "That will be all, Jason," he said in dismissal.

When he stood, Raines saw how tall he was and how handsome. He towered over her, eyeing her with an annoyed expression. Still not taking his eyes from her face, nor offering her a chair, he glared at her. Finally he spoke. "Miss Scott, I believe? I don't seem able to place our having met before . . ."

"We . . . h . . . haven't," stammered Raines, nervous, but not dropping her gaze.

"Yet you say that you have important business with me. How can this be?" His black eyes bored into her, but Raines did not flinch. She had no intention of being bullied by him, even if it meant being thrown out in the next instant.

"I . . . I suppose I do owe you an apology, Lord Kemp, but I did not lie when I told your butler that I needed to speak with you. I . . . w . . . wish to apply for the position which you mentioned in the *Times* last evening."

"If you were intelligent enough to read the advertisement, then you should have been clever enough to see that it said, "GENTLEMAN", not lady, or do my eyes deceive me? Are you not a lady?" he asked sarcastically.

Raines held herself rigid and her cheeks felt hot from the blood which rushed to them. She said, "I understood the advertisement."

"Yet you persist in interrupting my morning and wasting my time?" he snapped. The words were spoken curtly, but Raines got the distinct feeling that he was enjoying inflicting his sarcasm upon her. There was the slightest glimmer of amusement in his cold dark eyes.

"As I don't see any others waiting to speak with you, and as I don't see why I should not be given the opportunity to explain my qualifications, then I can't see that your time is being wasted."

He stared at her for a few seconds, then threw back his head and gave a deep, hearty laugh. "Well spoken, Miss Scott. If you care to move to the chair nearest the fire, perhaps you can warm a bit and explain your presence."

Thankful to be able to sit, since her knees felt as if they might give way at any moment, Raines walked gracefully to the chair and sank into it. Sitting ramrod straight, as she had always been taught, she clutched her purse in her lap and said, "I feel that I have the qualifications for the position you have spoken of, and I wanted the chance to discuss this with you. Please don't form an opinion until I have finished, if you will be so generous and kind."

"Oh, but you see, Miss Scott, I have already formed an opinion. I do not like females with their hysterics and weak constitutions, and vapors . . ."

"You will find none of those in me, I can assure you," Raines said, irritated at his patronizing manner. "My father had his moments, rest his soul, when he could be quite snappish and ill tempered, but it did not send me into hysterics, as you say, nor did it deter me from my duties."

He watched her closely, still not smiling. "Yes, Miss Scott, you do seem of the temperament to hold your own. I dare say you would make a marvelous governess."

Raines ignored his snide implication of her personality and continued, "I worked with my father for years, and until his recent death was involved in his trading and cataloguing of rare coins. You see, that was his occupation."

"There is little purpose in my asking if he was good at his profession. Needless to say, had he been, you would not now be upon my doorstep looking for work."

For the first time anger rose in Raines. If the man wanted to make derogatory remarks about women, and her ability, that was one thing, but to attack her father was unforgivable. "My father was more of a gentleman than you are capable of comprehending,

26

since you feel that manners are not required when addressing those you believe below you in station." She rose to leave, because she realized the interview and job were lost to her now.

Lord Kemp motioned for her to sit back down, and surprisingly she obeyed. His expression, which had been cynical up until this moment, seemed to soften the least bit, and he said in a gentle voice, "My apologies, Miss Scott. My retort was unforgivable. I can assure you that it was not justified and will not be repeated. It irritates me to find a young woman, alone and without proper funds, thrown into this predicament. Although, let me hasten to state, no doubt your father's death was sudden and unexpected, and he did not have time to prepare for your future. Is that correct?"

His voice had taken on a kind tone and what he said was so true that Raines thought she might cry, an act which she felt certain would definitely lose her this position. Struggling to fight back the tears, and annoyed that she should feel the urge to cry now when she had fought so valiantly to hold up these past few months, she cleared her throat. "My father was a kind, carefree man of a scholarly nature, who was so engrossed in the history and value of rare coinage that he sometimes forgot about the day to day importance of money." She smiled, her lips turning upward just enough for the dimples to peep into view on her cheeks. "Even if Papa had had warning of his impending death, he would have said, 'Raines? Why that girl can take care of herself. She has the brain of a man and drive to succeed. There's no need for me to fret about her future, and she probably wouldn't listen if I tried to decide it for her.' " Raines laughed aloud and added, looking straight at Lord Kemp, "And he was correct. I most likely wouldn't have listened to his advice."

Lord Kemp watched her closely and his expression registered amusement. "Well, Miss Raines Scott, so you think working for me is the position you want? Tell me, why do you feel that you are qualified?"

While Raines felt he might still be mocking her, for the first time she saw the slightest chance of her getting the job. At least he had not thrown her out of the house when she stood up to him. "I am familiar with numismatics, since my father was a member of the London Numismatic Society and often wrote and presented papers before that learned group. Although he was not able to own many of the more valuable coins, he was often called upon to identify and appraise coins for those who were. I wrote all his speeches for him and copied his writings into volumes which are still in my possession. My mother died when I was small and my father always took me into his confidence. We shared a mutual love for rare coins. It was a relationship which left me much richer than a mere inheritance." For the first time Raines's voice carried a note of self-confidence, because she was speaking on a topic she knew and loved.

"It seems, now that I've had time to think on it, that I have heard my father speak of a Scott. Was your father Roger Scott by any chance?"

Raines face broke into a radiant smile and she felt pride when she answered, "Indeed he was! Now do you understand why this job is perfect for me?"

He rubbed his chin and studied her, the dark black

28

eyes warmer yet still not friendly, as though he were wary of her. Suddenly he stood and strolled from his desk over to stand by her chair. "I'd like to explain the duties expected of the person who accepts this position. First, I want to be perfectly frank; up until this moment you appear to be the most qualified applicant, but I still prefer a man for the job. If no one more qualified applies before noon today, then my manservant will drop a note by your residence stating the time to be ready to leave on the morrow. I am most anxious to return to Balfour Castle, since I have numerous responsibilities there." Raines nodded, her hopes soaring, and he continued, "My father had a coin collection of some value and enormous size. I am heir to it, but have no interest in numismatics, much to my father's disappointment. My mother, realizing my lack of interest, feels that the collection should be catalogued, appraised, and then at the completion of this laborious task, turned over to the British Museum to be enjoyed by many. I am in accord with her in this desire, so long as I am not burdened with the task of the cataloguing and such. The job will take many long hours of work and I am willing to pay a reasonable salary to anyone who can carry out this business. I have taken into consideration the skill and knowledge required for this job, and the salary will be much handsomer than that which would be paid to, say a tutor or," glancing at Raines, he added, "governess." He moved over to the desk once more and sat down again, glancing at the papers on it. "So, now that you understand the duties and my attitude toward hiring a female for the job, would you still be interested should no one more qualified appear by noon?"

"Yes, sir, I would. Since my time will be spent going over the coins and carefully evaluating each, I see no reason for the two of us to come in contact, therefore whether I am male or female should really not trouble you greatly. I will do everything possible to stay out of your way," said Raines quickly.

Her last remark caused Lord Kemp's brows to lift, but if he thought she was being impertinent, he made no comment. She saw that the interview was over, so she rose to leave.

She had almost reached the door when Lord Kemp called after her, "Miss Scott, if I am not being too forward, what will become of you if you do not get this position?"

Raines stared at him for a moment, then decided to be honest. In a voice which betrayed her dislike of the idea, she said, "Go back to my Uncle Percival's manor where I will be forced into a marriage to the widower Rockhill. The arrangements have been made by my uncle and only await the outcome of my attempt to find employment."

"In other words, you have two choices: accept employment from an ogre who does not like women, or enter into a loveless marriage which undoubtedly is not to your liking. Is that a correct assumption of how you perceive your situation?" His voice was teasing and he appeared to be enjoying Raines's discomfort.

She looked him levelly in the eye, her chin held high. "Precisely," she retorted, liking this man even less for seeming to enjoy her predicament.

He threw back his head and roared with laughter. She turned to leave once more and he stopped her again. "And what do you think is to protect you from me, since I seem to be your preference of the two fates?"

At first Raines was stunned that he should ask so bold a question, then she realized he was deliberately baiting her to make her uncomfortable. "I . . . I . . . assumed your mother, Lady Kemp, or your wife would be present in the castle. Also, I had intended to ask if you might be in need of another upstairs maid. Nettie Ogg has been a faithful servant in my household since I was a child, and I wished to inquire if you were in need of her services. She is above reproach in character and none can attend a lady with more care and grace."

"So you think your old and trusted servant might protect you in my home, is that it? Well, should I hire you, then I'll be glad to have the services of another maid. In a household the size of Balfour Castle, there is always need for more servants than are available in the neighboring villages. Especially one so loyal as to protect her mistress's virtue, and do excellent cleaning chores, also."

"Thank you and good day, sir," said Raines, turning on her heel and leaving the room.

Outside, she put her hands in her muff and stalked down the sidewalk. Nettie had to run to keep up with her. "Lor, miss, but you do seem in a lather. Ye didn't get the job, did you, love?"

"I don't know yet. But Nettie, Lord Kemp is the most despicable man I have ever encountered. Even if I should get the position, I shall count the days until it is ended." Raines felt so fired by her anger that she did not at first realize that a light snow mixed with sleet had begun to fall. It was not until she stepped on an icy patch, and Nettie had to catch her to prevent her sprawling on the ground, that she grew conscious of the weather.

"Please slow down this breakneck pace, Miss Raines, or you will surely fall and injure yourself. Then where would you be?" admonished the maid, holding her arm.

"Oh, Nettie, I'm in such a dither. I've got to get this job, yet Lord Kemp is the rudest man I've ever encountered."

"Did you get the chance to mention a place for me?" inquired the maid, breathless and watching Raines with consternation. She had never seen the girl so agitated.

"Yes, and he has agreed to hire you, if I get the position."

"Then how can the man be so bad, if he consents to let a young lady bring along an old and valued servant? He must know that I'd protect your honor with my life," reasoned the older woman, still studying her charge's face.

"Oh, it isn't that, Nettie. He hates women! He as good as told me so."

"Then Lord Kemp is not married? It seems to me that I have heard of a Lady Kemp before," replied the maid, trying to place where she had heard the name.

"I don't know if he has a wife or not. I do know that his mother is living, and she is the one who is pressuring him to do something with his father's coin collection."

Suddenly Nettie gasped and stopped walking, clutching the girl's arm to halt her rapid pace. "And how old does this Lord Kemp appear to be?"

Raines frowned, trying to think about him. She had been so nervous that she had not paid a great deal of attention. "I did not study him too closely. He was so hostile and rude. About thirty or maybe thirty-five. Why?"

"I believe I have heard servants gossiping about the young Lord Kemp and the ladies. You know, lots comes to the ears of us that never reaches young ladies of your station."

"All I can say is that a woman would be desperate to show affection for the likes of him. It is possible that other ladies would consider his dark looks handsome, but his attitude is so loathsome that I can never imagine having the slightest interest in him. Now, come on Nettie, let's get to the inn and out of this weather before we both catch our deaths." In a brighter tone she said, "At least he admitted that I was the most qualified person to inquire about the job. Come along, let's have a cup of tea by the fire in our room while we wait."

They did not have to wait long, for the messenger's firm knock came shortly after one o'clock. Raines was finishing her second cup of tea when he arrived. "Answer the door, please Nettie," she ordered, setting her cup down abruptly.

Nettie turned to her and said, "Do you suppose it is Lord Kemp himself?"

Laughing, Raines said, "No, Nettie, he said he would send his manservant. Now hurry and get the door before he thinks we are out."

The maid rushed to the door and opened it. She accepted the message and thanked the man who had delivered it. "The master ordered me to stay to see if the lady wished to send a reply," said the man, blocking the closing of the door.

Quickly Raines read the note and a red flush crept up her neck, but she controlled her voice as she said, "Tell Lord Kemp that we will be ready as instructed."

When the door had closed, Raines jumped to her feet and began pacing the floor. "This is an example of the man's insufferable gall!" She waved the paper in front of Nettie. "He says, if I am sincerely interested in the job, it is mine. However, he is not positive that the widower might not be the better choice for me. The nerve! Nettie, it will be difficult to work for such an obnoxious person."

Trying to soothe her, Nettie inquired, "When must we be ready to leave? We have much to do . . ."

"That's another thing. He says we must be ready to leave by five o'clock in the morning. Can you believe such an unthoughtful person? Why that gives us scarcely time to pack, and what of Uncle Percival?" She stopped pacing the floor and grabbed a piece of stationery. Reaching for the quill, she quickly dipped it into the inkwell and wrote swiftly. At last, satisfied with what she had written, she instructed Nettie, "Take this down to Mrs. Hutchins and ask her to send a messenger to deliver it to Uncle Percival. Here are some coins for his trouble. I know Uncle will be shocked when I do not even return to the manor for all my belongings, but I have asked him to pack and send the things on to me at Balfour Castle. I tried to sound cheerful about this position, although I am filled with misgivings. There's no need for him to become suspicious, or Aunt Thea may force him to come for me. I

34

know she had her heart set on marrying me off so they would be rid of their responsibility." Raines leaned back and chuckled. "At least Lord Kemp has saved me from one fate, although he may live to regret this action."

The maid watched in silence. She knew her charge well and this behavior was typical of Raines when she had something mischievous or devious planned. Unless she was fooled, Lord Kemp had met his match in the strong-willed Raines Scott. Taking the note from her employer, she rushed to carry it to the innkeeper. There was much to be done, if they were to be ready by five in the morn.

Chapter 3

Raines was packed and waiting the following morning when the coach arrived for them. She had dressed in the same black dress and cape worn the day before. The cape was warm and she was not the least interested in impressing Lord Kemp, and she did not want to soil one of her better outfits. She could not remember where Balfour Castle was located, but thought it was a good distance from London. Again Raines had swept her hair into a most unbecoming bun and it amused her to look so plain. Let Lord Kemp think he had hired a drab, unattractive young woman who was interested only in earning a living and burying herself in his vast coin collection. What did appearances matter anyhow? She had given up any silly notions of making a suitable marriage now that she was penniless and without an opportunity for a coming out year. Also, she was intelligent enough to know that if she appeared too attractive, Lord Kemp's wife or mother might not approve of her, nor think her capable of the job she had been hired to do.

With all this in mind, a very unostentatious young

woman and her maid proceeded down the stairs of the inn and over to the waiting carriage.

Lord Kemp stepped from the coach as they neared it. He was dressed in a black greatcoat fastened with brandenburgs and trimmed lapel and wore Hessian boots. It irritated Raines to see how style conscious he appeared in such an outfit, although she had to admit that he cut a handsome swath with his black eyes and dark hair. Long sideburns were the mode and as she entered the carriage she came close enough to see that his were neatly trimmed to midcheek. She felt uncomfortable in her worn black outfit which was clearly out of fashion. Perhaps she had made a mistake in continuing to look so austere. No matter, she reasoned, it could not be helped now. She heard his loud, firm voice giving instructions on the loading of her meager belongings, then to her dismay he opened the coach door and climbed in beside her. Thinking he would probably ride with the driver, she had instructed Nettie to sit on one side and she the other so they might catch a quick nap. Now she was trapped in the same carriage with him for the duration of the trip.

"Lord Kemp, I apologize for having taken over the carriage. Nettie can move on this side with me and you will have the entire seat to yourself," she said primly, letting him know that she preferred not to be too near him.

"Excellent idea," he said, changing to the opposite seat. The coach began moving and once settled, he said, "It is a long way to Balfour and I had a rather late evening. It will be much more commodious to have the seat to myself." With that he dropped his head and slumped into a lounging recline and went to sleep.

Raines bit her tongue to stop the retort which rose to her lips. The insufferable man was actually going to sleep, while she and Nettie struggled to make do on the small crowded seat. Why, any gentleman would have ridden up front and given two ladies the privacy of the carriage so they might rest more comfortably. Well, let him be rude, she would manage in spite of him. Shifting her weight, Raines tried to find a comfortable position so that she might doze, too.

Resting her head on the side of the window, she managed to doze off for several hours. Upon opening her eyes she saw that it was daylight, and through the fog and mist, she tried to decide where they were.

"We're almost to Stonehenge. Have you been here before?"

Startled she turned to find Lord Kemp watching her intently. "No . . . no, I haven't. Papa promised to bring me to see it many times, but we never came. I have always been fascinated by what I heard of the place. Is it as awesome and spectacular as described?" His intense stare and look of amusement forced her to drop her gaze, yet she was so filled with curiosity about Stonehenge that she tempered her reply politely.

"Decide for yourself. I'll have Toby stop, if you would like to see the place up close."

"Oh! I would enjoy it!" She exclaimed excitedly, before she remembered that she was his employee and not a guest. Dropping her gaze, she stammered, "Th

. . . that is if it will not delay us too long. I do not wish to upset your schedule."

"It is time to stretch our legs a bit anyhow. The horses will enjoy the rest as they have raced at top speed this morning." With that he tapped on the roof with his cane and ordered the driver to halt at the next crossroads.

The carriage came to a stop and he said, "If you ladies would like, I'll escort you over to the ruins."

"No, thank you," said Nettie. "I have no intention of walking across that wet moor to see a bunch of stones heaped in a pile by a pack of heathens. I'll stretch my legs a bit and then climb right back into this nice warm carriage and rest, thank you, sir."

Raines was about to insist that she accompany them, then seeing how set she was against going, shrugged and stepped out. Lord Kemp took her hand in his and she felt the warmth of his strong fingers around her small hand.

"Well, it looks as though we are the only two who wish to view the site, so shall we proceed, Miss Scott?" He led the way as Raines looked about her in awe.

It was a dreary morning, with a wind blowing strongly and mist spraying Raines's face, but she was so intrigued by what stood before her that the cold did not penetrate. Also the duchess's secondhand cloak was woven of thick wool and the moisture did not seep through its thick fabric. Raines chuckled as she wondered what Lord Kemp would think if he knew his employee wore a rag store garment which once belonged to one of his peers. The situation amused her and she smiled.

"That is the first smile I have seen from you. Stopping to see the ruins must indeed please you," he commented, watching her closely.

"That is not why I am smiling, but I must confess that this place is fascinating," remarked Raines, looking around her.

The 3,000 year old monument stood before them in all its massive mystery. A circle of stones each weighing approximately 28 tons and thirteen and a half feet tall stood silently, telling of a different era. A ring of equally large stones rested on top of the outside circle.

Leading Raines by the arm, Lord Kemp walked into the circle. "Do you know anything about the history of Stonehenge?"

"Not a great deal. I know that the stones were once in a perfect circle and that another smaller circle of blocks was inside. I had no idea that the stones were so large in size. How did they get the boulders on top of the tall markers?"

"No one knows for sure. They do know that some of these stones are only found in western Wales.

"Why that's over three hundred miles from here!" exclaimed Raines.

"Yes, so the workers must have had some means of transporting them here."

The wind whipped through the circle of stones, making whistling, eerie sounds, and Raines found herself staying close to Lord Kemp.

"Scientists think this was probably a sacrificial stone used by sun worshippers to offer sacrifices," said Kemp, touching a sixteen foot long stone marker which was in the center of the circle.

In spite of herself, Raines shivered. Lord Kemp noticed it and said, "Come, you are getting chilled out here. We must get you back to the coach and be on our way. Perhaps you can visit this site again next summer when the weather is more suitable for sightseeing."

Raines did not argue. Tucking her hand under his arm for support on the rough terrain, she walked briskly back to the coach trying to match his long strides. The stroll had invigorated her, and she felt warm and happy for the first time in days. Everything was going to be all right, she decided.

They started on their way again, and Raines stared out the window until the huge stones could no longer be seen through the haze.

"Is it much farther to Balfour Castle?" she inquired.

"You're not tiring already are you?" Lord Kemp asked, a hint of sarcasm in his voice.

"Of course not," snapped Raines. "I'm accustomed to long carriage rides. I was merely inquiring." He had turned back into the ogre again, and she did not intend to address him for the rest of the journey.

They stopped at an inn for food and again for high tea, and still Raines kept her vow to remain silent. She addressed her few words to Nettie. The annoying thing was that Lord Kemp seemed to be enjoying this silence. He either slept or stared out the window at the passing landscape, or even more irritatingly, stared at Raines. Several times she almost ordered him to study something other than her appearance, but checked herself. She did not want to lose this job before she had the opportunity to at least see if she would enjoy it. However, of one thing she was positive, Lord Kemp was determined to irritate her any way possible. The only time on the entire trip that he had acted civil was at Stonehenge, and there he had been so pleasant that for a moment she had forgotten how rude he truly was.

Night had fallen and the travelers were growing weary when Lord Kemp finally announced, "Ladies, Balfour Castle will come into view in a few moments."

Raines sat up straight and began fussing over her cloak. She reached up with her hands to sweep her blond hair into place, then caught herself when she remembered that it was now tightly wound into a bun. Lord Kemp, who was still rudely watching her, smiled, then glanced away, but did not speak.

Staring out the window, Raines was impressed at the view ahead. The towering stone castle rose out of the fog and she saw torches flickering on braces at the entrance to the hall. The carriage rolled across uneven brick paving and down a winding drive, then around a curve. Braking, the driver inched onto the bridge which covered a moat and into a courtyard. At last the carriage came to rest before massive wooden doors ornately carved and bearing the brass crest of the Kemps.

Lord Kemp assisted the two women down from the carriage and Raines was thankful to stretch and move around. It had been an extremely long day and she was ready for the comfort of a soft downy bed.

Their party entered through the massive doors and came to stand in an enormous flagstone hall. Sconces lit the hallway and Raines saw that rows of gloomy looking men's portraits lined the hall. Even in the dimness she saw a striking resemblance between several of the noblemen and Lord Kemp. He had the same high forehead, strong profile and piercing black eyes.

Raines guessed it to be nine o'clock or later and she was exhausted. She hoped Lord Kemp would order a small meal to be sent to her room. Instead, she could not believe what he was saying.

"Miss Scott, after you have been shown to your room by Jeanie and have refreshed yourself, please come down to the library. I would like to explain your duties."

"To . . . tonight?" Raines stammered.

He looked startled. "Is there anything wrong with tonight? You are not tired from the trip, I hope. Why any man would have endured it as a day of relaxation."

Raines gritted her teeth, but held her temper. "I will meet you in the library in half an hour. I am as anxious to start this job as you. The sooner it is begun, the quicker it can be completed." Her eyes shot sparks as she faced him.

"My thoughts precisely." He turned on his heel and walked out of the room.

Once he was out of hearing Nettie said, "Oh, Miss Raines, you are exhausted and I'm sure he could have put off the business until the morrow."

Climbing the stairs, Raines thought she would drop before she reached the top, but she kept doggedly moving. "It doesn't matter that I'm tired. Lord Kemp is determined to show me that I can't do this job as well as a man, and I shall surprise him if it kills me."

The maid made grumbling sounds as she followed her mistress down the hall. The servant from Balfour was a pleasant enough sort and chatted cheerfully, seeming unaware of the two disgruntled people who trailed behind her.

When Raines entered the bedroom her spirits rose for the first time. It was a very pleasant suite with a large inviting looking bed which had been carefully turned down to expose clean linen. A brisk fire burned in a grate located in a small sitting alcove. The blue and gold blended into a rich color scheme that resulted in an appearance of subdued elegance.

"Will you be needing anything else, ma'am?" the maid asked shyly in a thick brogue.

"No, thank you. Nettie will see to my comforts tonight, before she assumes her duties in the household tomorrow." Raines added quickly, "Unless Lord Kemp has instructed otherwise."

"No, ma'am, Lord Kemp sent word to fix a room for your maid. I think he intends for her to continue serving you. Also, she is to aid me in such duties as I see fit."

"Well, at least he hasn't ordered her to scrub the floors or polish the silver before she goes to bed tonight," Raines retorted, taking off her cloak and sinking down on the bed.

"No, ma'am. Watson, the butler, is in charge of the silver and two women come in from the village to do the hard scrubbing," the girl said, mystified at the young woman's sarcasm.

Waving her away, Raines drew a deep breath and said, "Never mind, I'm just tired tonight. That will be all, and please show Nettie to her room." Turning to Nettie, who looked equally as strained, she said, "Get a good night's rest, because I can't promise what lies in store for you tomorrow."

Nettie was clearly angry at the way her mistress was being treated, yet she knew there was nothing she could do to remedy it. Giving Raines a quick look, she inquired, "Are you sure you will be all right?"

"I'll just rest here for a few minutes and then go down to see what he wants done tonight. I'll be revived in thirty minutes. Now, go on to your room and don't fret over me. Remember that I am a young working woman and there will never be any more privileges for me." She turned her head aside so the maid would not see the tears forming.

"Good night, Miss Raines," said Nettie. "Don't you worry your pretty head. Something good will come of all this. I am positive of it." While she spoke the words, her tone lacked conviction.

Once the door had closed, Raines rolled over and gave way to her tears of weariness and frustration. It was not that she wanted to renege on her duties. It was simply that she could not believe any man could be so inhuman as to expect her to begin work tonight.

Finally, after a good cry, she felt somewhat better and walked to the washstand to pour a pitcher of water. Quickly she dabbed at her tear stained eyes. It would not do for Lord Kemp to see that she had already dissolved into tears. He had made it quite clear that he had no patience with weeping women.

After washing her face, and the short rest, she felt much better. Straightening her dress, she stood back to inspect her appearance. She had dark circles under her eyes from lack of sleep last night, and her eyes were still a little puffy, but otherwise she looked presentable. At least, she chuckled, she looked the role of the destitute spinster.

Walking briskly, she retraced her steps to the first floor where a manservant stood waiting to show her into Lord Kemp's office. A look of surprise crossed his face when she entered the room, only to be replaced by a hint of amusement in his eyes.

"Well, Miss Scott, I see you did make it back after all. I was about to give you up." He had taken off his greatcoat and wore a tweed jacket with leather patches on the elbows and was smoking a pipe. He offered her a chair near the fire and said, "I hope my pipe doesn't bother you. I like to have a smoke for relaxation after a long day."

"As you please," replied Raines, primly. She had no intention of being overly civil to this brute ever again.

"Would you like a glass of Madeira? It might help you to relax," he suggested.

"No, thank you, I don't care to drink during working hours." She sat erect and unsmiling. "Now, if we can discuss whatever it is that must be taken care of tonight, then I would appreciate so doing. It is getting late and I don't believe many employers would require their workers to labor past midnight."

Again Raines saw a flicker of amusement cross his face, but his voice was strictly business-like when he said, "I regret having to impose on your time tonight,

46

Miss Scott. I do not expect hours of this length after tonight. It is just that tomorrow I must leave early, and I thought you would be anxious to have your duties explained."

"Indeed I am," said Raines with a touch too much enthusiasm.

"Then let me show you where the collection is kept," he replied dryly. There was no humor in his eyes now.

He walked over to a massive bookcase near the fireplace and stopped. Raines watched in astonishment as he pushed inward on the bookcase and the wall swung forward, revealing a smaller room. Motioning for Raines to follow, he lifted a candle from a sconce. The two moved quietly into an inner room where shelves held vast stacks of coin containers.

Raines was surprised at the size of the collection and felt a thrill of excitement at having the opportunity to examine it.

"Miss Scott, you may begin wherever you like, and I assume you have some idea in mind as how you plan to catalogue this collection."

"I must admit to being overwhelmed at the size of your father's collection; however, I will devise a systematic approach for the inventory."

"You may work in the adjoining room, and I will instruct the servants to carry out any wishes you might have for working tables or materials. Each day when you have finished, please lock the room and carry the key with you at all times." He glanced at her, then added, "perhaps you need a ribbon and you can attach the key. We do not have thieves at Balfour

Castle, yet a wise employer does not put temptation in a man's way."

"I understand. The key will remain in my possession at all times." Raines nodded. "Yes, the ribbon sounds like a suitable mode for managing the key. I will take care of the matter in the morn."

Leading the way, Lord Kemp left the vault room and locked the heavy door, then pushed the bookcase around on its pivot.

Raines wondered if at last the meeting was over and she would be allowed to go to her room. She tried to conceal how tired she felt and struggled to stifle a yawn.

Once back in the library Lord Kemp gestured for her to sit by the fire again, and he moved to the deep cushioned chair opposite her. "I apologize for not introducing you to my mother, Lady Kemp, this evening. As I mentioned in London, she has not been well and retires very early. In the morning I hope you will seek her out and make her acquaintance. She is the one who will direct you, since it was her desire to have this task undertaken."

"I will do as you suggest. When would be an appropriate time for me to visit Lady Kemp?" The fire made Raines warm and she fought the urge to let her eyelids droop. Trying to stay alert she shifted her position in the chair.

"Mother usually rests abed until ten, then eats a light brunch in her room. I would say eleven o'clock would be the best time for your visit. In the morning, check with Mrs. Carlton, her nurse, to make sure Mother is well enough for company."

Trying to sound polite, although she wished to snap at him, Raines said, "Although I may be ill endowed financially, Lord Kemp, I have not lacked in proper upbringing. I understand the correct principles of etiquette without prompting from you." She glared at him and to her delight, Raines thought she detected the slightest blush. She had pricked him with that remark and it pleased her. To temper her words, which had been a bit curt, she added hastily, "My father was an invalid on the last, and I understand how a guest can tire one."

Standing abruptly, Lord Kemp said, "I will show you to your room, Miss Scott. Your temper seems short from lack of rest, or is this a trait we will have to learn to live with?"

Anger rising, Raines started to reply, then realizing this would only confirm his belief that she was an ill-tempered shrew, she closed her mouth. She walked past him without further comment, determined not to rise to his bait. "I am sure I can find my way back to my room without your assistance, Lord Kemp. My mind is not short, even if my temper is."

He threw back his head and laughed again. It was a deep resounding rumble which filled the quiet castle. "You may be a thorn in my side, Miss Scott, but I admit that you are equal to any sparring partner who has set foot in Balfour in many a day." Reaching out, he took her arm to guide her through the door.

Most of the lights had been extinguished and the hall was now lit by one lone torch. If Raines had not despised her companion so intensely, she would have rejoiced in his companionship through the dark cas-

49

tle.

He held the candle high to light the way down the silent corridor, while his other hand still rested on her arm. Raines grew uncomfortable at the idea of them walking unescorted toward her bedroom. She had no idea what might be going through his mind. Suppose he tried to take advantage of her? If he tried anything beyond the realm of chivalry, she would scream until she raised the household, she decided. Feeling confident that she could handle any situation with him, she relaxed her guard.

"I have ordered a light supper to be sent to your room, since I did not think you would care to dine so late. However, after tonight I expect you to take all your meals in the main dining hall. We breakfast at eight, lunch at one and sup at eight. And I do not hold with tardiness, so be forewarned."

"I will make an effort to always be on time," replied Raines. Until this moment she had not known if she would be relegated to the kitchen with the staff or be allowed the privileges of family. In any other circumstances she would have felt comfortable with her position, but with this man who did not hide his scorn for women, she had been uncertain.

They walked briskly up the stairs, their shoes making soft sounds on the stone steps, and the sounds echoed down the hollow halls. At night the castle seemed awesome to Raines and in the future she did not intend to venture out of her room after the evening meal.

At the top of the stairs they turned and continued their walk down the long corridor. "Tomorrow my solicitor, James MacBain, will be coming for an extended visit. He has some details to discuss with Lady Kemp. I imagine he will be interested in talking with you about your plans for the coin collection. I think you will find him a pleasant fellow and I hope he can be of some assistance to you."

"I look forward to meeting him." They had reached her door and Raines said, "I believe this is my room. Thank you for being kind enough to escort me through the castle. It turned out to be farther than I remembered, and in the night it was pleasant to have someone lead the way with the candle."

She turned to enter her room and he touched her arm to stop her. "Tell me, Miss Scott, after seeing Balfour Castle and finding yourself in my company, which you plainly detest, do you still think this better than marrying the widower?" His eyes mocked her and in the light she saw the demonic smile which crossed his face.

"That, Lord Kemp, will take some thought. Good night, sir!" She pulled free and moved into her room, shutting the door with a loud bang. She heard his laughter echo through her chambers.

Pacing the floor she fought to control her temper. She had accepted employment from the most despicable man she had ever known. How was she to endure the ordeal? And even more frightening was the thought of what lay in store for her, if she did not succeed in this position. Her uncle would not humor her in another attempt to find employment. Of that she was certain. There was nothing to do but endure this rude man and his taunting attitude. From the size of the coin collection she estimated the task would take at least six months if not longer.

Perhaps Lord Kemp would busy himself away from the castle and she could work in peace. Surprisingly, Raines found herself wondering if there was a young Lady Kemp, and if so, when would she meet her?

Chapter 4

Raines learned the answer to her question about a young Lady Kemp sooner than she expected. The following morning she dressed quickly in a navy, high waisted gown with snug fitting sleeves. Already she had discovered the castle to be damp and drafty, even with a fire blazing in every hearth. She wanted to look presentable when she met the elderly Lady Kemp because the matron's impression of her could go a long way in preventing Lord Kemp from dismissing her.

Finding her way through the castle, she entered the large dining hall where a place was set for her, and a young maid stood ready to serve. Seeing only one place, Raines inquired, "Are there no others to have breakfast?"

"Lord Kemp left at dawn and Mr. MacBain hasn't arrived yet," explained the maid, placing a plate before her.

"What about Lady Kemp?"

"No, ma'am, she never comes down anymore since she fell and injured her hip last summer."

"And Lord Kemp's wife . . ."

"There ain't no Lord Kemp's wife. Not at the moment. There's some that says Lady Charlotte will soon be the new mistress, and then there's others that say Lord Adam won't never settle down to one woman again." The maid seemed to enjoy this bit of gossip, because she continued, " 'Tis good that you be a plain woman, Miss Scott, or you would not be safe from the likes of him."

"Well, you can rest assured that my reason for being here is purely business, and I haven't the slightest interest in the romances of Lord Kemp." Raines was clearly piqued that the maid considered her too plain. It wounded her vanity to be so described, yet it was one of those things to be endured. At least she would be free from his lordship's advances.

"You know he had a wife. Them who seen her said she was a beauty, too. In fact, they says it was her looks which caused her death."

"You mean Lord Kemp's wife is dead? What happened to her?"

"That I can't say, ma'am, since it happened before my time. I've only been with the family for three years."

"Nobody has mentioned how she died?" Raines pressed harder for information. From the young girl's caution, Raines felt she regretted having broached the subject. Determined to learn more, she urged, "Surely you've heard something."

The girl shook her head vigorously, "No, ma'am. When I was just hired the housekeeper warned me that Lady Alexandra was never to be discussed."

"Why?"

Now the maid appeared visibly shaken and ready to flee the room. "Please, ma'am, I can't say no more. I need my job and I've said too much already."

Raines patted her arm. "Don't fret. I won't repeat what you have told me."

Finishing the meal as quickly as possible, Raines decided to go next and arrange an appointment with Lady Kemp's nurse. On the way to the nurse's room she encountered Nettie, who was dressed up in a new servant's uniform of light gray with a ruffled pinafore of white linen.

"Lor help me, Miss Raines, but don't I look the ticket?" she asked, turning for Raines to see her new finery. "And this don't be the only one I gets. There's two for the week and a right proper gray smock for wearing when ashes are to be emptied. This Lord Kemp knows how to treat servants, don't you agree?" Her face flushed with excitement and she stopped chattering when she saw Raines frown. "What is the matter, Miss Raines? Have I said something to upset you?" She rushed on, "I didn't mean to imply that your father was not a good and kind employer. 'Tis just that I've never worked in a position where the master was as rich as Lord Kemp."

Patting her arm, Raines reassured her. "I understand, Nettie, and your uniform looks splendid. I only wish I shared your delight at being employed here."

Watching her closely, Nettie whispered, "Nothing has gone wrong, has it Miss Raines? You ain't fixing to leave or nothing are you?"

"No. And it's silly for me to behave this way when I have a nice job and Lord Kemp's wages are more than generous. So let me be on my way. I'm probably just a trifle homesick and in a few days everything will be fine. Now, would you care to show me to Lady Kemp's suite or do you have any other duties to be performing?"

"I'm suppose to be readying the guest rooms. Seems we've big important company coming today," whispered the maid, in a conspiratorial tone.

"I know Lady Kemp's lawyer is due, and I must go and arrange my visit with Lady Kemp before his arrival."

"Now that you've seen Balfour, how do you like it, Miss Raines? Is your job pleasing?"

"It is the only reason I can tolerate Lord Kemp. The Kemp coin collection is fantastic and will be a joy to catalogue." Raines glanced around her to make sure no one was in sight. "Have the servants said anything about the Lady Alexandra? There seems to be some scandal surrounding her death."

"There's been whispers and innuendoes aplenty, but nobody has said more. The first thing cook told me was that I was never to speak of her to his lordship or any of the staff."

"Nettie, let's find her portrait. I'm curious to see what she looked like." Raines started off down the hall. "I noticed all the Kemps and their wives' portraits are in the foyer and line the corridor."

The maid put out her hand to stop her. "You won't find her there," whispered Nettie.

Stopping abruptly, Raines whirled to face her. "What . . . what do you mean?"

"She ain't there." Moving ahead, Nettie led the way. "I know where her picture should be, but it ain't there."

"How did you find this out so quickly?" asked Raines, amazed.

"Company is coming and my first task was to dust all the portraits. Well, I got interested in them and when I got to Lord Kemp's, I saw the blank space beside his. "See," she ordered, pointing to a blank space on the wall where the paint was slightly darker. The outline of a frame was clearly visible.

"You're right!" said Raines. "Why would he remove his wife's portrait?" They moved farther down the hall so as not to be seen staring.

Before they had gone ten steps, Raines heard her name called. She turned and saw a manservant walking rapidly toward her.

Bowing quickly, he said, "Miss Scott, I'm Watson, the butler. Lord Kemp asked me to give you a message for him. He said that Mr. MacBain would be arriving this morning and would you please entertain him until Lady Kemp is ready to see him."

"Of course, when do you expect him?"

"He's here now, Miss, and is downstairs in the study waiting. I missed you when you left the dining room and have been searching the castle for you."

Raines felt a flutter of nervousness, while outwardly struggling to appear calm. "Fine, I'll go down and greet him. Please tell Mrs. Carlton that I would like an appointment with Lady Kemp when convenient. I was on my way there now."

"I'll show you down to the library, before I come back and deliver your message." He moved off ahead of her.

Following briskly along, Raines caught a glimpse of her reflection in the mirror. Quickly she smoothed her hair back and frowned at how bland she looked. She wished she had applied a bit of rouge to color her pale cheeks. One day she intended to surprise this household by wearing her prettiest dress and fixing her hair in the latest style, swept up and held in place with a bone comb. It was most annoying to have to hide one's best features. Before she had time to dwell further on her plainness they had reached the drawing room, and Watson stood back for her to enter.

The man who had turned to greet her was younger than she had expected. He held out his hand in greeting. "You must be Miss Scott, the brave young lady I've heard so much about since arriving. I understand your father was the honorable Roger Scott, the famous numismatist?"

When he smiled Raines warmed to him and began to relax. His dark blond hair was carefully brushed back from a high forehead, and his green eyes shone with friendliness. He was attractive without being exactly handsome.

She smiled. "Yes he was."

"Then I can understand the logic in Adam hiring Scott's daughter for this important task. He was quite lucky to engage the talents of one so able. How did he ever convince you to accept this job?"

"I'm afraid that it was I who answered the advertisement and sought him out."

She saw his right brow rise slightly in question and decided to be honest because she found herself at ease with him. "I completely forgot my manners, please be

58

seated. I'm afraid I am a bit rattled this morning. You see, I only arrived last evening myself and this is a new role for me."

They moved to chairs near the fireplace and faced one another. "I don't wish to bore you with my life's story, but to sum it up briefly, I needed employment and this seemed the logical job." She laughed, hoping at least her smile was pretty. She had never felt duller. "So here I am."

"I think it is an excellent arrangement for all, and more especially for me, since we shall be working together."

Seeing her surprise, he continued, "I am Lady Kemp's solicitor and therefore have a vested interest in seeing that the collection is properly catalogued. She wishes to see it presented to the British Museum while she is still alive to attend the ceremonies. You realize that Lady Kemp has been in declining health for some time."

Before Raines could answer, Watson appeared and announced that Lady Kemp wished to see both of them at this time.

Raines accompanied MacBain into Lady Kemp's suite, silently apprehensive about meeting the woman. She felt it was imperative that she please Lady Kemp or her job would be terminated.

Lady Kemp, a slender woman in her late sixties, watched their entrance with warm interest. She reclined on a rose colored chaise lounge and gestured for them to sit in the two chairs facing her. Lady Kemp wore a ruffled gown of pale lavender and though she wore a light scent, the room still had the odor of lingering illness. Even with the mist of heather Mrs.

Carlton had sprayed, the smell of infirmity prevailed. Raines recognized it and it brought back memories of her own father's confinement.

"Good morning, James, it is good to see you again. Henry was not able to come?" Lady Kemp extended a bird-like claw for him to shake. This small gesture appeared to tire her and she let her arm fall quickly to her lap.

"My uncle sent his regrets. He is suffering from the gout again and asked you to forgive him for sending me in his place."

Lady Kemp nodded in understanding. "Poor Henry is wearing out, just as I am." Then she turned her attention to Raines. "You must be Miss Scott. Adam told me you had arrived, and he regretted having to go off on business this morning before we were introduced. I hope you have not been at loose ends for assistance around the castle. Since my stroke I do not rise early and there is no one else here to assist in managing the household. If only Adam would follow my advice and take a wife." She shrugged as though to dismiss the subject. "Oh well, enough of that. Have you seen the coin collection?"

"I have, Lady Kemp, and it is much larger than I dreamed. Lord Kemp showed it to me last night, since he thought I might wish to start work today."

The matron's eyes twinkled as she studied Raines more carefully. "It is interesting to see that you are a female and young at that. I never would have believed Adam would hire a woman."

Raines blushed. "Lord Kemp made it clear that he hired me only because I was the most qualified applicant. My father was—"

"Yes, Adam explained all your credentials to me." Lady Kemp interrupted. "My late husband often spoke of your father, so I am satisfied that you can do the job. I find it amusing, however, that Adam turned down Mr. Phelan Tilmouth who has held the office of secretary in the Leeds Numismatic Society for the past twenty years."

Stunned, Raines sat in puzzled silence. He had seemed so hostile about accepting a woman. To discover that a more qualified, or at least as qualified a gentleman had applied, and still Lord Kemp had chosen her, did indeed, amaze Raines.

The conversation moved on to business between Lady Kemp and MacBain. Since the business was of no importance to her, she let her mind wander to other things.

It was not until she heard her name mentioned that she turned to listen. "I'm sorry. Were you addressing me, Lady Kemp?"

"Yes, I wanted to know if there were any supplies or special items you needed for your work? James is going back to London tomorrow and will be glad to purchase them and have them sent to you."

"That is most kind," she said gratefully to James. "I'll make a list and give it to you before tomorrow, if that will be early enough."

"That is fine. Lady Kemp and I have several business matters to go over, but I plan to return to London by late afternoon."

"Then if you will excuse me, Lady Kemp, I will return to the library and begin work. I have not had time to go through the vault and I still don't know all it contains. This will be such a thrilling job! My father and I spent many nights looking at pictures of some of the world's oldest coins and now I will have an opportunity to see and touch them." Her voice was animated with the excitement she felt.

"Miss Scott, there is one other thing I should mention. You will be taking your meals in the dining room with the family, although Adam is the only one who will be present. I regret that I do not undertake the stairs unless it is an emergency or an extremely rare occasion such as Christmas. I hope you do not find my son too curt or unfriendly. He seems to have taken a distinct dislike to all young females, although I see a ray of change in his hiring one. I merely say this to prevent your being offended by his abrupt manner at times."

"Don't worry, I understand temperamental men, since my father could be an absolute bear at times," replied Raines, rising to leave.

As Lady Kemp nodded her eyes seemed to twinkle mischievously. "I think you may be able to handle Adam," she said, smiling. "But please come to me if any serious problem arises."

Raines thanked her and took her leave, rushing back to the library. Her spirits soared at having an ally in Lady Kemp. She had fretted that being a woman would upset the matriarch, but the opposite appeared to be true.

Once back in the library, she found a pad and pen in the desk drawer and with them in hand opened the bookcase door. Quickly she used the key Lord Kemp had given her last evening to unlock the door.

The vault room was small and windowless, so Raines lit a candle and placed it on the shelf. It soon grew obvious to her that she would have to carry the heavy coin books out into the library to see clearly. But before she did that, she wanted to inspect the contents of the room. Blue leather bound coin books with gold lettering identified the years or countries represented inside and the shelves were lined with dozens such volumes. Some coins were framed in glass cases and one section contained boxes of coins which were not marked or identified. She knew most of her time would be spent in this section. Satisfied she had probed and investigated every facet of the room, Raines returned to the library and sat down to make her list. Writing swiftly, she dipped her quill into the inkwell and wrote without a smudge. Her penmanship was excellent because her father had demanded perfection. At last finished, she sat back and studied her list, pride rising as she surveyed its neatness. Then quickly she folded the stationery and slipped it into an envelope.

"Writing a letter to your sweetheart, Miss Scott?" inquired a voice from behind her. The speaker's tone was mocking and carried a hint of irritation.

Jumping to her feet, Raines turned to face Lord Kemp. "No, I w . . . was making a list of supplies to be ordered when Mr. MacBain goes back to London." She saw the scowl on his face relax a little. "I thought you were out of the castle for the day."

"Oh, would that have been preferable to you?"

Her cheeks flushed with anger. "Of course not! I meant that you startled me. If you have been here long, you know that I've been engrossed for several hours in this collection and did not hear you enter." She flushed at the thought of being spied upon. "A gentleman usually makes his presence known, Lord Kemp." She hoped she had not gone too far with this reprimand. He seemed to relish goading her until she grew annoyed.

He ignored her retort and casually sat on the edge of the desk. "And how is the inventory progressing?"

"This is the largest private collection of coins that I have ever seen," she said, her voice softening. "It is thrilling to find such treasures. I included a ledger in my order of supplies, and when it arrives I can begin the tedious job of listing coins by years. I noticed that your father already had many volumes organized in this manner."

Lord Kemp walked to the fireplace in long swift strides before he spoke again. "Please stop your work for a few minutes, Miss Scott, and come sit by the fire. I need to discuss several things with you and it is drafty near the window."

Obeying, although his manner puzzled her, she moved to the chair he indicated.

"How did my mother appear to you? Did she look well?"

"I really can't say. She looks like any invalid who has been ill for some time and . . . and her color is very pale. But I was not privileged to know Lady Kemp before her stroke, so I cannot judge how she is now."

"But you have seen sick people before, haven't you? She doesn't look well, does she?" he pressed, his voice sounding anxious. Raines saw how troubled he was and felt a pang of sympathy for him. Her own father's illness, and the fears it had created in her, moved her to be kinder.

"My first reaction was that your mother was weak and tired, if that is what you mean, Lord Kemp." Her expression warmed and her eyes said silently that she understood his anxiety.

"I've been worried about her for some time. She appears to be growing weaker. The responsibilities of this household are too much for her."

"Couldn't you hire a housekeeper to relieve some of the burden?" she said gently.

He shrugged and cleared his throat. "That isn't what I'm referring to. I might as well be specific—we need a hostess here at Balfour, and I'm asking you to consider accepting this role. Your pay will be increased to compensate for the added duties, of course." He paused and watched her reaction through his dark hooded eyes.

Raines was caught off guard. "Why . . . why I . . . had not dreamed of such an offer, and I need time to think of the ramifications it might entail."

"Surely no one could think it was anything other than respectable with my mother ill and I . . . I not having a . . . a . . . wife," he faltered. For the first time he seemed ill at ease, but he continued to watch her carefully.

"I have known many instances where a relative moved into a household and assumed this role. Do you not have a cousin or aunt or . . ."

He shook his head. "No one that I would consider." His voice had an edge to it. Just as quickly his manner changed and he said, "When I saw you in London this idea first took form, but I planned getting to know you better before approaching the subject. However, my mother is worrying about forthcoming obligations, and I must decide hastily on some solution to ease her mind."

"The household has been most pleasant in the short time that I've been here." She saw that he wanted an immediate answer and to her surprise, Raines heard herself saying, "All right, I accept."

Jumping to his feet, Kemp moved to the table and raised a wine container. "Excellent! Will you join me in a glass of wine to seal our bargain?"

Raines laughed, catching his excitement. "It is too early in the day for me, and I already feel heady with this new responsibility. I think I'll retire to my room and rest for a while. This decision has left me quite shaken." She stood to take her leave.

"One more thing, Miss Scott. Your duties will include a good deal of entertaining, and I will include a clothing allowance in your salary."

Unable to hide her delight, Raines looked at him and exclaimed, "That's most generous!"

"When I go to London, I'll select several fabrics and have Mother's dressmaker stitch them up for you, if that is acceptable with you, of course."

Raines preferred choosing her own materials, but she did not want to offend him, so she replied, "That will be fine, sir."

"And one more thing, Miss Scott. When your new gowns arrive, I hope you will do away with that black monstrosity you wore to my house for your interview. It is most hideous."

In spite of Raines's indignation, a slow blush crept into her cheeks. The nerve of this insulting man to criticize a lady's wardrobe! Her eyes sparked fire as she controlled her temper and asked, "Will there be anything else my lord requests, since my appearance doesn't seem to please him?''

He strolled casually over to her, while she stood rooted to the spot, fired with anger, yet uncomfortable with his close scrutiny. Slowly he circled her, before he touched her tight bun of blond hair which was pulled back severely from her high cheekbones. "Yes, take your hair out of that silly chignon and let Arlette fashion it in the style the young ladies are wearing in London this season." A look of mischief twinkled in his eyes as he chided, "Really, Miss Scott, how could you be so blind to the fashion around you, and yet be such a bright young lady?"

"I had my reasons," retorted Raines, determined to respond, even if he discharged her for it.

Lord Kemp reached out as though to free her hair from its net, and Raines stepped back quickly. "Miss Scott, you aren't afraid I'm going to seduce you, I hope," he chuckled, dropping his arm. He was clearly enjoying himself and her discomfort.

"Indeed not! I would have to be weakened by your attentions for that to happen, and you can rest assured that I haven't the slightest interest in you as a suitor." With that Raines spun on her heel and strode toward the door, his deep laugh echoing in her ears.

When at last she reached her room and had shut the door behind her with a loud bang, she burst into tears. The insufferable clod! The nerve of him to criticize her clothes and hair style! Even if she became the most gossiped about person in England, she intended to look her loveliest from this moment forward. With tears still streaming down her cheeks, she snatched the bone hairpins from her chignon and threw them on the dresser, letting her golden curls cascade down onto her sobbing shoulders. This was the last anyone would see of the dowdy Raines Scott, she vowed.

Chapter 5

Dressing for dinner that evening, Raines took extra care with her appearance. She had bathed in scented bath oil and Arlette had shampooed her thick blond hair. Patiently she had followed the maid's advice and sat by the fire toweling her hair until it dried.

After much deliberation, she and Arlette had chosen a strawberry silk dress with high waist and silver trimmed vandyked borders. Once the dress had belonged to her cousin, but fortunately for Raines, the young lady had gained too much weight to squeeze her plump figure into it, and Aunt Beatrice had reluctantly given it to her.

"Arlette, I want you to fix my hair in the latest French fashion—swooped up in ringlets and tied with this matching strawberry velvet ribbon. Do you know how to make the small dangling wisps of curl on either side? I want to look the fashion plate tonight." She eyed the girl in her mirror, her blue eyes twinkling from excitement.

"Yes, ma'am, I've done it often." The girl sensed Raines's happiness and skillfully added her talents to helping accomplish this miraculous change from duckling to swan. After an hour of patient curling, the two stood staring at Raines's new appearance in the mirror, the maid with a look of awe and admiration in her eyes and Raines with a smile of satisfaction. The figure who stared back at them looked like a young debutante. It was the reflection of a tall, regal looking girl with patrician chiseled features and periwinkle eyes sparkling with mischief as she thought of the surprise Lord Kemp had in store for him.

At precisely eight o'clock she walked into the dining hall and followed Watson to her place. She was delighted to see that James had not left for London as scheduled. And he did not hide his pleasure at the transformed Raines. "Miss Scott! You look ravishing tonight! I knew you were pretty; however, in that shade of pink there is none fairer in all of England than you tonight."

Sitting next to him, she gave him a dazzling smile. "Why thank you, Mr. MacBain, and please call me Raines. After such a pretty compliment, I think you are entitled to be on a first name basis," she flirted, ignoring Lord Kemp who sat at the head of the table and remained silent. She felt a stir of disappointment that he showed no sign of noticing a change in her appearance.

"Raines it shall be, and you must call me James. Now that we are finished with formality, I look forward to getting to know you better, my dear." He did not take his eyes from her face and clearly had fallen under her spell.

Raines reveled in this new-found admiration. Leaning forward she murmured, "And I you, James."

Kemp cleared his throat. "Now that you two have settled on what you will call each other," he said acidly, "may we continue with the meal? I am not fond of cold roast beef and Watson has been ready to serve for a good five minutes."

He proceeded to serve Raines's plate with a lavish slice of beef.

"If Lord Kemp doesn't stop piling potatoes on my plate, I shan't be slender enough to wear this dress long," said Raines coldly.

"Adam, you have not commented on Raines's appearance tonight. Aren't you as pleased as I to find such a lovely guest at our table?" James was puzzled at his friend's curtness for he knew Kemp to be quite the rake when he set his mind to it.

Kemp's only reply was to inquire if MacBain wished gravy over his thick slab of meat.

Raines picked at her food while she listened to the men talk. She was piqued that Lord Kemp had not shown any sign of approval at her improved appearance, especially after his remarks in the afternoon. Although why she should seek his approval she couldn't say.

Once the meal was finished, James turned to Raines. "Since the weather is pleasant, would you care for a stroll out of doors? I'll send Watson to fetch a light wrap for your shoulders, if you care to join me in the garden." He smiled at her invitingly.

She opened her mouth to accept the invitation, when Lord Kemp interrupted. "I'm sorry James, but I need to discuss some business matters with you in the library, since you will be going back to London in the morning."

"Really, Adam! Couldn't it wait until after we take a brief stroll down to the lake and back? You could have your after-dinner brandy while we're gone," said James, not hiding his irritation at being summoned to discuss business so soon after the meal.

"My dear James, neither you nor Miss Scott are hired to socialize on my time, while I sit idly by awaiting your presence. Now, if you wish to continue in my employ, I suggest that you and I remove ourselves to the library. Miss Scott may go into the green parlor and entertain herself on the piano or with a good book until I have finished. If the two of you then wish to rendezvous, it will be your privilege and of no interest to me whatsoever."

James's face had gone white at this cutting speech. Raines, fearing a confrontation and not wishing to be the cause of any trouble, spoke up quickly. "I appreciate the invitation, but I must retire to my room and read about the coins of the Roman age, since that is where I will be starting tomorrow. Goodnight." She turned on her heel and left both men staring after her. It amused her to see how her friendship with James annoyed him. Tomorrow she'd make an effort to be with James alone.

But the following morning she learned that James had left earlier for London and her disappointment was acute. She walked to the library to see if he had remembered to get her supply list. Rushing down the empty hall, she dashed into the study and seeing it unoccupied, walked straight to the desk where she had laid her list. There it rested, just as she had placed it the afternoon before.

Stamping her foot she muttered, "Drat it! He forgot!"

"What has you perturbed so early in the morning, Miss Scott?"

Whirling, Raines faced Lord Kemp, who had entered the library from the vault. His entrance had been so quiet that she had not heard his approach. "Must you always slip up behind people and spy on them?" she retorted, angry that he had startled her.

He seemed unoffended by her sharp tongue, instead a hint of amusement crossed his handsome face. "Are you always so disagreeable early in the morning, or is there extra cause for your bad temper today?"

"James has left for London and . . ."

"My! My! I didn't know that his departure would upset you so greatly. You must have taken quite a liking to him in the few hours he was here," he teased, still grinning sardonically.

"Lord Kemp, I know you find this difficult to believe, but my mind has better matters to occupy itself with than some sweetheart or lover. I am not some lightheaded girl with her first crush."

"You could have fooled me last evening the way you flirted and fussed over him. I thought you'd burst into tears when I stopped your little walk in the garden."

"Why you . . . you insufferable! . . ." Raines stammered. She snatched up the ink well to hurl at him and a strong hand seized her wrist in a vise-like grip.

He stopped her other hand in mid-air and pinned it behind her, moving closer so that their bodies almost touched. He stared down at her through cold black eyes and Raines thought her breath would stop. She

73

gazed into the deep recesses of his eyes and, annoyed at the stirring she felt within her body, she glared and turned away her face. "Ah, Miss Scott, why do you not honor me with the same adoring expression that you bestowed upon James last night? Perhaps you are angry because you missed your little stroll, and no doubt a moonlight embrace. I apologize that I am but a poor substitute."

Raines's furious cry was stifled as his lips crushed hers in a hard kiss. He moved closer, pressing her body tight in his embrace. She grew angry at herself for her body's betrayal as it responded to his caress. Never had she been kissed this way before and instead of feeling repulsed, she found her nerves tingling with a sensation quite new to her. Just as suddenly as his lips had touched hers, he abruptly broke away and held her from him, studying her expression.

Color rose to her cheeks. She averted her eyes, but not before sensing that he was as shaken by the kiss as she. The mocking smile crossed his face again. "Well, Miss Scott? Was I a satisfactory substitute for James?"

She glared at him without speaking. Wisely he removed the inkwell from her fist and placed it out of her reach before finally setting her free.

Raines moved skillfully from within his grasp and turned to face him. Her face burned with shame and she was frightened at what she had to say, yet she had no choice. "Lord Kemp, I'm afraid that I must resign!"

"Resign? Was my kiss so terrible?" he teased. "Perhaps I should try again."

He chuckled as she backed hastily away from him.

"Please do not make light of this, sir! I am a lady, alone, and do not intend to find myself compromised." She held her head proudly erect. "I may be in your employ as a coin curator, but I have no intention of selling my virtue as well."

He stared at her in wonder. "Good Lord, I believe you are serious about leaving."

"Of course I'm serious. I cannot continue working for an employer who—who is bent on seducing me!"

Kemp seemed struck by her words. "Will you go back and marry the widower with the many children?" he inquired.

She shook her head, and still angry, checked her retort, tempering it instead to, "I will travel back to London and find other employment." Even while speaking her mind raced on to her dwindling supply of funds. "If all else fails, then I suppose I can accept Mr. Rockhill's offer."

"Well, we certainly can't have that," Kemp said gravely. "If you are going to marry just anybody who will provide you with a comfortable home, then I suppose you might as well marry me."

Raines stared at him in stunned silence. "My lord, I don't think I could have heard you correctly."

"I was not aware that you suffered from a hearing deficiency, Miss Scott," he snapped irritably. "I said that if you are planning to marry for security, and not love, then you might as well marry me."

"Marry you?"

"My dear Miss Scott," he said annoyed at the expression of horror on Raines's face. "Surely the idea is not so repulsive as that."

"But you scarcely know me and have appeared

from all outward signs to find me unattractive and . . . and unsatisfactory in every way." Raines struggled for words to explain the situation. "Why . . . why there has been no courtship."

"Really, Miss Scott! Scarcely five minutes ago you gave me to understand that you were over that girlish romantic nonsense. Have I misunderstood you?" He watched her closely.

"I hardly think the two things are the same, sir." She paced over to the sofa as she tried to think where this conversation was leading. Her head swirled from the mere shock of it.

Before she could say more, Watson knocked on the door and rushed in the room. Clearly agitated, he exclaimed, "Lord Adam, 'tis your mother—She has been taken ill. You must come at once!"

"Good heavens, Watson! Send Roland for Doctor Reilly!" Lord Kemp raced from the room and took the stairs, two at a time. Raines followed close behind, anxious to see if she could be of help.

It was over an hour before Roland returned with the doctor following behind in his trap. When the doctor entered the room he ordered everyone other than Nurse Carlton out. Raines walked to her own quarters to await news. She wanted time to think of all that had happened to her since morning. She saw Lord Kemp go into the library and knew he would wait there for the doctor's opinion.

Being too nervous to work, she tried to read a book which she had brought with her. It dealt with the identification and values of ancient Roman coins and was a period she knew she needed to review. Drawing her chaise lounge nearer the fire, Raines tried to rest and concentrate on the text, but her conversation with Lord Kemp continued to enter her thoughts. Finally she flung down the book and let her thoughts wander to Lord Kemp. Why had he proposed and was he serious? How would she have answered had Watson not interrupted? Why would a man of his wealth want to marry a girl he did not love, when there must be dozens of young debutantes who would welcome the opportunity to merge their wealth with the Kemp fortune? He was young, handsome and Raines felt he could be kind and charming when he chose to be. None of the events made the slightest sense to her. She sat quietly thinking of how different her life would be if she agreed to marry him.

About thirty minutes later a soft knock sounded on her door. It startled Raines out of her thoughts and she rushed to answer it.

A maid said quietly, "Lord Kemp instructed me to inform you that the doctor says his mother suffered a severe heart attack, but she is resting comfortably. He thought you would wish to know."

"Thank heaven she is living! I appreciate Lord Kemp thinking to tell me. Did his lordship say there was anything I could do to help?"

"No, ma'am. The doctor said that Lady Kemp must have complete rest." The maid eyed her, as though trying to decide if she should say more.

"Is there anything else I should know?"

Twisting her hands nervously, the girl shook her head. "No, ma'am. 'Cepting the doctor don't think madam will make it this time. He told Lord Kemp that her heart was damaged bad."

"I'm sorry to hear that. However, Lady Kemp

recovered before and she may rally again."

Each day, Raines worked quietly in the library. She did not see Lord Kemp, other than at meals, and then he was often silent. A daily check on Lady Kemp's health revealed that the elderly woman was failing rapidly. There had not been the hoped-for turn for the better as in the past.

Lord Kemp made no further mention of his proposal, and Raines had ceased to think of it. Instead, she had dismissed it as a joke on his part, although it was a strange one.

One day, while checking the calendar, Raines was surprised to discover that she had been at Balfour only a month. Her daily schedule had become so routine that it seemed she had been here for years. It was a quiet household and no one interfered with her work. Since Lord Kemp avoided her now, she had not brought up the discussion of her resignation again.

So the day Watson came into the library where Raines sat bent over a small pile of Egyptian coins, she scarcely looked up from her work.

"Miss Scott, I thought you should know Lady Kemp has just died," he said in a quiet, somber voice.

Jumping up from the chair, Raines cried in a shocked voice, "Oh, I am so sorry! Does Lord Kemp know?"

"A stable boy has ridden into town to fetch him."

During the days which followed Lady Kemp's death, Raines found herself assuming many of the roles of hostess to the visitors who came to pay their respects. Along with Lord Kemp, family friends, and

78

the staff of Balfour, she attended the quiet services which were held in a small stone chapel on Balfour grounds. Lady Kemp was laid to rest in the family cemetery located in the churchyard.

It was while Raines stood listening to the vicar's droning voice as he read the scriptures that her eyes strayed to the tombstones. Idly she read the names and inscriptions on those nearest her. It was easy to determine which was Lord Kemp's father, his grandfather and so on; even back to the fourteen-hundreds. Only half aware of the vicar's voice now, Raines scanned the area for Lord Kemp's wife's grave. She knew it must be the newest marker in the graveyard, yet she couldn't find it. She surreptitiously edged to one side to read the names on the granite stones which had been out of her view. At last she was satisfied. There was no stone for Alexandra Kemp. She was not buried at Balfour!

Raines heard the vicar giving the benediction and feeling guilty at her lapse of attention, bowed her head to pray, the puzzle of Alexandra Kemp, for the moment, forgotten.

After the services were over and the last guest had departed, Raines went to her room to rest. It was then that she had the first opportunity to wonder what would happen to her now. She realized the cataloguing of the coins had to be completed quickly, because it was not proper for her to remain in this residence unchaperoned.

The following morning Raines arrived downstairs early, prepared to begin work again. Walking quietly, she entered the library which had been hers exclusively since the day she and Lord Kemp had had their

79

discussion nearly six weeks earlier. But today the room was not empty. Standing by the window, gazing out over the estate, deep in thought, was Lord Kemp.

"Excuse me," Raines said. "I'm sorry, I didn't expect anyone to be in here." She turned to leave, but Lord Kemp swung around to face her.

"Come in, Miss Scott. I was waiting for you, since I knew it was your habit to come here first thing each morning." He moved over to the sofa and gestured for her to sit across from him. "We have a conversation to finish, and I think you should sit for our discussion."

Not arguing, she moved swiftly to the chair he indicated and sat down. "What do you wish to discuss? I have plans to complete the coin inventory as quickly as possible, if that is what is troubling you, sir."

"I believe we were discussing marriage the last time we were in here together, Miss Scott. Surely you have not forgotten so soon?" He looked tired, yet his voice held a trace of irritation which surprised Raines.

"I thought that subject was closed."

"Indeed not. It merely had to be postponed. You see, Miss Scott, I am aware of the fact that a young lady of your upbringing cannot stay unchaperoned in this house with me. So to protect your reputation we must come to a decision today." He studied her face intently. "I have realized for some time that my mother could not get well, and I knew that preparations had to be made in the event of her death." He spoke in a low, business-like tone. "Here is what I propose. I have business to attend to in London and can go and live at my town house until you finish the inventory. I don't see how even a clergyman could object to a plan of that nature, do you?"

She felt a sudden twinge of disappointment at being left alone at Balfour. The place was huge and she knew she would get frightfully lonely, yet his plan was the only sensible one. "No, I don't think anyone could object to that arrangement, sir."

"It troubles me to have to make these plans but there are always those who wish to fabricate tales for the sake of gossip, and London is full of such idle people." He paced the floor as he talked as if he had forgotten her presence.

Suddenly he stopped in mid-stride and turned to face her. "Miss Scott, I have not been completely honest with you."

"How so, Lord Kemp?"

"It is imperative that I marry within the year, and I have known this for several weeks. My father left such a stipulation in his will. You see, I was somewhat of a rake in my youth, and he was determined to see me married to a woman of excellent reputation before his estate was turned over to me. This requirement was thus placed in his will. He gave me until my thirty-fifth birthday to accomplish this feat. During my youth I wed the Lady Alexandra Rafferty, but she died unexpectedly." His face hardened and his jaw seemed to tighten in anger and grief. He waved aside this fact by saying, "The details of the marriage are unimportant. The point I'm trying to make is that I thought this marriage fulfilled my part of the bargain. On James MacBain's last visit he informed me that a distant cousin was challenging this stipulation, since the will read that I must be involved in a solvent marriage. So James advised me to marry again immediately. This would put an end to any efforts on my relatives' part and would avoid the possibility of a long and expensive court case." He watched Raines closely as he said the next words, "There are things in my past that I'd prefer to remain buried and not be dragged out for public airing." He drew a deep breath and sighed, then of a sudden his mood changed and he grinned rakishly. "Miss Scott, again I am asking you to marry me."

Raines had listened quietly, and now she said, "But you don't love me. Would you not prefer to marry someone for whom you cared deeply?"

"Absolutely not!" he thundered. "My next marriage will be a purely legal arrangement. All I ask of you is that you remain respectable, maintain the houses, and in return you may spend your time as you please. I will furnish you with a large household allowance . . ."

Blushing, Raines stammered, "Wh . . . what of the other obligations of marriage, sir? In a loveless contract I . . . I don't see how I can agree to . . . to . . ." Her eyes centered on the carpet and she felt the heat of a blush creeping into her cheeks.

"You have my word that the marriage need not be consummated longer than to produce an heir, if that is what you desire." He spoke easily, as though this was of no importance to him.

She watched his face closely. "Lord Kemp, what of other heirs to your title? I'm not saying I agree to this absurd arrangement, but I do think you should take into consideration several heirs before you enter into such a plan."

He nodded. "I have given that some thought.

82

Perhaps after we have agreed to this arrangement, we should specify a number of children to be born from the marriage. Do you think three would be a sufficient number? That is, if one should be a male child in good health."

Raines could not believe they were discussing marriage and a future together in such a cold and calculated manner. Suddenly she stood and walked to the bookcase, trying to understand what was happening. Had he loved his wife so dearly that her death had killed all feeling in him? Hesitantly she turned and said, "I'm sorry, sir, but I think the offer is out of the . . ."

A knock on the door interrupted her and Lord Kemp ordered the butler to enter.

"I am sorry to interrupt, sir, but there is a messenger here with a note for Miss Scott. I thought she should have it immediately." He handed the envelope to her.

Quickly she read the message and gasped. She turned to Watson and said, "Thank you. There will not be a reply for the messenger."

Watson bowed and departed while Kemp stood waiting for her to explain. Seeing how startled she had been, he inquired in a sympathetic tone, "It isn't bad news, is it Miss Scott?"

She had grown quite pale and agitated. Turning to face him, her eyes filled with tears, she said, "Uncle Percival has heard of your mother's death and has ordered me to be packed at once. He is coming to fetch me back to Rosewood Manor. He says that he has investigated your reputation and that your character is besmirched. And he does not intend for me to spend one more night unchaperoned and under the same roof as you."

Lord Kemp's face burst into a wide grin and he threw back his head and roared with laughter. "I never thought the day would come when my reputation as a black sheep would be an asset, but today it has proved such. Well, Miss Scott, which shall it be, the dastardly Lord Kemp or the good widower Rockhill? It seems that you have little time to decide, because, if I'm not mistaken, that is your uncle's carriage making the bend. The messenger must have stopped at the local tavern and tarried too long."

Raines rushed across the room to stare out the window to where Kemp gestured. She gave a small cry of distress and her hand went to her mouth. "It is my uncle! Oh, dear! And I've no time to think of an alternate plan."

The first hint of sympathy sounded in his voice. "My dear, if the choice is so distasteful to you, can't you refuse to go with him?"

"No! You don't understand! I'm not of age yet, and if my uncle chooses to have me returned, and he surely would, then the law would see that I went home with him." She watched the carriage pull up out front. Her mind was filled with reservations, but she did not think she could stand to return to Rosewood Manor, and marriage to the widower forced an involuntary shudder to shake her body. At least with Lord Kemp she could bargain for her rights. She turned to face him and cried, "You win! I accept your offer of marriage."

His lordship, who seemed to be enjoying her predicament, said, "Splendid! I think you have made a wise choice. Just leave everything to me, and I will explain to your uncle. We can get his blessings."

They did not speak again and remained silent until the loud boom of her uncle's voice echoed down the hall. "Show me to my niece! And if that scoundrel has touched her, he'll answer to me!"

Rushing to the door, Raines nervously smoothed her skirt and pressed her hands tightly to her sides. She ran to kiss his cheek and said, "Uncle Percival! It is such a surprise to see you! Did you have a pleasant trip?" Her voice filled with concern and sweetness to cover her nervousness. What if he should refuse to grant his permission?

"Let me look at you, child. Are you all right? I came as soon as the news reached us that the Marchioness had passed away. Your aunt insisted I come at once. Are you packed?"

"Please come over to the fire and sit down, Uncle Percival. I'll ring for tea and then answer your questions." She tried to remain calm, but his insinuations embarrassed her, and out of the corner of her eye, she saw that Lord Kemp appeared to be enjoying the entire scene. He actually had the gall to wink at her.

Kemp came forward and offered his hand. "Welcome to Balfour, Mr. Scott."

Remembering his manners and seeing that everything looked respectable—at least his niece was fully clothed—Percival said, "So sorry to hear of your mother's passing. Mrs. Scott and I offer our condolences." Then to Raines, he said, in a scolding voice, "My girl, why didn't you let us know?"

"Really, Uncle Percival, there was so much to do with the guests arriving hourly, and arrangements to be made that I didn't have time. I intended to write and inform you. I try to write every month. Doesn't Aunt Thea show you my letters?" She managed to keep the quality of innocence in her voice. In truth she had not written of Lady Kemp's death because she had feared just such a confrontation as this with her relative.

"Are you packed to leave? It is threatening to snow and I want to be away from this area before nightfall, since the nearest inn is past Stonehenge."

Lord Kemp spoke for the first time, "Please be my guest for the night. The weather looks far too stormy to return today and you must be tired from your trip."

The tea tray arrived and Raines poured, adding an extra lump of sugar to her uncle's cup, since she knew how partial he was to sweet tea. Handing him the cup, she explained, "I haven't packed for several reasons. First your messenger must have stopped along the way, because he only delivered your message minutes before you arrived."

"That scoundrel! I thought that rider who passed me in the drive looked familiar. I'll see that his wages are docked for tarrying." Relaxing, he sipped his tea and settled back by the fire, propping his feet on the ottoman to warm his toes. "Well, in that case it seems I'll have to accept Lord Kemp's offer of lodgings until the morn. You can be packed by then, can't you?"

"Sir, I think there is a matter which I need to broach with you at this time. You see, I have asked Miss Scott—Raines—to be my wife. We had intended to discuss this matter with you before my mother's untimely death. Out of respect I did not feel we should concern ourselves with such matters until after my mother's funeral. We were again discussing the situation when you arrived, weren't we, Raines?" She nodded without speaking, amused to hear the smooth way Lord Kemp was placating her uncle.

"Marry, you say?" A gleam of approval flickered in his eyes, as he contemplated this. It would surely enhance his position in the community to have his ward wed one of the wealthiest bucks in England.

"Yes, I have asked for dear Raines's hand in marriage, and she has graciously consented to be my wife. That is, with your approval of course."

Scott glanced at his niece for her confirmation and she added, "Uncle Percival, I hope you aren't angry with me for not telling you and Aunt Thea, but as Lord Kemp says, his mother's sudden illness and death made it improper for me to do so." She looked innocently at her uncle and asked, "Do you think Aunt Thea will forgive me for not telling her the good news first?"

Her uncle cleared his throat and it was easy to see that he was warming more to the idea each moment. He reached out and patted her hand. "Your aunt is a very understanding woman, and I know she will excuse you."

"Then we have your blessings?"

Looking pleased with himself, Percival swelled out his chest and said, "Indeed you do! I gave my three daughters nice weddings, and I will be most happy to represent my dear brother in consenting to this marriage of his only child, who is like another daughter to me." He held out his hand to shake Kemp's hand vigorously. "By jove! So my niece is going to be Lady Kemp. Congratulations, my man!"

Putting down his tea cup he turned to Raines and said, "We must be off early in the morn, so we can tell your aunt the good tidings, my dear."

Kemp cleared his throat. "I was hoping that Mrs. Scott might travel to Balfour for the wedding, and we could have a quiet service in my family's chapel. With my mother's recent passing, I feel in due respect we should bypass the usual parties and celebration."

"Whatever you say, my lord. When did you have in mind holding the ceremony?"

"I thought Friday would be a good day."

Raines sucked in her breath in shock, since that was only four days hence. Both men turned to face her. Blushing she covered her surprise by saying, "I . . . I . . . was thinking of the wedding dress and all the preparations which I need to make."

"Nonsense," said Lord Kemp, waving his hand in a gesture of dismissal. "My mother's wedding gown is packed away upstairs and I believe that it will be a perfect fit for you. If your uncle sends one of my servants to summon your aunt, I don't see why we can't have everything ready by Friday." He looked at Raines as though to explain, "We can't impose on your good uncle too long. I'm sure he has pressing business at home, and you can understand his reluctance to leave you here unchaperoned, now that our betrothal has been announced."

There was little Raines could say. She was committed to this marriage and what did it matter, since either date it would be merely a marriage of convenience? "You are right as usual. Friday will be fine, if you think we can get the arrangements made."

Kemp put his arm around her shoulders and drew

her to him in an embrace of approval. "Splendid! Now that it is settled, let's have a toast to our wedding."

Raines felt like she was in a dream. A short while before she had been worrying about money and her future; and now, here she was, planning on Friday to wed England's most notorious womanizer, Lord Adam Kemp.

Chapter 6

The remainder of the week was a whirl of preparations, and in the castle, servants scurried to bake in haste for the wedding. Since the house was in mourning, no outside guests were invited and the affair took on a hushed mysterious atmosphere. It was not as Raines had always envisioned her wedding week would be, and when alone, she shed from time to time, a tear of disappointment.

Aunt Thea had arrived on Thursday morning in a huff of joy mingled with anxiety, and was trailed by her three ugly daughters, who though acting sweetly toward Raines, failed to hide their resentment and jealousy over her coup. It was almost beyond their comprehension for their poor cousin to have fared so well even if his lordship did have a slightly tarnished reputation. The man had gone a bit wild with the ladies after the death of his wife and there'd been vague rumors of a scandal surrounding that event.

Margaret, Ellen, and Glenda were seated in Raines's bedroom as Thea and the seamstress studied the stylish gown which Raines wore. The dress was of magnificent heavy satin with an inset of delicate French lace around the neck and on the cuffs of the long satin buttoned sleeves. The candlelight shade of the aged satin gave it a mellow hue which looked breathtaking on Raines with her fair coloring.

Touching the dress at the waist, Mrs. Scott instructed the seamstress. "Nip it in here to accent Raines's small waist, and I think it should be shortened about a fourth of an inch. Otherwise, everything seems to fit perfectly." Looking at Raines she commented, "You certainly are a lucky girl to have this exquisite gown to wear. It is such a shame that his lordship is in mourning and we can't invite his friends and ours. Many of London's finest *ton* may feel slighted at not receiving an invitation." She fussed with the train of the dress.

"Aunt Thea, I'm certain everyone will understand the need for this to be a quiet wedding, with Lord Kemp's mother just put to rest last week."

"Still, you'd think that his lordship would have postponed the wedding for a few months, so that all could have been invited," she said in a miffed voice.

"Aunt Thea, he doesn't have a relative to be hostess and manage the household during that time. This is the most practical and logical solution." Raines restrained the irritation in her voice, although it took strength of will to do so.

Glenda, the plump cousin, licked the chocolate

bonbon off her finger. She replaced the lid on the box of delicacies and studied her fingers before she said, "Raines, what happened to the first Lady Kemp? Isn't there some scandal surrounding her?"

"I really don't know. It has not interested me enough to inquire, but if you care to ask Lord Kemp, I'm positive he would enlighten you," said Raines sweetly while anger rose in her. Even if she did not love her future husband, she felt an obligation to be loyal to him and not enter into this idle gossip. Turning her attention to the seamstress she asked, "Are you ready for me to take off the gown? I've stood at attention for hours and my shoulders ache from having to remain so still."

The seamstress stopped her pinning. Raines quickly slipped from the dress and into a warm wool robe. She shooed her family out of the room and told them she planned to rest for a few hours, since she had risen at early dawn. The main reason she did this was to be alone and have time to think about what she had gotten herself into.

They reluctantly left, each under protest, and Raines walked over to the dresser and sat down to brush her hair. The girl who stared back at her in the mirror had large eyes which looked tired and frightened. Putting down her hairbrush, Raines thought, This is nonsense! I shan't behave like this the day before my wedding. Why, I'm suffering from typical bridal jitters. The idea made her laugh and instantly her face was transformed into a radiant, beautiful one.

There was a light tap on her door and at first she thought she had imagined it, but when she called for the person to enter, the door swung open and Lord Kemp walked into the room.

He wore a gray tweed suit with a white cravat which accented his dark piercing eyes. He scanned Raines's appearance with his cold probing glance, and she drew her robe tighter as she stood to greet him. A slow blush crept up her neck because she felt he was appraising her as his future bride.

"Your hair is long," he said in greeting, as though surprised.

"Yes, I wear it up because that is more fashionable."

"Was that unbecoming chignon more fashionable?" he teased.

Her cheeks flamed with anger. "I did not want to appear young or stylish, for I feared you would consider me too frivolous for the position."

"I saw through your charade instantly, but I let you go on since it seemed to please you." A grin slowly crossed his lips and his face was transformed into a devilish one. "Now that you are to become the future Marchioness of Balfour, I hope it won't be necessary for you to look quite so dowdy when we go out in public. That black dress deserves a place in a rag store."

Raines laughed merrily, but refused to tell him what she found amusing. Finally, wiping her eyes she asked, "You came to see me about something, Lord Kemp?"

He cleared his throat. "Don't you think we should begin calling each other by our first names now that we are betrothed, my dear Raines?" His voice carried a mocking note in it.

"Whatever you say . . . Adam." It was the first time she had allowed herself to think of the intimate relationship she had agreed to become involved in and a shyness crept into her voice.

He reached into his pocket and withdrew a velvet box. "The reason for my visit is to give you this. All Kemp brides have worn this necklace and earrings on their wedding day and I thought the tradition should be continued." He opened up the lid and held up a diamond and pearl necklace with matching earrings for her inspection.

"They are gorgeous," Raines cried, unable to remain aloof about the jewelry.

Taking out the necklace he instructed her to turn around, which she did without argument. Gently he draped the necklace around her neck and fastened the clasp while she watched in the mirror. He skillfully manipulated the catch and she felt an odd sensation as his fingers lightly brushed the nape of her neck.

Touching the necklace, she turned to tell him how much she loved it and realized that he stood only inches from her. Lifting her head she stared into his deep, black eyes which showed a hint of emotion for the first time. Slowly he put his hands on her shoulders and gently drew her to him. His head bent forward and his lips sought hers as she closed her eyes to accept his kiss. The warm touch of his lips sent a thrill through her body and a stirring began deep within her. The pressure on her mouth became more intense and frightened by her own feelings of desire, she put her palms on his chest to push him away.

Abruptly he freed her and stepped back. Gasping for breath, she quickly moved further from him and said, "Lord Kemp . . . Adam . . . I don't think it is proper for you to be in my room. I . . . I'm dressed so scantily." She faltered for words. "Su . . . suppose someone saw us?"

"Do you think the bride's reputation would be tarnished even if it was the bridegroom kissing her the day before her wedding?" he taunted, his eyebrows raised skeptically.

Still flushed from the kiss which had affected her more than she cared to admit, she said, "I . . . I understood this was to be a platonic marriage—at least, for the most part." Her eyes began to fill with tears of nervousness and frustration, because she did not want to fall under the spell of a man who so clearly would never love a woman again.

The smile on his face disappeared and his features hardened into a blank expression. "I'm sorry if my impulse of the moment offended you. I give you my word I will not force my affections upon you." His voice had a hard ring of anger to it.

Stung by his abrupt change in manner, Raines's own temper rose. "Indeed you must think you are marrying a wanton woman, if you think you can come into my bedroom at your pleasure and have your way with me. That was certainly not my understanding of

95

our bargain."

"Do you find my attentions so offensive?"

The conversation was out of hand and Raines felt she would be lost if he knew how deeply his kiss had stirred her. She did not intend to allow him to make love to her at leisure like some trollop. "This conversation has gone far enough. Please leave my bedroom at once, my lord."

For a minute Raines thought he was going to strike her, and she inwardly cowered, but outwardly she stood her ground. "If you don't leave I shall call my uncle immediately!"

At that he laughed sarcastically. "My dear Raines, if you think your uncle would make one move to halt this wedding, you are sadly mistaken. He cannot wait for his niece, of limited funds, to become the next Marchioness of Balfour."

"How cruel of you to say such things to me!" cried Raines. "You are no gentleman at all."

He looked as though she had struck him. "You are no lady either, my love. You enjoyed my embrace immensely and will enjoy love-making equally as much, or I'm very mistaken." His face broke into a wicked grin, which to Raines's consternation made him even more desirable.

"I will never become one of your women!" she hissed, her eyes blazing angrily.

"We'll see about that, my love." He turned to leave, then stopped, facing her once more. In a quiet voice he asked, "Do you still wish to go through with this wedding farce?"

Her heart almost stopped and she stared at him a few minutes before she dropped her gaze and replied softly, "Yes, I . . . I really don't have much choice."

He seemed to take pity on her then and moved closer, lifting her chin with his hand, forcing her to face him. She avoided his eyes by looking down at the floor. "Look at me, Raines," he ordered and waited until she obeyed. "I have never had to force my attentions upon any woman; there have always been those willing and anxious, so do not fret. If you find my advances offensive, then I will make a point of staying out of your sight."

She opened her mouth to protest and to admit she had quite enjoyed the kiss, but before she could speak, he whirled on his heel and left the room.

Staring at the closed door, a sudden realization seized her. She was falling in love with her husband to be, and they had agreed this was to be a loveless marriage!

Removing the necklace, she flung it into the velvet case and slammed the lid closed with frustrated anger. Finally giving vent to her nerves, she burst into uncontrollable tears and for some time cried. First she cried for her father, whom she missed so terribly, then she cried from anger and frustration. At last, when there were no more tears to be shed, she slept quietly in the exhausted sleep of one who has lost the will to fight any longer.

Surprisingly, upon waking she found her strength renewed and her plight less frightening. Dressing for dinner that night she vowed simply to forget about the childish dreams of love and settle into her role as Marchioness of Balfour with all the advantages the title brought with it. If Lord Kemp lived up to his part of the agreement and sought his pleasures elsewhere, then what did she have to fear? He would never discover that she loved him.

Chapter 7

The following morning the sun burst into view, and Raines slid from her bed and ran to the window. Drawing back the curtain, she gazed out on the snow covered landscape which stood decorated in sparkling white as though for her wedding. She whirled to greet Nettie who had entered and cried, "Just look at the world today, Nettie! This must be a sign that everything is going to be all right." Her voice had a light, gay note in it.

"I hope you know what you are doing, Miss Raines. This seems a whirlwind courtship to me," sniffed the maid. "I've known you all your life, and for the likes of me I can't believe you loved Lord Kemp last week." She began picking up Raines's scattered clothes and hanging them on hooks in the wardrobe.

"Love, Nettie? That's nonsense! You must admit that Lord Kemp is a better catch than Mr. Rockhill. So if I must marry one of the two, at least he is handsome and young."

"Humph! You forgot to add that he has the

99

reputation to put the devil to shame in the bargain."

"Now, you don't know that for a fact, do you? You know how servants love to gossip and I'll bet you're the worse of the lot," scolded Raines. Suddenly she didn't want anything to spoil this day for her. A girl did not get married but once, or at least she didn't intend to, so she wanted to make the most of the whole affair. "Don't tell me a word that you've heard. I'll wait and find out for myself what Lord Kemp is like."

Nettie stopped her work and looked at her young mistress carefully. "There's one good thing about this marriage. Neither of you may know what you are getting. I have a suspicion that you'll prove a handful for Lord Kemp."

"You don't think I'll become a shrew, do you?" teased Raines.

"I think you may snare Lord Kemp's heart and that's something I understand no woman has accomplished in the past. There's only one thing which brings down the mightiest of men."

"Pray continue, Nettie. You have waxed so poetic this morning that I dare not stop you," laughed Raines. "And what, may I ask, is this secret thing which will make Lord Kemp my slave?"

The maid studied her carefully for a few minutes, a small frown of disapproval showing on her face. Finally she said, "Love. You just be careful, Miss Raines, that it's the Marquis who falls in love with you and not the other way around. I wouldn't want to see so lovely a chit as you fall hopelessly under his spell. The talk is that he can be extremely cruel to women who fall at his feet."

"I will take my vows today, but only I will know which are just mere ritual, and which I intend to keep," retorted Raines, her curls bobbing as she nodded her head defiantly.

The seriousness of the mood was broken by the arrival of Aunt Thea and her girls. "Raines! Why are you idle when there are a thousand things to be done before the wedding?" Thea clucked in disapproval. Then she turned to Nettie and instructed, "Hurry woman! Send for the large portmanteau so we can pack it. Lord Kemp has instructed us to be at the church at noon. He wishes to depart for London while there is plenty of daylight."

Whirling, Raines asked, "He has what? How dare he change the time of my wedding without even consulting me!"

"Now, now, he instructed me in the hall, and since you were sleeping, I agreed to give you the message. It is bad luck for the bride and groom to see one another before the ceremony, so you must understand his reluctance to speak with you."

"That's foolish! It's my wedding and I certainly should have been consulted. I have a good notion not to be ready," snapped Raines, feeling the anger build within her.

Quickly her aunt put a reassuring hand on her shoulder and said, "Dear, you are merely suffering from bridal jitters. Now compose yourself and let's hurry. I sent for the hairdresser and she should be here in a minute. Once you are dressed, then the girls and I can slip into our dresses and everything will be

ready. There's no need for you to get in a dither."
Leading Raines to a stool, she said calmly, "Now sit
down here and let me brush your hair. I think it would
look nice up today, since the veil has a tiara of pearls,
don't you?"

Raines did not bother to answer, but she did follow
her aunt's instructions without argument. The room
became such a whirl of activity that time raced along
at an unbelievable pace.

However, at precisely twelve o'clock Raines entered
the chapel on her uncle's arm. Her aunt had fussed
over her until she now was the epitome of the glowing
bride. She moved serenely in her long satin gown, and
the veil hid her pale face. Obeying Lord Kemp's
instructions, the diamond and pearl necklace adorned
her neck, and the matching earrings glittered in the
candlelight of the chapel. Those who did not know
better thought Raines the most radiantly happy bride
to wed at Balfour. And, in spite of her irritation with
Lord Kemp for changing the hour of the wedding, and
the fact this was supposed to be a loveless marriage,
she felt the excitement of the moment and was filled
with an overwhelming joy. As she neared the altar
Lord Kemp turned to watch her approach and she saw
the flicker of approval in his eyes. He smiled at her
and his black eyes seemed to soften.

Adam stepped forward to stand beside her and the
vicar began the ceremony. Raines repeated her vows
in a soft, solemn tone and Adam added his in a strong
clear voice which rang through the chapel. Before she
realized it, he was slipping a wide gold band on her
finger, and she trembled slightly as their hands

touched. Then the ceremony was over and the minister told Adam he could kiss the bride. Expectantly she raised her face for the kiss, but Adam's lips brushed hers for only the faintest second, before he took her arm and firmly led her from the chapel.

She knew he was still angry about her rebuff the evening before, but now it was her turn to feel rejected. What little significance she must be to him, that he should choose to kiss her so coldly at their wedding.

He did not speak until they were outside the chapel. "Get dressed quickly," he said tersely. "We'll be leaving for London within the hour."

Raines glanced at him in surprise. "Aren't we going to dine with our guests before our departure?"

"Cook has been instructed to pack a hamper for us and the carriage will be around front shortly. I see no need for the nuptials to last any longer. Our guests can entertain themselves and—"

"It's rude for us to leave so quickly," Raines argued stubbornly.

"My dear, honeymooners are exempt from the formalities of the day. If we decided to shut ourselves in your bedchamber for the afternoon, no one would utter a word." His eyes mocked her.

"You wouldn't dare!" she gasped, blushing. How little she understood this demon she had married. One minute he was kind, and the next he taunted her unmercifully.

He grinned rakishly. "I might, if you are not at the carriage in a short time."

"You . . . you are insufferable!" she hissed, but

103

could not continue because she saw her aunt approaching.

"You were absolutely lovely, dear," gushed Aunt Thea. Taking her arm she said, "Come, tell Lord Kemp goodbye for a short while and let's get you dressed for your honeymoon. According to your husband's instructions, he wishes to leave within the hour. We do not want to keep the anxious bridegroom waiting, now do we?" She steered Raines toward the castle and away from the group that milled outside the chapel. Raines threw Adam a murderous look and moved away without a word. She heard him laugh as she swept down the path beside her aunt. The impossible man enjoyed making her angry!

Promptly at one o'clock Raines kissed her aunt and uncle goodbye and stepped into the carriage with her new husband. She was happy to know that Nettie had already left with several other household servants to make ready for them at the townhouse.

Raines deliberately sat opposite Adam rather than beside him, and she stared out the window and waved to the small group until they were out of sight.

"Now that you are married, you have certainly developed an interest in your family," said Lord Kemp.

"Did you wish me to jump into the carriage and ignore them, just as you seem to have done?" she snapped. There was no use thinking she could be civil to this man. He did not attempt to be gracious toward her.

"It is a long journey into London and I have no intention of sparring with you all the way, so if you will excuse me, I shall go to sleep," he announced. Stretching his legs leisurely, he forced her to sit sideways to avoid them resting against her own.

The carriage bounced over the rough terrain, and it was impossible for her to find a comfortable position without touching Lord Kemp's legs, and this angered her even more. There simply was no alternative but to lean back against the side of the carriage and rest her head on the leather padded wall. This meant that her thigh had to touch his, and she gritted her teeth angrily as she watched to see if he would make any response. But he appeared to be sound asleep, so she drew in her breath and tried to get some rest too.

She slept until her neck became so cramped that it got a crick in it, and she sat up to rub away the cramp. Glancing out the window she saw that the sun was low in the sky and it was getting late. She realized she had managed to sleep for several hours. The carriage had grown quite cold and she fumbled with the heavy lap robe, pulling it over her. Feeling guilty about not sharing the blanket with Lord Kemp, she tossed the corner carelessly over his legs.

To her distress he stirred and opened his eyes. "Are you cold, Raines?" he asked in greeting as she watched, wide-eyed.

"I was, but this blanket will help."

"Are you hungry? Would you care for some wine?" He opened the basket which rested on the floor and removed a bottle of wine and two glasses.

"A glass of wine sounds delightful. A cup of tea would be even better, but I hardly think that's possible out here." She tried to keep her voice cool and polite.

He carefully filled her glass and handed it to her. "There are cheese and sandwiches here also."

"Wine will be enough for now." She sipped the liquid and felt it begin to warm her body. Surprisingly she found she was very thirsty and soon held her glass to be refilled.

Beginning to relax, she stretched leisurely, trying to shift her weight on the poorly cushioned seat. "Lord Kemp . . ." she began.

"Don't you think it is time you called me Adam, my dear? After all, we are married," he said mockingly. "I find it most distasteful to be addressed as lord anything by my bride. For appearance, and to avoid the gossiping tongues in London, I suggest you try to respond a little more warmly toward me. There are those who would delight in discovering this marriage is a farce."

His words stung her, but warmed by the wine and irritated by the mixed feelings she had for him, she smiled sweetly and mimicked, "Adam, dear, may I please have another glass of wine?" She batted her eyelashes coquettishly as she held her goblet to be refilled.

He scowled and dropped the wine bottle, quickly moving beside her on the carriage seat. She watched in stunned silence as he lifted her onto his lap while drawing a pistol from his pocket. "What do you think you're doing?" she hissed in indignation. He drew her closer and she struggled to get off his lap.

Softly, he whispered in her ear, "The carriage is slowing. Can't you feel it? The road must be blocked and only highwaymen would close this route. Now keep quiet! And for God's sake, don't fight me, or we may wind up dead!"

The driver had been giving the horses free rein and they had been pulling at full gait, but now she realized the carriage was coming to a grueling halt. Voices called out to the driver who shouted back that this was Lord Kemp's vehicle, and the owner was traveling to London on his honeymoon. The latter brought boisterous laughter from the group.

"Tell his lordship to step out of the carriage," ordered a gruff voice.

"I . . . I . . . th . . . think his lordship is asleep," stammered the driver.

"So, he can't wait for the marriage bed to begin his frolicking," hooted the man. " 'Tis a pity to have to interrupt his sleep or is he doing something more enjoyable? If so, we'll be glad to finish the task for him won't we, Jock?"

Raines leaned against Adam, trying to stop her trembling. She blushed at the crude suggestions and innuendoes the highwaymen were making.

"Kiss me," ordered Adam, putting his hands inside her cloak and around her waist. She could feel the cold metal of the pistol pressed against her back.

She leaned closer and obeyed his command. Touching her lips to his she kissed him passionately, aware that her heart beat faster more from his touch than from fear. To her surprise he responded to her, by drawing her even closer and his lips moved sensuously and relentlessly on hers. She slid her arms around his neck and touched the soft velvet collar of his coat and

107

his long hair.

"Look at the little love birds," said the highway-man, sarcastically. "Jock! Guard the driver while I take over for his lordship!" ordered the man who opened the carriage door.

Raines felt the explosion before she heard it, and the next thing she knew, she was on the floor and the highwayman was lying slumped half in the carriage. Blood oozed from his head and he stared at her with glazed eyes. She scrambled to her feet and moved as far away from him as possible. Adam had flung open the other door and was outside the carriage in one graceful bound.

Then she heard the second man shout an oath and another shot rang out. Her hand flew to her mouth and she bit on her finger to prevent a scream escaping her throat. Peering cautiously out the window, she searched for Adam. Silently she prayed that he was not injured and that the bloodchilling scream had not come from him.

"Raines! Are you all right?" called Adam from the front of the carriage.

Instantly she was out of the carriage and running away from the dead robber. "Yes . . . yes. Are you hurt?" she cried, rushing to the front, trying to locate Adam's voice.

She found him safe, stooping over Toby, the driver, and relief swept through her. "Is he dead?" she clutched Adam's arm as she stared down at the unconscious man.

"No, he took the ball in his chest though, and there's a great deal of bleeding. Tear off a piece of your slip and give it to me. I'll try to stop this hemorrhaging." Adam lifted the driver's head and wiped his face again with his blood-stained handkerchief.

"Th . . . this is the best slip I own!" cried Raines, ever practical and shocked at such an extravagance. "Shouldn't I try to find something else? How about the table cloth in the picnic hamper?"

"Raines, for heaven's sake! I'll order you a dozen more slips. Here! Take my knife and cut me a bandage." Then seeing her strained, pale face, he added softly, "Darling, you aren't poor anymore. You can order a dozen new slips tomorrow. Now, hurry and do what I say." He handed her a pocket knife and she pulled up her dress and cut a long strip of her petticoat off, then handed it to him without further comment. She ran to the coach and dragged the wool blanket out, averting her eyes from the dead man who stared up at her with leering, sightless eyes.

Handing the blanket to Adam, she asked, "Why did the robber shoot poor Toby?"

"He's a good fellow and he wouldn't have been shot, but he tried to block the robber's aim as I stepped from the carriage." He gently wrapped the blanket around the coachman, who still looked gravely ill to Raines, regardless of what Adam said.

"I hate to do this to you, but I'm afraid you will have to nurse Toby in the carriage while I drive the horses. Do you mind?"

"Of course not—I'll look after him." Then her eyes rested on the second dead highwayman. "What about these two? They won't have to be in there too, will

109

they?" She wasn't sure how she'd hold up, if this proved to be the case.

"No, I'll drag that one out of the carriage and leave both the devils here for the constable. When we reach London I'll send for the constable and explain everything to him." He rose and turned to face her, putting his hands on her arms. "Now, wait here until I get him out of the carriage, and we'll get Toby inside."

"Nonsense! I'll help you."

His grip tightened on her arm. "Raines, do what I tell you," he instructed sharply.

Tears pricked Raines's lids and she blinked to hold them back until she turned away from his view. She had only wanted to help and it was hateful of him to be so curt with her. Wiping away the tears which now coursed down her cheeks, she knelt to check on Toby. His color resembled the gray soil of the hinterlands, and she feared he would die before they reached London. Gently she adjusted the blanket, pulling it closer around his neck.

She heard Adam's footsteps returning, but she did not look up from her patient. There was no need giving him the satisfaction of knowing that his words had hurt her.

Adam lifted her to her feet and turned her to face him. Removing his handkerchief from his pocket, he wiped her tears, and when she tried to protest, he lifted her chin, forcing her to face him. "I didn't intend to be harsh with you a moment ago, but that simply wasn't a job for you to take part in doing. You've been a brave girl through this whole affair, and I shouldn't have been so abrupt." It was the closest

110

he'd ever come to an apology and Raines nodded in understanding.

He drew her to him and his face was close to hers. She thought he was about to kiss her and her heart raced rapidly. It would be so easy to fall prey to his charm, and Raines knew that to love him and not be loved in return would make her plight even more painful. Skillfully she pulled away from him and said, "Let's get poor Toby to the doctor quickly. He looks terrible."

Adam lifted the unconscious driver into his arms and carried him to the carriage. The move caused Toby's wound to bleed profusely again and Adam turned to Raines. "Take off what's left of your petticoat and use it to make a tourniquet. The gash is at a difficult place to slow the flow of blood, but do the best you can."

Looking around, Raines blushed. "Where shall I go to undress?"

Adam sighed deeply, then grinned a rakish grin. "Dear, you will be much safer undressing here before me than behind a boulder where more highwaymen might blunder upon you. Now, do as I say and forget your modesty." As an afterthought, he added, "My dear Raines, I am your husband. Now, quickly! Hand me your cloak and I'll hold it in front of you, so that should anyone come round the bend, you'll be hid from view."

Turning crimson with embarrassment, Raines mumbled, "You will have to help me with the buttons, since this dress fastens in the back." She turned to face the carriage and did not offer any other

111

comment. Skillfully, he unfastened her gown and she marvelled at his skill and speed, for she was certain he had had much practice. Once the gown was unfastened, he held the cloak around her, and she hurriedly slipped out of her dress and then the petticoat. Glancing around nervously, she gasped, "Aren't you even going to turn your head?"

"No," he said curtly, staring at her appreciatively. Blood rushed to her face and she clenched her teeth together to avoid a retort.

Quickly she flung the slip in the carriage and snatched up her dress and slipped it over her shoulders. Without a word, he hooked her bodice and dropped the cloak back around her shoulders. By now she was trembling from the cold, .and her teeth chattered as she snapped, "You are the lowest, most despicable . . ."

He moved closer and interrupted her by saying in a calm voice, "Save your anger for later. Toby needs your attention." Even as he ordered her to do his bidding, he seemed to rally in her anger. Raines felt helpless to understand this man she was now wed to, for better or worse.

She studied him, her face aflame with indignation. "A gentleman would have turned his head," she retorted.

"I would show you once and for all that I'm no gentleman, if poor Toby wasn't bleeding his last drop." His eyes twinkled with mischief. "Now be a good girl and sit in the back and nurse him until we get to London. I'll drive the horses for all they are worth. I apologize for having to force such an arduous task upon you, but someone must stay with him and try to stop the bleeding."

She felt faint, yet held her chin high and said, "I'll do the best I can for him; however, the wound looks ghastly, so please hurry." He took her arm and aided her in stepping up into the carriage.

Pulling a flask from a small compartment inside the carriage, he instructed, "If Toby regains consciousness, give him as much of this as he will drink. We should be there within a few hours if all goes well."

She grasped the bottle and nodded.

Soon the horses were galloping full speed toward London, while Raines sat watching Toby and thinking of this man she had just married. It amazed her how little she knew about him, yet she felt a growing interest in him with each passing moment. If all she had heard rumored was true, and she had little doubt to the contrary, then she must guard her heart against him. From all reports, he romanced and discarded women like fast horses or outmoded clothing.

They traveled along without further interruption for several hours. It grew dark in the carriage, making it difficult for Raines to see the wounded man. Occasionally, when the carriage hit a pothole in the road, he groaned in his sleep; however, when she called his name, he did not respond.

And, so it was that Raines Scott Kemp, Marchioness of Balfour, entered London town on her wedding night, alone in a carriage with an unconscious servant. The entire episode would have struck her as humorous if the man whose head she cradled in her lap did not hover so near death. Silently she prayed that the events on which her marriage had begun were not an omen of things to come.

By the time the lights of London came into view, Raines saw that her petticoat was soaked through with the driver's blood. Relief flooded her body as she realized that they would soon reach the townhouse where skillful servants could take over her task.

The carriage slowed, then swung in between iron posts and came to rest in a lighted courtyard. Before Adam jumped down from the driver's perch, he was shouting instructions. The door of the carriage flew open and a footman was assisting Raines out of the vehicle in seconds after the carriage halted.

Adam's voice rang out in the night as he ordered a young servant to fetch the doctor, while two strong servants lifted the wounded Toby gently from the trap. Raines heard Adam instructing Nettie to take her inside, and she followed without comment, glad to have the comforting support of her trusted family servant. She was too exhausted to say anything to Adam, and he seemed too occupied to notice her departure. Her mind was numb with fatigue, and she followed obediently.

She scarcely noticed the design of the tall, brick three-storied house which she entered. All she remembered was that the courtyard was cobbled and an ornamental fence surrounded the property. It looked like one of a series of townhouses lining Marlborough Street. She thought she had passed this section of Kensington before with her father when they had gone to the affluent shopping area of Knightsbridge.

Following Nettie, she entered a large foyer where a

114

chandelier with its branches holding at least a hundred candles, lit the hall. The flooring was polished parquet and a Persian rug covered the center of the area. Quietly Raines trailed behind Nettie, barely glancing at the rooms they passed on their trip down the long hall.

Nettie kept up a steady stream of chatter, glancing anxiously at Raines, as they climbed the stairs to the second floor and moved on to the master bedroom.

"I've lit the fire and tried to make everything comfy for you," said Nettie, standing back for Raines to enter the huge bedroom.

"I want to warm my hands and feet," said Raines, rubbing her hands together. "I feel like a block of ice." She walked over to a green chair which was drawn near the fireplace and sank into it. "I have never been so frightened in my life. The shock didn't hit me until we arrived here and I realized we were safe."

"Would you like some tea or chocolate?" asked Nettie, poking the fire, causing sparks to fly at an alarming rate.

"Nettie, for heaven's sake stop punching up the fire or you'll burn the place down. We're here and everyone is safe, so there's nothing to be alarmed over, unless it's the possibility of you setting fire to the house." Then more seriously she added, "I need a warm bath and a hot cup of chocolate, then . . ." She blushed. Then what, she wondered. What would Adam expect of her?

Nettie scurried off to instruct the upstairs maid to bring hot water while she prepared the chocolate.

115

Alone, Raines stood and moved around the room inspecting its contents to occupy her mind. The far corner held a huge walnut bed with a massive tapestry tester and a satin, down-filled comforter. It looked so inviting that Raines would have fallen into it instantly, had she not feared Lord Kemp would arrive and think she was anxious to begin her duties as a wife.

It was late and she hoped he would stay with Toby until they had some word from the doctor. Perhaps she could bathe and be in bed before he came. She could pretend to be asleep and thus postpone an encounter for the time being.

Satisfied with her scheme, she moved back to the fire to await her warm chocolate and bath, ever conscious for any sound of approaching footsteps.

Chapter 8

Upon waking the following morning Raines glanced over in the huge bed to see if Adam had arrived during the night. To her surprise his side was just as it had been the night before. A hint of irritation coursed through her. She couldn't decide if she was relieved or insulted that he had not shown up.

Nettie bustled around the room fixing her breakfast tray and fluffing the pillows. She made no comment about the unslept-in bridal bed. Raines relaxed, knowing Nettie would not pry and that the matter would not be discussed downstairs over morning tea.

It had been the same last evening when Raines had undressed for her bath. Quickly she had explained that her petticoat had had to be used for bandages. While Nettie had stood stonefaced, without a flutter of her eyebrows, Raines had stepped out of her traveling dress. It had been most comical to watch Nettie's stoic expression.

"How is Toby this morning?" she inquired as she placed her cup back on the breakfast tray. Perhaps Adam had stayed the night with him, if his condition was critical.

"He is awake this morning and filled with details of his heroism," said Nettie with scorn in her voice. "Ye'd think the man rescued you himself, and single handed in the bargain," sniffed the maid.

Laughing, Raines said, "Well, he certainly did contribute his part. To be honest, Nettie, I was so frightened I don't know exactly what did happen. All I remember is that Adam shot one highwayman and then jumped out of the carriage and ran to Toby's aid."

"Toby claims that while Lord Kemp reloaded his pistol, he fired at the second robber, thus drawing the highwayman's attention. That's when the ball hit him and he fell to the ground. After that he says the master finished off the culprit for him."

"What about his wounds?"

"The doctor said that he got a ball through the chest and, although he bled like a stuck pig, and ruined your good dress, it was a better injury than had the ball lodged in him. It seems that it went straight through him." She moved to pour Raines another cup of tea. "The doctor said that Toby lost a lot of blood, and once we feed him plenty of broth he'll be as good as new again."

"That's good news anyhow. Did someone summon the constable last night?"

"Yes, after the doctor left, Lord Kemp went back to the scene with the sheriff to show him where to find the culprits' bodies." She dropped her gaze and busied herself with straightening the dresser as she continued, "They left around two last night and the master hasn't come home yet this morning."

118

Raines blushed slightly, but continued eating without further comment. So at least she knew Adam had not slept in the townhouse last evening. She wondered where he had stayed.

When breakfast was out of the way, she began the exploration of her new home and was delighted with everything she saw. There were a few changes she wanted to make in the front parlor, and perhaps she would have several large chairs replaced, otherwise she thought the residence most tastefully decorated.

It was early afternoon before she finally heard a carriage arrive and saw Adam stroll up the front steps and into the hall. He carried a large package in his arms and she watched him shake his head when the butler tried to take it from him. In a loud voice which carried into her sitting room, he asked Watson where the new mistress could be found. Hurriedly she checked her appearance in the mirror and straightened the blue ribbon she had tied back her hair with. When he entered the room she went to meet him.

"Good afternoon," she said in greeting, smiling as he moved toward her. He was attired in a black suit with Hessian boots and looked every inch the handsome lord of the manor as his eyes swept over her.

Bowing, he offered her a huge white box, saying, "This is for you."

Surprise mixed with delight crossed Raines's face and she accepted the package. Moving to the sofa, she sat down and began opening the gift, while he stood by the fireplace and watched her silently.

Drawing back the tissue paper, she saw what was inside and laughed. Running her finger over the beautifully embroidered silk petticoats and their soft

119

French lace on the bodices and hems, she blushed. It was such a personal gift and it recalled to her her embarrassment of the afternoon before. "Thank you. These are lovely." For the first time since his entry into the room she looked directly at his face, and saw the look of amusement and pleasure in his eyes.

"Am I forgiven for making you tear up your other one yesterday?" Teasingly he continued, "I was not sure that I would ever be forgiven. You gave me such a murderous look after I told you to make bandages out of it."

"You must admit it is most unconventional to ask a lady to remove her undergarments." Her face dimpled as she tried to remain indignant, but she couldn't prevent an impish grin.

"Run upstairs and put on one of your new petticoats and get your cloak. We have more shopping to do this afternoon. It would never do for all of London to see my bride looking like a destitute relative. We're off to the dressmakers to order you some new dresses, my dear."

Delighted, Raines rushed to obey and within minutes they were off to the millinery and dressmaker's shop to begin a long and exhausting afternoon of shopping.

Adam helped Raines select yards and yards of fabric, and if she hesitated because of cost, he would insist upon her buying it.

Madam Raymor, the dressmaker, bustled around excitedly, unable to suppress her delight at such customers. A young assistant cut swatches of material and matched it with a pattern while the madam measured Raines's tiny waist and height.

"Lady Kemp has such magnificent coloring," cooed the designer. "My new pastels from Paris will be excellent for her. *Oui!* Yes, we must make her a white brocade for the duke's ball. You will be going, won't you?" she asked Raines who immediately turned to Adam for an answer.

"My invitation arrived before I announced my engagement to Miss Scott, but I'm certain one will arrive for her when the news travels to the castle," replied Adam, who lounged in a chair with his legs crossed, perfectly at ease in this world of women. "By all means make the white. I think it will look splendid with the Kemp diamonds she will wear that night."

"Then we must cut the decolletage low to accent the jewels," purred the seamstress while Raines stood mutely listening as the two discussed her.

When at last the final bolt of material had been draped and measured to Madam Raymor's satisfaction, Adam stood to leave. Taking Raines's hand in his, he helped her down from the model's bench. "Deliver the first dresses to my townhouse by Wednesday," he instructed.

"Oh, but Lord Kemp, that's an impossibility," said the little French woman, shaking her head.

"Hire extra help, if you want this commission," he ordered, taking Raines's arm and leading her to the door.

"*Oui,*" sighed the seamstress, "but not a word of this to the other ladies, or they'll have my head for putting your bride ahead. Some have been clamoring for their gowns for weeks now."

After they were out of hearing, Raines, who still had not turned loose of his hand, squeezed it excitedly and exclaimed unselfconsciously, "I have never owned so many dresses in my entire life! My head is whirling. Oh, Adam! Thank you for being so generous!" She looked into his eyes and smiled, trying to show him that she wanted to call a truce on their aloofness with each other.

At first his expression warmed and he seemed genuinely pleased, then suddenly the smile faded and in a cool tone he replied, "Think nothing of it, Raines. The clothes were a necessity. I could not let my society see Lady Kemp dressed like a pauper."

She immediately withdrew her hand from his, turning to prevent him seeing her disappointment. Without comment they climbed into the carriage and started off down the street. Neither of them spoke for several blocks and she sat in stoic misery. Suddenly a tear trickled down her cheek, and she turned her head to wipe it away, but another and another followed.

Adam slid over beside her and took his handkerchief from his pocket. He leaned over and wiped away her tears. "Raines, why are you crying?" he asked in an impatient voice, yet it was tempered with softness. "I thought I made it clear that I can't abide simpering women."

"I'm sorry if I'm such an embarrassment to you. I . . . I . . . had no idea you felt my clothes were that objectionable," she stammered.

"I apologize for my rude remark. You are a lovely girl and you look stylish in your blue gown and cape this afternoon. That is not the point. What I am trying to explain is that the Marchioness of Balfour must wear originals adorned with furs and jewels. Now dry your eyes and I'll take you to Swann House for tea. That should prove to you that I'm proud to be seen in public with my little country bride." He waited for her to comment and finally she nodded that she understood.

He rapped on the carriage and instructed the driver to circle Hyde Park for fifteen minutes, before taking them to Swann House. "We will have to drive around Hyde Park until the redness leaves your eyes," he said, "or all of London will say that I've already taken to beating you."

At that Raines laughed and put away his handkerchief. She hoped that he did not realize she had cried more from disappointment at his aloofness than from his remark. He seemed comfortable with her only when they were on politely cordial terms, and became hateful when the conversation took a more personal turn. She must remember in the future to hide her true feelings from him, although it was growing harder to do so. He became more charming daily. For her, the marriage was no longer merely a convenient arrangement.

By the time they drew up in front of the tearoom, Raines had regained her composure, and when Adam took her hand to assist her from the carriage, she glanced at him and smiled.

A doorman hurried to open the door for them and several patrons spoke to Adam as they walked inside. Adam put his arm possessively on her waist as he steered her to the table where the waiter escorted them.

Adam ordered tea and biscuits for them before his attention was distracted by someone calling his name. A woman, dressed in a stunning black afternoon outfit, came toward them and threw her arms around his neck. Before he could stop her, she had kissed him soundly on the lips.

Raines sat in irritated silence watching the spectacle. The jealousy rose in her as she studied the tall, large bosomed woman. Her hair was black and piled high on her head and she had one of the new black beauty moles pasted on her cheek, just like Raines had heard the French women were wearing. Even in her pique Raines conceded that the woman was the most beautiful creature she had ever seen.

Adam removed the woman's arms from around his neck and stood. "Charlotte, such a warm greeting took me by surprise. Please let me introduce my lovely wife, Raines." He gestured toward Raines who had never felt more plain than under the scrutiny of this enchantress, whose eyes grew wide with shock, then closed to mere slits of jealousy.

Adam sensed Charlotte was about to say something cutting and added, "And darling, I want you to meet Charlotte Brownlees, Duchess of Sandberry and the widow of the late Duke. She and I are . . . er . . . are old acquaintances." It was the first time Raines had ever sensed him to be at a disadvantage.

Raines nodded and mumbled a polite remark, knowing instinctively that Charlotte Brownlees was or had been Adam's mistress.

Charlotte, who looked about twenty-five, stared back at Raines with hatred in her cold brown eyes. Suddenly she turned to Adam and said, "Adam, you scoundrel, when did you marry this quaint child? Is she some distant cousin you married to save the family honor, or have you been naughty and gotten caught by an irate papa?" She tapped him playfully on the shoulder.

Raines felt the heat rise in her cheeks as she sat quietly listening. Why, the despicable woman! Eyes sparking anger, she retorted, "Neither is correct, madame. It was love at first sight for Adam, and he swept me off my feet. I wanted a long engagement, but darling Adam would not hear of postponing our marriage. He was about the most anxious bridegroom I've ever known." Laying her hand possessively on his arm, she asked coyly, "Weren't you, darling?"

Taken aback and clearly uncomfortable with the verbal barbs being hurled by both women, Adam grinned at Raines, who flashed him a knowing smile. Never would she have dreamed of displaying such affection in public, but Charlotte Brownlees brought out an animal instinct in her to protect what was hers.

Charlotte's cheeks burned crimson and she stood for a moment silently glaring at them. "Let's see how long Adam finds the adulation of a child amusing enough to keep him home nights." Whirling, she made a dramatic exit from the room, the sound of black taffeta skirts rustling in the air.

Neither of them mentioned Charlotte, but for Raines the afternoon was ruined. She had sensed the danger of a tigress in pursuit of its prey and knew that she would have to be on guard against this woman from now on. Above all else, Raines did not want Charlotte Brownlees to discover that this marriage was for convenience only.

The tearoom was unusually quiet and Raines knew that most of its patrons had watched the proceedings with relish. Lifting her cup to her lips to hide their trembling, Raines glanced over its brim at the group. She stared them down and most dropped their gazes and resumed their conversations. Several other people strolled by their table and stopped to be introduced to Raines.

Finally, sighing deeply, Adam pushed back his chair and said, "It is impossible to have a private conversation in this place. If you are ready, dear, let's be on our way."

Leading her out of the restaurant, he said, "I see now that we must give a party to introduce you to London's *ton*. What do you way to an affair on Saturday, the fourteenth?"

Raines drew in her breath sharply at the thought of hosting her first dinner party so soon. "First I must have a new gown to wear. I know Madam Raymor agreed to put me ahead, but can even she deliver the gowns on such short notice?"

"I gave her a few extra pounds, so I feel confident your wardrobe will arrive within the week."

"That soon? If she sews only for me, how can she possibly finish my large wardrobe so quickly?" gasped Raines, unable to imagine such speed.

"Darling, you are innocent," he teased as he lifted her into the carriage and followed. They moved cautiously out into the busy traffic. "She hires extra help for a sizable order like yours. Why, for the price she will charge me, she can engage five more seamstresses and still make a huge profit."

"Adam! Is it wise to spend money so foolishly? I could do with the dresses I have until she can make the new ones herself." Raines was not accustomed to throwing money around carelessly.

"Listen, pet, don't trouble your mind about money matters. You just learn to enjoy your new situation in life and I will handle all the business expenses. When I see that you are spending too much, I will certainly be the first to call it to your attention. Which brings up a personal matter. I want to give you a household allowance that will be yours to spend as you please."

Brightening, Raines looked over at him and asked, "Will it truly be mine to do with as I please?"

"Indeed it will."

"And I may even save it if I so desire?"

A frown crossed his handsome face and he answered without facing her, "Why would you want to hoard it away?"

She shrugged and shook her head. "I don't know. It would just be comforting to have some money of my own. I have been the poor relation for so long that I think it would be nice to have an independent cache."

"Knowing that you now have access to my wealth isn't sufficient?" He pretended to look out the window, but he watched her from the corner of his eye. His anger mounted rapidly and he took her arm in his grip, pressing tightly. "You aren't thinking of saving a nestegg and disappearing one day, are you?"

Shocked by his anger, she tried to pull her arm from his tight grasp, but without avail. "Don't be silly! Of course that isn't what I intend. We have a bargain and I'll live up to my part." Then as an afterthought she warned, "As long as you keep your part of the agreement."

They had arrived back at the townhouse and the horses came to rest at the hitching post. Adam let his hand drop and put his other hand on her shoulder and drew her near. She was so close that their lips almost touched as she saw the flick of anger in his dark eyes. She stared back at him in innocent surprise as she felt her heart flutter at his nearness. His touch aroused an ache in her and she wanted to put her hand on his brow and rub away the scowl, yet she dared not.

"Raines, get one thing perfectly clear. You are now Marchioness of Balfour and my wife. It is a bargain that you entered into willingly and with thought, so never, never, think you can leave me. Do you understand that?" His eyes bored into hers and he waited until she nodded meekly.

"I may be your wife, but I can't see the need for you to be so boorish about it," she snapped. "If you don't want me to save my money, then I shan't, but for heaven's sake, Adam, don't treat me so possessively." She tried to pull away from him.

Instead of releasing her, he drew her nearer and with brutal force pinned her arms behind her and bent her head back with the pressure of his lips on hers. He kissed her long and hard and when she stopped trying to fight him, he released her arms which she gently placed around his neck. Gasping for breath she broke away from him and set about straightening her dress. "Adam, please behave yourself," she scolded.

He took her chin in his fingers and turned her to face him, his eyes mocking her. "You are my wife and I shall kiss you when I please."

She jerked away from him and stepped from the carriage. Her fury over being treated like a piece of property erupted, and she whirled around to face him once more. He sat watching in the carriage, an air of haughty pleasure on his face.

"Let me tell you one thing, Lord Kemp, I may be your wife in name, but you do not own nor possess me yet!" she cried, throwing back her head in a proud gesture.

Softly he said, "I will, my pet, I will. It is just a matter of time until I collect my end of the bargain."

She turned her back on him once more and stalked into the house. To her relief he did not follow, and when she crept to the parlor window to look out, he and carriage were well down the street.

Touching her fingers to her lips she traced gently over their surface, still feeling the sensation of his lips upon hers. He had the ability to stir her emotions to peaks she had not dreamed possible, yet she must never let him know how much she loved him, or she would be a victim of his love. Raines doubted he was capable of love. Not the warm, affectionate emotion which she so desired. Though at times he could be kind and tender, it was true, when she showed the least reciprocation, he seemed to withdraw and became an arrogant, hateful person.

As Adam did not return for dinner that evening, Raines dined alone. Afterwards, she went into the drawing room to read, and finally, convinced that he did not intend to come home early, she retired to her room where she lay awake listening for his arrival. She lay in bed and through a nearby window watched the moon dart in and out of the clouds until the clock struck three times. Then she turned over and tried to sleep. But the thought which continued to plague her was whether Adam was with Lady Charlotte.

Disgusted with herself for letting this jealousy gnaw

at her, she slid from the bed and lit a candle. Finding her robe, she donned it hurriedly and taking the candle, eased out the door and downstairs. She had decided to slip into the parlor and have a small glass of wine in hopes it would help her to sleep.

As the candle wavered in the breeze and flickered, she cupped her hand around it to make a shield. Softly she crept down the hall and into the parlor where the red coals of the dying fire glowed, throwing a dim light into the room. She paused at the threshold to scan the room and listened to hear if any of the household was still about. Satisfied that she was alone, she tiptoed over to the liquor cabinet and removed the bottle of Madeira. The bottle tapped another and made a sharp clinking sound. Quickly she placed the candle on the table and reached for a glass with her free hand.

She poured a stiff drink, watching the liquid rise in the glass until it reached the brim. After taking a sip, she recorked the bottle and smiled.

At that moment a voice rang out behind her. "What have we here? A bride who tipples in the night? Tsk, tsk," scolded the voice in a mocking tone.

Giving a startled cry of alarm, she whirled around to face in the direction of the sound. As her eyes adjusted to the darkness she could make out his rakish features. He was dressed in evening clothes and had, no doubt, only been home a short while. "You scared me half to death," she hissed, trying to keep her voice low.

He stood and walked over to where she was and grinned down at her. "Do you always drink alone in the middle of the night?"

"Of course not!" she snapped, thankful that it was too dark for him to see how flustered she really was. "I c . . . couldn't sleep and I thought a glass of port would calm my nerves."

He reached out and took her arm, leading her to the sofa. "Then by all means come closer to the fire and we'll have a drink together." He reached into the cabinet and withdrew a bottle of scotch. "I was just about to have another one myself."

She smelled the liquor on his breath and from his slurred speech knew that he had already had a considerable amount to drink. Pausing, she said, "I . . . I don't think I should stay down here."

"Why not? You are my wife, even if I haven't sealed the marriage vows. If we choose to sit in the dark and sip our toddies at three a.m., then it is our perrogative." He eased her down on the sofa beside him.

Raines was uncomfortably aware of his nearness, but could do nothing about it, since she sat as close to the arm rest as possible and he blocked her escape in the other direction.

"I propose a toast to us," said Adam. "May our marriage produce enough heirs to satisfy the solicitors!" He tapped his glass to hers and chuckled. Taking a deep drink, he frowned as he studied her face in the reflection of the fire. "What's the matter, my dear? Didn't you like my toast?"

She started to reply, then changed her mind and took a sip of wine instead. What was the point of arguing, she thought. To him the marriage was a joke and a farce, so she might as well play along with it and never let her true feelings show.

Quickly she drank the glass of wine, and a warm, relaxed feeling began to settle through her body.

"Have you ever had a drink of scotch?" he asked, reaching on the floor for the bottle. Taking her glass he filled it with the clear liquid. "Here, try this," he ordered, handing her the goblet.

Obeying, she sipped the liquid and coughed. Adam put his hand on her back and rubbed it gently. "Just sip the drink slowly, dear. Don't try to gulp it."

Feeling giddy and no longer caring what he thought of her, she obediently drank the liquor, enjoying the warm glow that suffused her. Relaxing, she leaned back against Adam and felt the pleasant sensation of his muscled chest against her back. She shivered as a new tingling began to rise within her, and Adam put his arm around her and drew her closer.

"Are you cold, my dear?" he whispered in her ear, so close she could feel his warm breath on her neck.

"No . . . yes . . . I . . . I don't know," she giggled in confusion. Turning to face him, she said, "You know we shouldn't be down here like this. I'm not behaving as a lady should." This sent her into peals of laughter once more, and she cupped her hand over her mouth to stifle the noise.

Taking her empty glass from her, Adam said, "I think you've had enough for one night. Now, let's go up to our room, shall we?"

He stood and pulled her to her feet. The drinks were having their effect and, steadying her when she swayed, he gently led her up the stairs. Raines did not know what was going to happen next, and she was so relaxed that she really did not care. All she wanted to do was find her bed and fall into it. Suddenly she was terribly sleepy. Stifling a yawn, she giggled as they tiptoed down the hall toward her room. Adam followed her, and softly closed the door behind them, snapping the bolt into place.

Skillfully, and without a word, he slipped the robe from her shoulders and let it fall to the floor. Leaning over, he kissed her gently and her arms went around his neck. At first she shyly returned his kiss, then the blood coursed to her head and she began to match his breathless ardor.

She tried to protest as the gown slid away from her shoulders, but he stilled her attempt with his lips and swooped her into his arms and lay her on the bed.

Knowing what was to come next, she waited quietly, thankful for the darkness while she listened to him undressing. A moment later he slid into the bed beside her, and she gasped with delight as his warm flesh touched hers.

Slowly he stroked her body until she wanted to cry out for him to stop because she could not stand the growing flame within her. It was as though her desire would engulf her, and suddenly she found herself matching his kisses and seeking out his mouth when he moved away.

Laughing gently, he whispered, "You are a little witch underneath that cool exterior, aren't you? You are as passionate as I suspected."

His hands caressed her breasts gently and a moan escaped her lips. He kissed each one playfully and she urged him on by pressing her body closer. She knew that she was acting wantonly, but the liquor and the skillfulness of his hands made her abandon all pride.

"Love me, Raines," he whispered hoarsely. "Give

yourself to me. Don't fight me, darling."

When at last he entered her, she gave a small cry of joy and matched his ardor rhythmically with her body. After an interminable time of rapture, their bodies became satisfied and they fell back in exhaustion.

Gently Adam cradled her in his arms and she snuggled close, happier than she had ever been. She waited for him to tell her that he loved her, and she knew that she was ready to confess her love for him. She lay quietly in his arms waiting, until she heard his methodical breathing and thought that he was asleep. Shocked and angry, she tried to withdraw from his arms, but he tightened his grip on her. He had been awake all the time!

Now she felt confused and cheapened by the experience. She had behaved disgracefully and he probably thought she was no better than the whores he was reputed to spend time with.

Raines's eyes misted and she let the tears trickle down her cheeks as she thought of how her body had betrayed her. She had enjoyed his lovemaking and knew that having experienced this new awakening, it would be more difficult to hide her emotions from him.

As she eased off into a fretful sleep she planned how she would react to Adam in the morning. Perhaps when he was awake he would confess his love and everything would be all right.

But when Raines woke the following morning to find the sun shining in her eyes, she was shocked to discover that Adam had slipped from the bed and was gone.

Dressing hurriedly, she rushed downstairs to find Nettie. The maid came rushing out of the kitchen upon hearing Raines shouting her name.

"What it is, Lady Raines?" Nettie asked, drying her hands on the dishtowel she carried. Holding it aloft, she explained, "I was just helping cook with the morning's dishes. Is something the matter?"

Realizing how foolishly she was behaving, Raines shook her head and tried to sound calm when she asked, "Where is Lord Kemp this morning? Has he had breakfast?"

"Yes ma'am, he has. He instructed me that he would be working in his study this morning. He said that you were sleeping late and not to disturb you. He said no one was to interrupt him."

Ignoring the warning and feeling light with relief that Adam was still in the house, Raines rushed to the study and tapped softly on the door. A curt voice instructed her to enter.

This was the first time Raines had been in his office and she glanced around nervously, trying to locate where the voice had come from. The walls were lined with bookcases filled with rich leather bound volumes, a fire burned brightly in the marble faced fireplace, and the furniture was covered in deep green leather which looked comfortable and inviting. At last Raines saw the large mahogany desk which faced a wide French window. Adam glanced up from the papers he had scattered on his desk. He had been going over columns of figures before being interrupted. Seeing that it was Raines, a smile crossed his handsome face and he stood to greet her. "I didn't know you were up and about yet this morning. I

135

thought you might be suffering from too much Madeira," he teased.

Laughing selfconsciously, Raines waved aside his suggestion. "On the contrary, I feel marvelous this morning. In fact, I rested better than I have in days." Suddenly she blushed as she thought of what had taken place between them the night before.

Smiling, he came and took her hands in his and kissed her fingertips. Raines longed for him to kiss her again as he had last night, but he made no move to do so, and she tried to hide her disappointment when he moved back to his desk and sat down. Facing her, he asked absently, "What are your plans for today?"

"This morning I thought I would meet with the staff and see how competent Miss Hartnell is."

"I think you will find her extremely competent as a housekeeper. However, if you are not satisfied with her, you may come speak with me and I'll see that she is dismissed and someone else hired."

Raines looked aghast at such a suggestion. "Oh, no! I don't plan to come into the household and immediately begin making changes. First I'll watch to see how the place is running, and if I see where changes will profit either the help or us, then I'll suggest them. But, heavens, that is weeks away."

"And do you have any plans for the rest of the day? If not, would you like to go on a trip out of town with me? I need to ride out to see Squire Helms and I thought you might enjoy seeing the sights."

Raines sank down in the chair opposite the desk and frowned in disappointment. Shaking her head, she said, "Oh, I'm so sorry, but I can't go. Lady

Gossington is coming for tea . . ."

"Sybil Gossington?" he interrupted, his voice registering his disapproval.

"Yes," replied Raines hesitantly. "Is there anything wrong with that? She sent her card around, practically the hour of our arrival, and stated that she wished to come and welcome me to London."

"She would," said Adam, standing and moving over to the windows. "I don't like it. She is up to something."

"Darling, have I committed some faux pas in accepting her gesture of friendship? If so, please tell me and I will try to remedy it." His cold anger confused her. "I should have asked you first, but . . ."

He turned back to face her and said in a tone of dismissal, waving his hand, "No, you needn't consult with me before you have visitors. There is nothing wrong with Sybil's social standing. She is the widow of one of London's richest men and of fine family herself."

"Then whatever is the matter with her?" asked Raines in a perplexed voice.

Adam studied Raines's face a moment as though he might be trying to decide how much to tell her before he spoke, "My dear, you are such an innocent and Sybil is London's worst gossip. I am positive that she is coming to inspect you, so she can make a report back to the town's wags later this evening. Let's face it, our marriage was sudden, and she is bound to be curious as to why it took place so quickly."

"I certainly shan't tell her, if that is what is worrying you."

"No, it isn't that. I know you would never tell her

137

that this is a marriage of convenience that would not have occurred had the solicitors not been breathing down my neck."

Raines felt her heart lurch and a sick feeling filled her stomach. "Adam, after last night, do you still feel that ours is just a marriage of convenience?"

His face hardened. "I believe I owe you an apology. I'm afraid both of us had a little too much to drink last evening." His voice grew colder as he said the next words, "I was honest with you when I offered you the security of my protection in return for your agreeing to be my wife. I should never have taken advantage of you last night. I'm afraid I was temporarily overcome by your charms. Please forgive me."

Jumping to her feet, Raines's face turned crimson with suppressed anger as her temper and humiliation grew. "I accept your apology," she said bitterly. "As you say, we both had too much to drink or I would never have consented to your entering my bed." Her eyes flashed as she faced him and her voice was filled with contempt and loathing for the man who made her feel so cheap.

"Raines," he said and reached to take her hand. She pulled away quickly, turning her back on him, and he dropped his arm.

Abruptly she left him. She made no effort to prevent the door slamming as she left the room. Racing frantically into the front parlor, she sought refuge in a secluded corner. Her anger mounted and she picked up a Dresden figurine, about to hurl it across the room, then suddenly slammed it back down on the table and ran to get her cloak.

She was far down the street when she heard the

front door slam and Lord Kemp's horses approaching. At first she thought he was coming to collect her, and stubbornly decided that she would refuse to enter his carriage.

Instead, the matched chestnuts raced past her at full gallop as Lord Kemp angrily snapped his whip in the air. He didn't glance in her direction, and she saw from the set of his jaw that he, too, was furious.

Moments after he passed from view, she heard her name called. "Lady Kemp, wait!" came the cheerful voice and she turned to face the fair-haired man who strode toward her.

"James! It's so good to see you!" she cried in greeting. Here was a friend and she seized upon the moment to take her mind from her troubles.

Chapter 9

Raines grabbed his hand in greeting and flashed him a radiant smile. "Oh, James! I can't begin to tell you how happy I am to see you," she said.

He was obviously flattered by her exuberant reception, and grinned broadly. "How's the lovely bride?" He studied her carefully, a slight question in his eyes.

Cautious not to say the wrong thing, since he was Adam's solicitor, she said guardedly, "I'm fine." Her voice did not hold a note of conviction, so she hastened to add, "To be perfectly honest, I suppose I'm a little homesick for my family. The wedding took place so quickly and I scarcely saw my aunt and uncle before we left for London." She smiled again and paused for him to interpret this as he liked.

Patting her hand, he placed it under his arm and said, "I've just the remedy for that, my dear. We'll go shopping. I don't know a woman alive who doesn't love to shop and spend money."

She held back, since she did not have her household allowance yet, also she did not know what gossips might say about her going shopping with James.

"I . . . I . . . don't think it would be wise." She said this reluctantly, because she did hate to part company with him.

Sensing her hesitancy, yet seeing how badly she wished to go, he argued, "Nonsense. I have not bought you a wedding present and what would be more appropriate than for you to select it yourself."

"Oh, James, I couldn't do that."

"Why not? I already know the store where we must trade, and I see no harm in you showing me which item you prefer." Watching her carefully, he continued, "We can go find Adam and take him with us if you like. I'll explain to him that you were hesitant to go alone."

She shook her head. "That won't be possible. He had to go see Squire Helms this morning and he just rode out of town. Maybe we should wait until he returns." Her expression grew somber, and her lower lip began to tremble when she again thought of her earlier conversation with Adam.

James, mistaking her distress for disappointment, patted her hand once more and announced in a firm voice, "That settles it. We are going shopping. If Adam has anything to say about it, I'll scold him for leaving his bride alone so soon after her arrival. This business with the squire could certainly have waited another week."

Feeling she must defend Adam, she hastened to add, "Adam invited me to accompany him, but I have a guest arriving this afternoon and couldn't make it."

"There will be no more discussion on the matter. It is resolved," he said. "I'll take you shopping, out to lunch at Swann's and deliver you home in time for

141

your appointment."

Several coaches and carriages passed while they stood with heads together and the occupants leaned forward to observe the two people so engrossed in conversation. To anyone who did not know better, they resembled lovers having a very serious discussion.

Raines, oblivious to the stares they received, soon forgot her troubles as she listened to James's easy chatter. James was delightful company and soon they were talking like two old friends. Raines felt safe and comfortable in his presence.

Once they were in Picadilly Circus, James led the way into Hager's Silver Shop. Here they found row upon row of magnificent silver trays, tea services, bowls, goblets and hundreds of small serving pieces.

"All right, my dear, look around and pick anything your heart desires," he whispered close to her ear so the shopkeeper would not hear.

She gasped, looking around in amazement. "I couldn't. Everything here must cost a fortune. Let's go somewhere else."

"Good day," said the proprietor, who entered from a back room. "What can I do for you today, Mr. MacBain?"

"This is the Marchioness of Balfour and I brought her to select her special wedding present. Please show us what you think is appropriate."

The shopkeeper flushed with joy at the good fortune of having such an excellent customer, for business had been slow of late. Moving to a cabinet, he gestured toward an ornate silver punch bowl with ladle and several dozen cups. "This is a useful gift for entertaining, and I'm sure Lady Kemp will be doing much of that now that she has arrived in London."

"Oh, I could never accept such an elaborate gift as that," Raines protested. Glancing around for something smaller, she spied a silver brush and comb set. It was something she had always wanted. Picking up the silver handled mirror, she ran her fingers over the smooth surface. "This is a gorgeous dresser set," she said.

"That has been a very popular item with the ladies. With madam having such long and lovely hair, perhaps she would like this for her gift." The man picked up the brush and held it for her inspection.

"No, that would be out of the question. I want to select something less personal—it should be a gift for Adam and me." Nervously she glanced around, until her eye caught a pair of silver horses standing on a small platform. She moved over to the pair and picked up one, turning it to inspect the work more closely. "These bookends would look striking in Adam's study, that is, if James thinks they are what he'd like to choose."

"I think you have made an excellent choice, my dear," said James. Turning to the proprietor, he instructed, "Put them on my bill and send them around to Lord Kemp's home."

Raines moved discreetly away so they might finish the sale, and she busied herself in studying the fine picture frames and ornate nut sets. Two women entered the establishment and nodded casually to her. Since she knew neither, she merely tilted her head and smiled but did not speak.

Taking her by the arm possessively, James said, "Come along, my dear. Let's be off in search of lunch. I am starving."

Suddenly she felt lightheaded and happy and said, laughing, tucking her arm under his unselfconsciously, "So am I, James. This has been the most fun I've had in months. I'm so glad that I ran into you."

"If you want to know a secret, I intentionally came by your street this morning in hopes of seeing you." He hailed a cab and once they were seated in the carriage, he turned to her again and looked grave. "Raines, why did you marry Adam so quickly? I . . . I thought you weren't too fond of him and your sudden marriage shocked me. I know it's presumptuous of me to be speaking this way, but I must know."

Startled, Raines suddenly realized the conversation was leading in a dangerous direction. "It isn't like you to pry, James, and I'm shocked at you." She saw her words caused a rush of color to his cheeks and she tried to soften their effect by adding, "My marriage to Adam is quite advantageous and he has shown me nothing but kindness." While this was not completely correct, Adam did deserve her loyalty.

James changed the subject and for the rest of their visit things went pleasantly. He did not broach the subject again.

James returned her to the house shortly before Lady Gossington was scheduled to arrive. She was in the foyer affectionately bidding him good-bye when the carriage pulled to the curb and Lady Gossington stepped out.

Quickly Raines checked her appearance in the hall mirror and was sorry she did not have time to run upstairs and change, but the hours had slipped away and now it was too late. She heard James and Lady

Gossington exchanging pleasantries on the front stoop as she slipped into the parlor to await her visitor.

When the plump woman bustled into the room, Raines went to meet her with outstretched hands. "Welcome to my home, Lady Gossington. You are my first official visitor and I want to extend a special welcome to you." She kissed the older woman's cheek and led the way to the silk upholstered sofa.

Once she was seated, Lady Gossington glanced around her and with an approving nod remarked, "Lord Kemp has kept the place up, I see. He so seldom entertained after . . ." she paused as though hesitant to continue and glanced at Raines.

"Do you mean after his first wife's death?" she offered, determined not to show offense at the mention of the other woman.

Lady Gossington cleared her throat before speaking. "Please forgive me, my dear. I know that it was thoughtless of me to mention Alexandra."

"I am fully aware of the fact that Adam was married before and I am not in the least uncomfortable concerning any mention of his first wife." She saw the look of surprise on Lady Gossington's plump face and to change the subject, she continued, "I'll ring for our tea." She smiled to confirm her sincerity and hoped that she was performing her role convincingly.

"Do you plan to make changes now that you are lady of the household?"

Having rung for the maid, Raines settled back on the sofa and faced her guest. "I suppose in time I will make some changes. After all, my taste cannot possibly be exactly the same as anyone else's. However, at the moment there are so many other things to learn that I haven't had time to give it much thought."

"You said I was your first official guest, yet I passed James MacBain leaving as I came up the steps," Lady Gossington said simperingly.

Raines knew the woman was prying, and she was determined to squelch any gossip concerning her friendship with James. "He and I are old friends. We ran into each other this morning when I went out for a walk. I was so delighted to see him that we spent the morning chatting and I'm afraid the time slipped away."

The older woman's eyebrows rose in a questioning gesture, but she made no further mention of the matter.

Fortunately Nettie entered with the tea service and Raines busied herself with serving.

She was beginning to regret having allowed Lady Gossington to visit so soon after her arrival, before she had been able to get settled into her new role. She needed time to learn of London's society. Although, how was she to learn if she did not mingle?

As they sipped their spiced, lemony tea, Raines studied the plump woman who sat across from her. She wore a rose colored silk gown, trimmed with rows of lace at the neck. On a slender woman it might have been attractive, but on Lady Gossington's figure it was gaudy and ridiculous. A stunning diamond and ruby necklace graced her neck, and her fingers were laden with similar gems. It was quite obvious to Raines that Lady Gossington was vain about her hands, which fluttered continually about her like two white doves.

To steer the conversation away from James, Raines said, "I am looking forward to meeting the young hostesses of London. Adam says that we must give a dinner party soon. Do you have any suggestions as to whom I should include on my invitation list?"

"As a matter of fact, I'll be happy to help you with the list. One of the reasons for my visit today is to discuss having a social event at my home for you. I want to give a ball in your honor to introduce you to London's finest."

Clapping her hands, Raines could not hide her excitement. "What a lovely gesture! I wish Adam were here so we could tell him immediately."

"We need to set the date for this affair. Do you think Saturday two weeks will be satisfactory?"

"I don't have anything scheduled for that date, and I don't know of anything Adam has planned. Let's say that time and if it isn't satisfactory with him, I'll send a note around to you immediately. Also, by that time I should have my new gowns from Madame Raymor."

Raines's newfound happiness met an early death with Lady Gossington's next statement.

"I thought Adam would take you to her, since she does all of Charlotte's work—which he would know, of course." She gave Raines a boldly conspiratorial glance.

Almost hating herself for taking the bait, yet wanting to be certain she understood, Raines asked, "Charlotte?"

"Yes, my dear, Charlotte Brownlees. I believe you met her yesterday, although I imagine it put Adam in a most awkward position."

"I didn't notice that it bothered him," replied Raines, determined to end any gossip.

The older woman seemed to enjoy her discomfort,

147

yet she retained a semblance of friendliness. "I'm sure you are aware of the fact that she and Adam were once a pair. Why, when word reached her ears that Lord Kemp had married you, she literally went into a rage and—"

"Lady Gossington, I really don't wish to hear about this. What happened between Adam and Lady Charlotte is of no concern to me. My husband was a single man at the time and naturally he had flirtations."

"My dear, you are a sweet and innocent child and I like you. I don't say this to offend, but to warn you: Lady Charlotte is not accustomed to losing any man before she tires of him, so my dear, watch her. Everyone knows that she and Adam were lovers. She had been his mistress for over a year. In fact, her husband having been forty years older than she, it was rumored that she and Adam were lovers long before the poor man's death."

Standing, Raines tried to halt this talk, because it did disturb her. She felt a rising jealousy of Charlotte Brownlees, and had since the moment she first met her. "Please, I understand your intentions are good; however, now that Adam and I are married, I see no reason to be concerned." Shrugging, she gestured with her hands, "After all, he was free to marry her before he met me. Had she been his preference, I believe he would have done so."

Lady Gossington set down her cup and reached for another rich pastry, being careful not to get the sticky substance on her fingers. "I must confess that all of London was startled by Adam's sudden decision to marry. He had made no secret of his intention to remain single." Watching Raines from the corner of her eye, she continued shrewdly, "Or is there some other reason for his hasty marriage?"

"I agree it must seem strange to those who know him," Raines felt forced to admit. She didn't understand why she continued to try to justify their marriage, yet she did. Although her pride refused to allow her to admit the truth to this woman or any other person, she loved Adam. "You must remember that his mother died recently and after a long confining illness. He saw no need to postpone our marriage when it was advantageous for us to be married immediately."

The older woman bit into the creamy concoction and chewed slowly as though all her concentration was on eating. Raines stopped moving around the room and came back to sit across from her. They sat in silence until the sweet cake had totally disappeared. Then, wiping her fingers gingerly on her linen napkin, Lady Gossington at last said, "I've heard all the reasons which have been given, and still I'd wager a diamond necklace fit for the queen that there's something you are not telling me."

Acquiring her most innocent expression, Raines said sweetly, "I'm sorry to disappoint you, but that's all there is to tell. It was instant attraction for the two of us and with my uncle's permission, we married at Balfour." Warming to the story, Raines added, "I must admit that it took some pleading from me and Adam to get my uncle to consent on such short notice." Seeing the look of disbelief on the dowager's face, Raines feared she had gone too far.

"I can't see why he would object, other than perhaps because Adam has such a reputation as a rake." The woman chuckled, apparently thinking of some particularly succulent morsel of gossip.

"I know my uncle was convinced that Adam would give up his worldly behavior once we were married," argued Raines. "And I am convinced also."

Vigorously shaking her elaborately coiffured head, Lady Gossington frowned, leaning forward to pat Raines affectionately on the arm. "Let me give you some advice, my dear. I like you. You're smart, extremely attractive, and I'd wager a lot more clever than your innocent eyes betray. Therefore, I think you will appreciate what I'm about to say. Never trust Adam Kemp with your heart. He has loved many women, and some more beautiful than you, my child, but none has ever captured his heart and I don't think you will either." When Raines opened her mouth to protest, the older woman silenced her and said, "Oh, he may be affectionate and attentive for the moment, since you are a new plaything, but in time his eye will roam again. As long as you're not attached to him, it won't matter to you."

"I understand what you are trying to tell me," said Raines stiffly, wishing that she didn't feel there was some truth in the woman's words.

"If you had a mother, then she could explain all this to you, but I understand that you are orphaned."

Raines was surprised that the woman knew so much about her. "I have been motherless since I was a young child."

"Then let me give you some motherly advice. Turn your head the other way when Adam resumes his affair with Charlotte, as I am positive he will. Hold your head high and pretend it does not exist. You are

Lady Kemp, Marchioness of Balfour, and that is the one thing Charlotte cannot have as long as you live."

Raines sat in silence, unable to reply.

Putting down her napkin, Lady Gossington stood to leave. "It is getting late and I must be on my way. Remember what I've said and enjoy your new role."

Walking to the door, Raines felt a cloud of despair engulfing her. Adam had warned her that this woman was an insufferable gossip, yet she had not expected that her presumptuousness would affect her so deeply.

Once the door closed on her departing guest, she went to her room to try to sort out her feelings. Flinging herself upon the bed she lay in miserable silence. She had no reason to be angry with Adam, yet he was the one she felt most betrayed by. Why had he married her when he had vowed not to love again? Why hadn't he married Lady Charlotte, if what Lady Gossington said was true, and now she did not doubt that it was. What had made him so bitter? She grew even more frustrated because she knew that this was not a subject she could broach with Adam. He had never lied to her or misrepresented his feelings. She had simply been a fool to let her heart gain control over her head. Her cheeks again grew hot as she thought of the ardent way she had responded to him last evening. He must think her a common strumpet to have reacted as she did. Well, one thing she vowed—in the future, she would remain aloof and unemotional.

That evening she pleaded a headache and ordered her dinner brought to her room. She then addressed the possibility that Adam might resume his affair with his mistress. Standing up and stalking around the bedroom, she decided that she would not tolerate him flaunting his women before her, and if need be, she would tell him so in no uncertain terms. This marriage contract was not going to be one sided!

Chapter 10

Raines decided to inform Adam of her decision when she saw him. However this did not happen for several days and when she did encounter him again, the conversation took such a surprising turn that she forgot to broach the subject.

Raines was sitting in the morning parlor reading a novel when she heard heavy footsteps approaching. She knew it was Adam and he had returned from wherever he had been staying. She had not seen him since the morning of their argument and she didn't know if he had been detained at Squire Helms or had intentionally avoided returning home because of their quarrel.

Glancing up from her book, she did not smile or greet him as he strode into the parlor. She could see that he was furious and his dark eyes flashed like onyx when hers met his.

Holding out a neatly wrapped parcel, he said loudly, "Will you kindly explain this?"

Puzzled, she looked at him to see if he was drunk or deranged, and shrugged. "I can't say that I can. I don't know what it is that you are holding. Where did it come from?"

He thrust the package in her lap and stood glaring as she calmly opened it. Perversely she took her time breaking the satin ribbons and unfolding the wrappings, enjoying his fury. Placing the white box in her lap she opened the lid and gasped with delight, although she now understood some of Adam's wrath. Inside lay the ornate silver dresser set which she had admired in Hager's. She grew more nervous as she lifted the card and read the name on it, although she knew it was from James before she ever saw his neat writing.

"I want to know why James MacBain is buying you expensive gifts!" demanded Adam, moving closer, with his fists clenched by his sides. His brows almost met in the middle of his forehead and he looked as though he'd love nothing better than to wring her neck.

"Why, I haven't the least idea," she answered innocently, frowning at the implication in his tone. "I admired this set the other day, but I certainly didn't anticipate him buying it and sending it to me."

"Then you don't deny you met him secretly last week? The moment I was out of town." His scowl was so ugly that Raines feared he might strike her.

Suddenly his insinuations sparked her anger and she jumped to her feet, slamming down the box and looking him in the eye. "I most definitely deny any such thing! How dare you accuse me!"

"Then you didn't stroll all over London arm in arm like two lovers?" he shouted, his voice growing louder.

"Please lower your voice, Adam, there is no need to

154

alert the servants about your mistrust."

"Why not? They probably know more than I about your clandestine meetings."

Raines could not ever remember being angrier than at this moment. Her face felt hot and she knew she was on the defensive, yet she refused to cower before him. "If you had come home before today, then I would have told you about running into James while I was out walking. And, I would have explained about him asking me to pick out the wedding gift he was giving to both of us." She emphasized the words, both of us. "After I chose silver bookends for *your* library which are on *your* desk, he then suggested that we have lunch." She shrugged and said, "That is all there is to it. You have blown the whole matter out of proportion." She saw his face relax and the anger fade.

Still not satisfied, but in a calmer tone he gestured toward the box and said, "Send that back to him."

"Of course I will, but not because you order it. I'll return it because I can't accept such an expensive gift from a friend." She drew a deep breath and let it out. "Honestly, Adam, you act like I'm a shameless harlot or something." Now the tears began to brim and she turned away to prevent him seeing them. They were tears of anger and hurt, not remorse, for she was not ashamed of her conduct.

Awkwardly Adam stepped toward her and tried to put his arms on her shoulders. She jerked away quickly and moved from within his reach. Gaining control of herself she turned and faced him once more. "Adam, it seems that we are constantly quarreling about something, and I find it most distasteful.

Perhaps it would be better if you stayed where you have been the past few days . . ."

"I've been at my club. I wanted time to think over some things. And when the rumors began to reach my ears about your meetings with James, I continued to stay away." Watching her carefully, he continued, "I will not be cuckolded."

In a soft voice, Raines tried to say the next words as convincingly as possible, "You have my word, I will never have an affair behind your back. I'm afraid that a marriage of our type, without love, breeds doubt and mistrust. That's something we didn't foresee, isn't it?"

"Raines, I don't intend to move out of my own house. We must learn how to live under the same roof and be civil to one another. We had no difficulty communicating before our marriage."

Raines was about to dispute this statement, then thought better of it and remained silent.

"I have been very lonely here, away from my family and not knowing anyone. James was comfort and company for me. However, if you do not wish for me to be seen in public with him again, you are my husband, and I'll abide by your wishes, although I desire you to reconsider the matter."

"Raines, you are so naive about life in London. Your intentions may be good, but Londoners are infamous for their liaisons and you are leaving yourself open to idle gossip when you behave as you did the other day."

Holding her chin erect, she said proudly, "Then I shan't give them opportunity for a second chance to mock me."

"You are a lovely woman and our marriage was hasty, so there are bound to be those who are jealous and wish to hurt you."

It was on the tip of her tongue to ask if Charlotte Brownlees was one of those who might wish her harm. Instead she changed the subject and said, "Lady Gossington came for tea and asked if Saturday week would be satisfactory for her to give a ball in our honor. What shall I tell her?"

At first he frowned. After hesitating a moment he nodded. "I suppose that date is all right. Knowing Sybil, she is up to no good, but you must be introduced to the *ton* and she is one of the most famous matrons in London. Her introduction of you will be the endorsement needed to get you invited into every parlor in the city."

Picking up the comb and brush set, Raines said, "If that is settled, I'll send Watson around with a note to Lady Gossington's. Now I must take this to my room and rewrap it." In a strong voice, she said, "I'll return it to Hager's and ask them to credit James's account. Later I'll send a brief note of apology to him. Is that satisfactory with you?" Her voice remained cool and she did not smile.

Seeing how miserable she looked, Adam made a step toward her, but her frown stopped him. He dropped his arms to his sides and shrugged, saying, "Handle it any way you like. You understand those things better than I."

For the next two weeks Raines and Adam lived in the same house in cool politeness. She busied herself working on cataloguing the coin collection, anxious to complete the task and present it to the museum. At least while she worked she forgot Adam and the state of her marriage. When she had made the agreement with him, she had never dreamed that their personalities would clash so over almost every incident. That was not completely true, though. As to the household, Adam gave her complete rein, and she could come and go as she pleased now that the unpleasant incident over James was ended. She had not heard from James since she returned his gift and wrote the curt letter of apology for refusing it. When she wrote the letter she had feared Adam might demand to read it, so she had made certain it was cool and to the point. Now she was sorry she had not tempered the message with at least a warm feeling of regret. James had been her friend at Balfour, and she enjoyed his company in the same way she enjoyed a brother's friendship. Why couldn't Adam understand that?

She and Adam resided in mutual coolness, speaking only when it was necessary, until the day of Lady Gossington's ball arrived. Raines was dressing in one of her new gowns while she chatted with Nettie. Since they had moved to London, the old and trusted maid had become Raines's closest and only confidant.

As Nettie fussed with the tiny silk covered buttons on the blue gown, Raines said, sighing deeply, "Oh, Nettie, I should be looking forward to tonight's ball and instead I dread it more than you can imagine."

"Nonsense, Lady Raines, don't you go talking like that. You look a perfect picture with your hair fashioned in that new style with those curls twirling down on either side of your face. Why Lord Adam will be proud when he shows you off to all of London tonight."

"I'm afraid it's Adam and not the others that I dread being with. Nettie, I may have made a terrible mistake in marrying him. I thought it would be so simple and now I'm not pleased with the way things are turning out."

"That's foolish talk from someone who has a head as clever as you. Why, to be a lady and have this beautiful house and have Lord Kemp to care for you, 'tis a far cry from the life you were headed for as a woman who had to earn her keep. If I may be so bold as to say that," stammered Nettie.

"I know what you are saying and on the surface I tend to agree. It is just that I'm not positive I can continue living in a house without love and friendship. Adam and I treat each other like strangers who must share the same accommodations, but don't care to become acquainted."

"Now don't go getting silly notions. Here, stand straight and let me fix the bodice on this dress. It seems to me that the neckline is a mite too low for my liking," she added reproachfully, frowning at the dress which had a square cut neckline that ended just above the swell of Raines white rounded bosom.

"I know it is lower than those we wore in the country, Nettie, but Madame Raymor assured me that it was exactly the correct cut when I questioned her." Tugging at the shoulders, she tried to raise the neckline a little.

"Well, if that's what all the society ladies will be wearing, then just leave it be. I tell you, my lady, you are enough to cause Lord Kemp to burst with jealousy when the other men see you."

"Adam jealous?" Raines gave a little laugh.

159

"That's ridiculous. He hardly knows I exist and couldn't care less what other men think of me."

"Now there's one time you are wrong, Lady Raines. Why the day Mr. James sent you the gift and he intercepted it, he ranted and raved around the house for hours. Cook told me that she'd been with his family ever since he was a mere babe on his mother's knee and she'd never seen him act so jealous." She had finished her last minute adjustments to the gown and held out the new blue kid shoes for Raines to slip her silk stockinged feet into. The shoes had been dyed to match the exact shade of the gown and had tiny jeweled bows for buckles on the top.

Still not convinced Adam had really been jealous, not merely asserting his rights as a husband, Raines said, "The staff in this house gossips too much. They should be ashamed of themselves."

"That may be true, Lady Raines, but I don't think there's a lord living that can stop the maids from discussing their employers. Not even the good King can prevent it in the castle."

"Nettie, you're a wise old woman, if you do seem a bit incorrigible at times. No, you're right. I don't suppose talk can be stopped."

Nettie beamed under Raines's mixed compliment. Growing bolder she added, "Since we are mentioning the servants, I think I should tell you that they are sorry to see you and Lord Kemp going around looking like gloom and doom all the time. When you first married they thought you were just the one to pull him out of his misery and make him laugh again. They also liked your spirit and thought you'd take naught off him, which is the kind of wife they say he needs,

160

MORE PASSION AND ADVENTURE AWAIT... YOUR TRIP TO A BIG ADVENTUROUS WORLD BEGINS WHEN YOU ACCEPT YOUR FIRST 4 NOVELS ABSOLUTELY *FREE*
(AN $18.00 VALUE)

Accept your Free gift and start to experience more of the passion and adventure you like in a historical romance novel. Each Zebra novel is filled with proud men, spirited women and tempestuous love that you'll remember long after you turn the last page.

Zebra Historical Romances are the finest novels of their kind. They are written by authors who really know how to weave tales of romance and adventure in the historical settings you love. You'll feel like you've actually gone back in time with the thrilling stories that each Zebra novel offers.

GET YOUR FREE GIFT WITH THE START OF YOUR HOME SUBSCRIPTION

Our readers tell us that these books sell out very fast in book stores and often they miss the newest titles. So Zebra has made arrangements for you to receive the four newest novels published each month.

You'll be guaranteed that you'll never miss a title, and home delivery is so convenient. And to show you just how easy it is to get Zebra Historical Romances, we'll send you your first 4 books absolutely FREE! Our gift to you just for trying our home subscription service.

BIG SAVINGS AND FREE HOME DELIVERY

Each month, you'll receive the four newest titles as soon as they are published. You'll probably receive them even before the bookstores do. What's more, you may preview these exciting novels free for 10 days. If you like them as much as we think you will, just pay the low preferred subscriber's price of just $3.75 each. *You'll save $3.00 each month off the publisher's price.* AND, your savings are even greater because there are never any shipping, handling or other hidden charges—FREE Home Delivery. Of course you can return any shipment within 10 days for full credit, no questions asked. There is no minimum number of books you must buy.

him being stubborn and proud. In fact, there's some who argue you two are too much akin and too proud for yer own good."

"That's enough of that Nettie. You tell the kitchen staff to stop this prattle and concentrate on their chores."

Nettie nodded, uncowed by Raines's orders. "My lady, we just have yours and Lord Kemp's interest in mind. I know he loves you . . ."

Raines had been selecting the jewelry she planned to wear, but this proclamation caused her to stop and turn to stare in amazement at the maid. "Whatever gave you such an idea as that?"

"Oh, I'm knowledgeable in the ways of menfolk, even if . . . even if I ain't never had one of me own. And I knows of what I'm speaking. I watch the way he looks at you, even when you ain't aware of it. I know once I didn't think he was capable of loving a wife. Now I know I was wrong." She nodded her head vigorously and cackled at her joke. "Yes, ma'am, I know that he is eaten up with love."

"I hate to dispute your knowledgeable record, Nettie, however, about this you couldn't be more wrong."

"Ye think not, do ye? Well my dear, I know something more. I know that you are in love with him, also, and that be a true fact, too."

"Nettie, I don't wish to discuss this any more. Now either find another topic or just remain silent," snapped Raines. She did not like the way her feelings for Adam had been discovered, and worse yet, discussed by the entire staff. Why, she and Adam must be the topic of tea every day! She would have to call the staff together and instruct them to spend their free time in a more suitable pastime than prattling.

Nettie did not seem offended by Raines's curt remark. Instead she just smiled a sly grin and nodded. Curtsying she said, "I'll be going down to help with the kitchen cleanup, if that is all you'll be needing." Standing back to survey Raines, she nodded her head again and said, "You are a picture tonight. That blue dress is the exact color of your eyes."

"As a matter-of-fact Adam selected this silk. I think he's just partial to blue, since he selected five different shades to be made up into dresses and gowns."

"Humph! Think what you like, Lady Raines, but old Nettie knows some things better'n you do."

Laughing Raines said, "Shoo! Go on and get out of here before you have me believing the world is flat again."

Nettie left the room and Raines sat quietly thinking about what the maid had said. She heard the door between her room and Adam's room open and he walked in. He was dressed in a blue velvet frock coat with satin vest and breeches to match. The high white cravat was folded crisply and held in place with a huge diamond stickpin and he had never looked more attractive to Raines. His large, muscular frame prevented the outfit from making him look dandified.

Bowing elegantly, he smiled, boldly accenting his square jaw line. "Good evening, Lady Raines, you do look breathtakingly beautiful tonight." His eyes shone with his approval and Raines discovered herself glowing under his praise because she did feel fashionable and lovely tonight.

"Adam, we will look marvelous together, both dressed in blue. They'll think we planned it." She clapped her hands with joy as she envisioned what a handsome couple they would make entering the ballroom.

"It was planned, my dear," he said, grinning his devilish one-sided smile which made her heart skip a beat. When he tried, no man could touch him for charm, she thought.

Putting her hand to her bare neck, she asked, "Do you think this dress is cut too low? Madame Raymor assured me that it was the fashion; however, Nettie has scolded me for it."

His eyes traveled to her neckline and then lower, his expression growing even more rakish as he stared at her cleavage. "Ah, 'tis a pretty sight to behold," he teased.

Quickly she put her hand to her bosom and blushed crimson.

He moved closer. This was the first time they had been alone since the night they made love. She saw the flicker of desire in his eyes and swiftly moved away. Pretending to fuss with her hair, Raines watched him in the mirror. Her emotions were in a turmoil. Oh, why did his presence have such an effect on her? He did not move nearer, but if he should touch her again, she did not know how she would react. That night still burned in her memory and she blushed now at the wanton and shameful way she had returned his caresses. Since the morning after, when he had made her feel she meant no more to him than a mistress or a common tart, she had purposely avoided further encounters with him.

163

Adam moved a step closer and stood behind her, close enough for her to smell his spicy cologne. She tried to concentrate on placing a comb in her already perfectly arrayed hair.

After watching her silently for several minutes he said, "I have the perfect thing to accent your outfit tonight. Wait one minute and I'll be back with it."

Surprised, Raines turned and watched him stroll from the room. She loved gifts and waited as anxiously as a child for his return. When he came back, he was holding something behind him and he instructed her to close her eyes.

She kept her eyes closed and held her breath as he drew near again and draped something over her shoulders. His hands lingered. Realizing what the surprise must be, she gasped in astonishment and opened her eyes. Gently he turned her so that she saw her reflection in the mirror. There she stood, wearing an exquisite long white ermine cape.

Stroking the soft fur she cried, "This is the loveliest thing I've ever seen! Oh, Adam, I love it!" With tears of joy in her eyes she turned to face him. "I have never had any gift as wonderful as this in my entire life."

Softly he said, "Then I am happy that I chose it for you." A rakish grin crossed his deeply tanned face and he said, "Am I forgiven for making you return James's gift?"

Turning serious she said, "Adam, it wasn't a question of my losing a gift. It was your accusations which angered me."

"But now, am I forgiven?" He stared hard at her and refused to move away.

Unable to stay angry with him, she laughed and

nodded. "Yes, you are forgiven. Are you convinced?"

"Do I get a kiss for my gift?" His black eyes held so much merriment that she was not sure if he was serious.

"Yes, you deserve a kiss." She stood on tiptoe and lightly kissed him on the lips, her heart pounding so loudly she thought he must hear it.

"Is that what you call a kiss?" He gestured at her cape, running his fingers down the arm of it. "Surely, fair maiden, you can do better than that for a cape as fine as this."

"Honestly, Adam, you tease too much! What did you expect?"

"There's many a lady in London who'd pay far better than that peck for a coat of ermine."

"You drive a hard bargain, sir," she said, "but since I want this luscious coat, I'll pay a fair price." She stood on tiptoes again and this time she put her arms around his neck and drew his mouth down to her lips.

Suddenly his arms were around her waist and he drew her closer, forcing her head back and kissing her harder. His lips pressed into hers and his arms closed so tightly that she thought she would suffocate in his embrace. Her heart began to pump furiously and a warm glow spread rapidly through her body. For resist him as she might, his caresses had a way of awakening desires in her which she did not know existed. She felt his breath quickening and grew afraid of what might happen next, so she struggled to break free.

Pulling her head back, she gasped for breath before she cried, "Adam, we must stop! You're going to mess up my hair and my gown." She tried to pull away.

165

"Damn the dress!" He muttered, searching for her lips once more, his hand caressing her tingling breasts. "I'll buy you another."

Pushing him to arms length, Raines argued, "You can't get another tonight, and Lady Gossington is expecting us any minute. Please, we must go." She hoped her voice carried more conviction than her body felt.

At last he released her, an odd expression in his eyes.

"We must be on our way," she said, reaching for her fur muff. "Since we are the guests of honor, I don't want to be late." She slipped her arm under his and they walked out to the carriage looking like young lovers. Raines caught their reflection in the hall mirror and wished with all her being that the picture she saw were true.

The coach crossed the city with speed, and as it neared the house where the ball was being held, Raines noticed carriages lining the street while the coachmen stood around dressed in their bright livery. The men huddled in small groups, laughing and trying to stay warm, while their masters and mistresses were inside making merry. Raines knew that a scullery maid would come out soon and pass a mug of ale to each, to help warm them. All the men and boys seemed accustomed to the weather, which was windy but clear this evening.

Peering out the carriage window, Raines remarked, "Everyone who is anyone seems to be here tonight. I've never seen so many crested carriages parked anywhere other than at the palace."

Nodding his dark head, Adam said, "Even though

Sybil is the most notorious gossip in London, no one dares miss one of her affairs. She is the most sought-after hostess and women will resort to absurd efforts to obtain an invitation."

Suddenly Raines sobered and faced Adam. In a soft voice she confessed, "I am so nervous. Adam, please promise to stay close all evening. I don't know these people and . . . and no one may talk to me."

The carriage stopped suddenly and the blackamoor jumped down and ran around to open the door. Deftly Raines stepped out and pulled her cape closer, drawing warmth and courage from its softness.

They strolled up the steps of the brightly lit mansion and were greeted by a tall, slender butler who recognized Adam immediately and appeared delighted to see him. Raines knew Adam had been a guest here often for the man's jubilance at seeing him again was genuine. Bowing, the balding butler said, "Good evening, Lord Kemp, 'tis good to see you again. It has been dull around here since your last visit, sir." Then gesturing for them to enter, he addressed Raines, "Lady Kemp, I'll give your wrap to the parlor maid."

Raines let the white cloak slip from her shoulders reluctantly and was sorry that she could not wear it into the ballroom for everyone to admire. It pleased her to see the careful way the butler handled the fur, and it was evident that he realized its value.

They moved down the hall which was lit by hundreds of candles hanging from chandeliers and in wall sconces. The whole house was ablaze with the light from them, and Raines decided there must be more candles burning in this hall tonight than she and her father had used in a lifetime.

Their shoes made soft sounds on the marble flooring and when they neared the ballroom, footmen stepped forward and swung open the large white doors trimmed in gold. Music flowed softly through this wing of the house, and people could be heard laughing and talking.

A second butler stepped forward and announced in a loud, clear voice, "The Marquis and Marchioness of Balfour, Lord and Lady Kemp!"

Those standing near enough to hear swung around to stare at the couple. Raines saw the curiosity on their faces as they studied her closely, anxious to see this woman who had captured the unobtainable Marquis of Balfour. She smiled up at Adam as she took his arm and stepped into the ballroom. He pressed her hand reassuringly and she realized that he sensed her nervousness.

Scanning the crowd which watched her with open interest, she thought she detected a look of approval on most of their faces. Her eyes swept the group while she kept a smile pasted on her face.

Suddenly she caught sight of Charlotte Brownlees who was dressed in a red velvet dress, her hair piled high and held in place with a diamond tiara. Her white breasts were exposed almost to their tips and Raines was shocked to see so much cleavage exhibited by a lady. In the country, and in the circles she and her father had traveled, a more puritan morality still prevailed, although she had heard how daring many London matrons were becoming. When her eyes met Charlotte's, she nodded in greeting, but the latter stared back in cold unblinking silence. The hatred in those eyes made Raines shudder involuntarily.

"Are you cold, darling," whispered Adam. "Let's move closer to the fire until you become accustomed to the coolness in here. The ballroom is always cooler than other rooms because so many people will soon be dancing and the coolness will be relished then."

Lady Sybil broke away from a group of men to come and greet them, extending her hand for Adam to kiss. "So here come my honeymooners. I was so afraid you could not pull yourselves away from the boudoir long enough to put in an appearance."

Raines blushed at this insinuation, but Adam only chuckled as he bent to kiss Lady Gossington's plump, jeweled hand. "My dear Sybil, I would have torn myself away from the first nuptial night to attend one of your parties, and you know it. Now, let's introduce my beautiful wife around, so others may have the pleasure of seeing why I kept her a secret, until after I had marched her to the altar."

"By jove, Adam, you rake! You've done it again! You beat the rest of us to the most beautiful lady in these parts," cried a tall, attractive man several years older than Adam. Taking Raines's hand in his, he bowed and kissed it. "Daniel Melchett at your service." Straightening and running his eyes over Raines seductively, he continued, "My only regret madam, is that Adam found you first."

Laughing and enjoying the compliments, whether the men meant them or not, Raines moved around the room, until the orchestra started the first waltz. "I claim the first dance with my bride, gentlemen," announced Adam, with pride in his tone.

He led Raines onto the dance floor, and they began

gliding around the room. At first the others stood back and watched the attractive couple who looked up at each other so affectionately, and then they, too, began to join in, until the floor was filled with waltzers.

This was the first time Raines had ever danced with Adam, yet she found him an easy partner to follow. Of all the days since her marriage, tonight, at last, she felt totally happy. As she looked up into Adam's dark eyes, she felt the passion between them ignite, and he drew her even closer to him. "You are a very skillful dancer, Lady Kemp," he murmured in her ear.

"You seem to have a great deal of talent yourself, my Lord," she whispered back.

"Are you enjoying it?"

Her eyes sparkled with happiness as she smiled up at him and said sincerely, "Adam, I wish this dance could last forever. I feel like Cinderella at the grand ball."

He laughed and kissed her lightly on the cheek, and Raines thought her heart would burst with happiness. Adam must love her, or he would not exhibit such affection in front of his friends, she thought. She relaxed in his arms and she felt aglow with happiness.

When the music ended, she was claimed by a new partner and was whirled back onto the floor. For the next two hours she caught only fleeting glimpses of her husband. Sometimes he was dancing with the wives and sisters of friends. At other times he stood on the sidelines chatting with a group of gentlemen, but every time their eyes met, he smiled and she returned his greeting. It was as though they were the only two people in the room and had just discovered how much they loved one another.

It was nearly midnight when Raines walked off the dance floor and thanked a young army officer for going to get her a glass of punch. As she was tired and out of breath from dancing every dance, she moved over to sit on one of the tiny satin covered chairs which lined the wall. While she waited for her gallant to return, she searched the hall again for a glimpse of Adam.

When at last she located him, her heart gave a lurch and she felt a tightening in her chest. He stood, head bowed, attentively listening to something Charlotte Brownlees was saying to him. Charlotte's conversation must have been amusing, because he bestowed upon her the same affectionate smile which Raines had thought had been reserved for her. A pang of jealousy seized her and she felt the color drain from her face. How could he spend so much time with that woman? Raines felt insulted that Adam's ex-mistress had even appeared tonight. Charlotte could have shown the discretion to stay away knowing that the ball was in Raines's honor. Raines thought that everyone in the room must be watching Adam and Charlotte's behavior with the same curiosity as she.

When she saw Lady Charlotte take Adam by the hand and lead him out of the room, she felt the color drain from her face. Where were they going, and how dare he leave her alone to wander off with his paramour? Anger swelled in her and she glanced around to see if anyone had noticed her reaction. At that moment she caught sight of James MacBain, who stood silently watching her from across the room.

When their eyes met, Raines nodded in greeting

171

and James quickly made his way across the floor to where she sat. He looked dapper in his evening clothes, a rose wool coat with a white satin vest and breeches. His dark-blond good looks were accented by the rose color of his outfit and his green eyes met hers boldly. "Lady Raines, you are a perfect picture for sure. Always lovely, tonight you have captured the hearts of all the men here," he said, bending to kiss her hand. "May I join you?"

"Of course." Raines moved invitingly, to make room for him beside her, delighted to have a friend to help her through this awkward moment. Now she saw many people glancing toward her, curious to see her reaction to Adam's bold departure with his mistress. She hoped that none of her hurt and resentment was visible in her expression.

"James, where have you been keeping yourself?" she cried exuberantly. Although others who did not know her well might be fooled, she knew her voice was pitched too high and was a tell-tale sign of her nervousness. "I have missed you so much."

Apparently pleased with her warm greeting and rather taken aback by it also, James whispered, "I wasn't sure I was welcome in your home anymore."

"Not welcome, James! Whatever do you mean? You are one of my dearest friends—in fact, the dearest," she said, with a flirtatious smile. Even Raines was shocked at her own behavior, since she had never been a flirt. Yet, she determined that if Adam could take freedoms with the opposite sex, then so could she.

"Well, when you returned my gift to the silversmith and sent the curt letter of apology I thought you were angry."

"Oh, pooh, James! You know I could never be angry with you. I simply had to return your gift because you had already given us a lovely gift, and I couldn't accept something that valuable for myself." Deciding to tell the truth, she said, jokingly, "Why, Adam had a perfect fit when he saw the dresser set and insisted I return it immediately." She touched her fingers on his jacket gently, "I hope you understand."

Blushing with pleasure at her friendliness he offered his arm and said, "May I have this dance?"

Raines smiled up at him as they walked onto the dance floor and he took her in his arms for the waltz. He was an excellent dancer and Raines followed him easily as they glided around the floor. Glancing over his shoulder Raines saw Adam return to the room without Charlotte. He looked about the ballroom. This time when Raines's eyes met his she did not smile and she saw a frown cross his face. For several minutes he stared at her as she danced with James, then suddenly turned and strode back through the door. Raines knew that she was dancing too close to James and it had irritated Adam, but she did not care. In fact, it delighted her to think that he might be suffering as she had only minutes ago. Had he gone back to Charlotte? James spun her around the room, and she searched the crowd for Charlotte's red velvet gown, but it was nowhere to be seen.

At last the music stopped and she fanned herself, trying to catch her breath. "Heavens, James, I'm exhausted. I think I could use another glass of punch to help cool myself off."

They moved to the refreshment table which was

173

being filled with huge dishes of divine looking salads, meats and delicacies for the midnight supper. "Would you like a plate?" asked James, solicitously.

She waved away his suggestion while she patted her brow lightly. "No, just some cool punch to quench my thirst will be sufficient."

They accepted their goblets of punch and moved over to the corner to take seats away from those lining up to be served. Looking through the crowd again, Raines felt her anger rise. Adam was not back in the ballroom, nor was Charlotte, and they had been absent for fully thirty minutes.

"Are you looking for someone?" inquired James, watching her face carefully.

She sipped her punch before answering. She didn't want to sound like a jealous wife. Hoping her voice sounded casual, she said, "I was searching for the attractive Lady Charlotte. I can't find her anywhere. Do you suppose she became ill and went home?"

If James realized why she was interested, he hid the knowledge, and he glanced around the room as if searching for her also. "I don't believe I see her at the moment. Of course, she could have retired to the upstairs bedrooms to repair her makeup or rest for a few minutes. Many of the ladies do from time to time."

Still pretending to search the room for her, Raines said in an indifferent voice, "Oh, really? Perhaps that is where she has gone. I had intended to go over and speak with her a moment, but I will get another opportunity later, I suppose."

Still trying to sound casual, she asked, "Where do those doors lead or do you know?"

James studied her for a minute, before he decided to answer. "I do indeed know where they lead, since I've been to many parties here in the past. They open out onto the veranda. Lady Sybil has the most beautiful and well kept formal gardens, second only to Buckingham Palace. It would be worth your time to come one day and just walk through them."

Raines turned to face him, unable to keep the surprise from her voice. "The gardens! Well, for heaven's sake! I'd never thought of that."

"Would you like to go out? It's night and you can't see much unless the moon is full, but I would be glad to accompany you."

She jumped up and placed her crystal goblet on the table beside her chair. "Oh, let's do go for a stroll outside! It is so stuffy in here that I need a little air to clear my head. This punch is more powerful than I realized and this is my second serving."

Obediently James followed as she crossed the floor and headed for the doors. She saw several people stop talking and nudge each other, and she knew that her behavior would be the gossip of the tea curcuit in the morning, but at the moment she didn't care. Adam had gone out this way and so had Charlotte Brownlees. As she saw it, what was fair for her gallant husband was equally fair for her. Besides, she wanted to walk upon the two in a compromising position in the garden. It would be a delight to slap Adam's face and tell his strumpet off. With head held high she left the room, not the least concerned about what the others thought.

Once away from the crowd, though, her courage faltered. The cold night air struck her in the face and she shivered noticeably. James saw her clasp her arms tightly to try to warm herself and he put his arm around her. "Are you cold? Come closer and I'll keep you warm."

Raines knew that someone passing would misunderstand such a gesture, so she reluctantly rejected his offer, stepping gracefully out of reach. "We'll only stay out a few minutes and . . . and . . . I'll be fine for this short period of time. I should have worn my cape."

Since it was very dark and she could not see the path ahead, she moved slowly and James came up behind her again. Already she realized it had been a mistake to come out with him. As a married woman, she had left him no alternative but to think that she was inviting his attentions. If only she could catch a glimpse of Adam and Charlotte. She was beginning to think that it would be foolish for them to be out here in this weather.

She turned to tell James she wanted to go back indoors and bumped into him. Instantly his arms went around her and he drew her closer. Putting her hands on his chest to push him away, she cried, "James! Please, you mustn't! Someone might see us!"

"I love you, Raines," he said hoarsely, not releasing her. Bending, he attempted to kiss her and she struggled to prevent him, quickly turning her head away.

"James, please stop!" she cried, growing more alarmed as his hands groped to get inside her low cut bodice.

She struggled in his strong grip, shocked at his

refusal to listen, yet knowing that he probably mistook her resistance for feminine coquetry. Now he was holding her so tightly that she could hardly breathe and she gave a slight whimper of protest as his lips sought hers. Revulsion filled her and she pounded on his chest.

"Take your hands off my wife!" thundered a loud voice and she was instantly freed, as a startled James spun around to address Adam.

Shocked, James made no reply and she moved quickly over to Adam's side. He did not so much as glance in her direction. Instead he struck out with his fist and Raines grimaced at the sound of flesh striking bone.

Caught off guard James stumbled backward and lay sprawled on the ground. "Don't you ever come near my wife again or the next time I'll call you out." said Adam in a low voice filled with contempt.

Adam reached out, and taking Raines's arm firmly in his grasp, he led her to the house. She still had not spoken and remained silent as she followed along obediently. Once she tried to pull her arm away but his grip only tightened. At the door he instructed her, "We'll pay our respects to Sybil and then get your cloak. We are going home."

She gasped, "Adam, how will it look for the guests of honor to leave so soon?"

"What difference will that make? You've already disgraced yourself going into the garden with James."

Anger rose in her throat and she stopped in her tracks, and whirled to face him. "What is the difference between my going into the garden with James and you leaving over an hour ago with Charlotte

177

Brownlees?" She spat the words at him, her temper out of control.

For a second his face registered surprise, then he said, "I have no intention discussing this with you. Just do as I tell you." Seeing the look of rebellion in her eyes, he warned, "If you don't want the entire group to witness me turning you across my knee, you'd better do as I say and act civil when we get inside."

"You wouldn't dare strike me," she hissed.

Through clenched teeth, he said, "Don't try my patience much further, Raines, or I warn you, you'll regret it."

Seeing the fire in his eyes and the calm way he said each word, she knew enough not to push her luck much farther, so she lashed out in frustration, "I hate you Adam Kemp! I hate you!" Tears came to her eyes and she put up her free hand to cover her face.

He shook her gently and said, "Think what you like of me, but stop the hysterics until you get home. Now walk into that room and act like nothing happened. If you don't, tomorrow your reputation will be ruined forever. Don't give them the least reason to think anything took place out here tonight."

Knowing that he spoke the truth, Raines blinked away her tears and cleared her throat. "All right, I'm ready to go in now," she whispered.

Heads turned to watch their entrance and from the way the people averted her look, Raines knew she had been the subject of much discussion while she was gone. With her head high she walked past the people as she searched the crowd, hunting for Lady Gossington. Adam freed her arm and put his hand around her waist in an affectionate, possessive manner which gave no hint of the anger he felt.

They located Lady Gossington instructing a butler to bring more wines, and Adam explained their abrupt departure while Raines listened silently. "Sybil, please forgive our leaving early, but I just received urgent word that I am needed at Balfour. My dear wife doesn't want me to go without her, so we must go home immediately to begin preparations for our departure in the morning."

Sybil was a sly and clever woman and her brow rose inquisitively as her eyes raked over Raines for some clue of discord. "Nothing serious, I hope."

"No, just some farmer giving the bailiff a hard time. It's just one of those devilish situations where only the landlord can settle the matter."

Knowing how important it was to fool this woman, Raines stepped closer to Adam and lovingly placed her hand on his arm. "I can't bear to be separated from my husband for any length of time. He wanted me to stay and rest while he was away, but I absolutely refused. A wife's place is by her husband's side. Don't you agree, Lady Gossington?" She smiled sweetly and glanced at Adam with what she hoped passed for love in her eyes.

Uncertain whether she believed the scene she was witnessing, Lady Gossington had no choice but to go along with it. "I am sorry you must leave so early. I have not even had the opportunity to dance with the new bridegroom. You two disappeared right after supper and were nowhere to be found."

"Again, I take all the responsibility, Sybil, and I apologize," said Adam, making a graceful bow. "I had to go check on my coachman after I received word he was drinking too much ale and becoming rowdy in the bargain. Raines saw me leave and became concerned about me, so she had James help her search for me." He spoke glibly and although Sybil arched an eyebrow questioningly, he allowed her no opportunity to dispute him.

Raines and Adam left the ball smiling, but on the way home neither spoke. Raines was furious with herself. How had she allowed herself to get into such a compromising situation with James? And she was angry at Adam for disappearing with Charlotte. Slowly a tear of anger and frustration inched down her cheek. Adam sat in icy stillness, indifferent to her misery.

Chapter 11

Balfour Castle seemed bleak and lonely after the smaller townhouse in London. Since Adam had used Balfour as an excuse for their early departure from Lady Gossington's ball, they had been compelled to return here, much to Raines's annoyance.

The following morning she and Adam had ridden to the castle in silence. She had brought along *Emma*, Jane Austen's new novel, to read, and Adam had slept or pretended to sleep the entire trip.

Once back at Balfour he had ridden out to check his fields each day and she had been left to entertain herself. Though the incident with James was never mentioned again, it hung over them like a weight.

For the first week Raines spent most of her time on her work with the Kemp coin collection. Adam never had dinner, or any other meal with her, and since she soon tired of eating in the huge dining room alone, she had instructed Nettie to bring all her meals to her quarters. Each day she grew more depressed and knew that soon she had to make some type of decision concerning her marriage. The thought of spending the rest of her life living as she was now appeared unbearable.

On the seventh morning after they had arrived at Balfour Castle, Raines was deeply engrossed in a coin book trying to identify a rare 400 B.C. Greek coin when she heard the library door open. Looking up she expected to see Watson, when instead Adam stood watching her and her heart fluttered weakly. He looked thinner and his face had new worry lines etched into it. Truly he looked as miserable as she.

"Good morning," she said in greeting, wondering why he had come.

He didn't return her greeting. Instead he walked over to the fire and held out his hands to warm them. "I've been out checking the lambs in the north pasture and it's a rough day outside." She stopped what she was doing, carefully placing the coin back in its box, before she stood and moved over to sit by the fire.

"You have stayed busy since our return. You look tired. Are you getting enough rest?" he inquired.

She nodded, and he rubbed his hands together a few more minutes before he spoke again. She sat quietly watching, anxious to know what had brought him, yet afraid of what might lie ahead. At last he came to sit in the green chair facing her. "I might as well get to the point. My cousin Horace, who is next in line to inherit Balfour should I fail to fulfill the requirements of my father's will, is coming to visit. It is my guess that he has heard gossip in London that my marriage is not the blissful union it is broadcast to be and is coming to see for himself."

Raines gasped. "Why, Adam, that's terrible! Bal-

182

four is rightfully yours and you have complied with the requirements of the will. We married, what more do they want?"

"I'm sure it would help if we could announce the coming of a Kemp heir. There is no news of what type to tell me, is there by any chance?"

"No," she whispered, dropping her glance and fidgeting with her skirt, creasing the folds absently. "Is there anything I can do to help? I feel responsible for the gossip in London." She stood and moved over to him, putting her hand on his shoulder. "Please, is there anything that I can do to make amends? Adam, I'll do whatever is necessary for you to save Balfour." Her voice carried a ring of conviction and suddenly she realized how much she meant what she said. It was unimaginable to think of Adam losing this beautiful estate that he loved so much.

"There is one thing we can do." He sighed deeply before he continued, "We can put aside our differences and try to pretend we are happily married. I know it will take some play-acting on your part, but do you think you can do it?"

Raines laughed and replied, "I vow he will think this is a marriage made in heaven."

"It will mean that I will have to move into your bedroom with you. I'm sure Cousin Horace will bribe the maids to find out if we are sleeping together. Knowing his suspicious nature and what is at stake, he'll go to great lengths to prove that ours is not a true marriage."

"When is he due to arrive?"

"Day after tomorrow."

"Heavens! Day after tomorrow! This place is a

mess. I must get busy now or it'll never be ready in time." She reached to ring for the housekeeper, and paused with her hand in mid-air. Turning back to Adam, she said, "Adam I'm sorry for what happened at Lady Gossington's party. I should never have gone in the garden with James. I wanted to tell you this, but I've been too stubborn to do so. Regardless of what you may think, James MacBain means nothing to me. However, it is not his fault that he tried to kiss me. I must have led him to believe he could, so don't hold it against him. He has been your friend and solicitor for too long."

Without smiling, Adam said, "He is no longer acting in that capacity."

"Adam! You didn't discharge him, I hope."

"I did and the matter is closed." He clenched his teeth together and Raines saw that he was growing angry, so she did not pursue the issue.

He made no mention of Lady Charlotte and neither did she.

Reaching for the button, she rang for the maid. "If you will excuse me, Adam, I need to go over the many chores to be completed before Cousin Horace arrives. We want him to think I am the model wife and your home is perfect." She laughed to conceal her nervousness, yet she was delighted that Adam was again speaking to her.

That night he showed up for dinner and so did she. They had many things to discuss before his relatives arrived. She learned that Horace would be accompanied by his mother and his wife, and Raines knew how inquisitive women tended to be.

Already she had planned the menus to be prepared

and had instructed Watson to hire two extra village girls to help with the housecleaning.

The castle was aflutter with activity and when the day arrived for the important guests, Balfour Castle smelled of lemon wax and pine oil and all forty rooms glistened from their recent polishing and airing.

Dressed in a new day gown of yellow wool, Raines stood below the grand staircase and surveyed the castle with pride. Nervously she turned to Adam, who lounged with an elbow on the stair rail watching her. "I told Watson to light the fires in all the bedrooms, although I hope Cousin Horace and his wife will take the rooms I've chosen for them. Adam, do you think I've forgotten anything? I'm sorry there aren't any fresh flowers to be arranged. Do the vases of greenery look all right?" she continued talking rapidly, afraid that something would go wrong.

Laughing, Adam took her hands and turned her to face him. "Darling, stop fretting. We don't want to make Horace so comfortable that he moves in for the winter. A few inconveniences might help matters. Everything looks magnificent and Balfour has never appeared more elegant. In fact, you have probably made it so grand that Horace will be even more determined to lay claim to it."

Raines glowed under his compliments, noting it was the first time Adam had even called her an endearing name. Or was this just a warm-up for the performance they had to give later? Fidgeting with her dress, Raines glanced in the mirror and adjusted the neckline of the gown. "Do I look presentable? Does this dress look all right, or should I have worn the green one?"

185

She watched his eyes scan her seriously and there was a twinkle in them. Frowning she said, "I knew it. I should have worn the green. I'll just run back upstairs and change. It won't take but a minute." She turned to leave and Adam put out his hand to stop her.

"You look beautiful, as if you didn't already know it. Now, don't go and change, you've gotten your compliment."

Hurt, Raines said, "I wasn't hinting for a compliment. I'm sorry you thought so. I merely wanted to make a decent impression on your relatives." She dropped her gaze and blinked to prevent a tear forming. It seemed they constantly were hurting one another.

Still holding her arm, Adam lifted her face until her eyes met his. He spoke softly, "Raines, why must we always quarrel and misunderstand one another? I was teasing you a moment ago. You are lovely, and I'm proud to introduce you as my wife. Now stop fretting. Agreed?"

Silently she nodded, her heart aching from his nearness, and she thought for one fleeting second that he intended to kiss her. It was the most intimate moment they had had since the incident at Lady Gossington's. However, the sound of a carriage pulling up outside interrupted the mood.

"They're here!" cried Raines, in a whisper.

Watson appeared from a side door and went to greet the guests. Meanwhile Adam walked out with his arm lightly around Raines's waist in a possessive, husbandly manner, and said to the three people who stepped from the carriage, "Welcome to Balfour, Cousins. I trust your trip was pleasant."

Adam introduced Raines to the three and the two women embraced Raines and gave her a peck on the cheek. Horace Langley did not favor his cousin in the slightest and had Adam not informed her that they were related Raines would never have suspected it. For Horace was short and plump, with a large English nose and watery blue eyes which stared at Raines suspiciously. His wife, Velma, was just the opposite, being tall, a full four inches taller than he, and extremely thin, with a sharp beak of a nose and pale coloring. Mother Langley, who favored her son in stature and figure, was dressed to the nines, and wore a fur stole which looked to Raines as if it had molted.

After the initial pleasantries, the party moved into the parlor where Raines rang for tea to be served.

"I am so delighted to meet you, since naughty Adam didn't invite us to the wedding," said Mother Langley, as she sat down on the rose velvet sofa with a thud. Throwing off her fur, she said, "That was the worst carriage ride I've had in years. Ben, Horace's new coachman, is an idiot. He raced the horses at full gallop over every pothole between Leeds and here. I declare, every bone in my body aches." She rubbed gingerly at the back of her neck.

"Would you prefer to go to your room first and rest for a while before we have tea?" asked Raines, unsure what she should do for these grumbling, irritable people.

Waving aside the suggestion, Ardis complained, "A few hours rest won't help my aching body. It'll take several days for me to recover from that ride."

"Mother Langley doesn't travel well," explained

187

Velma, in her clipped, pinched voice. Obviously accustomed to her mother-in-law's temperament, she smiled at the older woman saying, "After your tea, Mother, why don't you go up and have a hot soak in a tub? I'm sure that will ease some of the pain."

Still not mollified for the discomfort she had been put through, Mrs. Langley said to her son, "If you would just repair those worn springs on the carriage, I feel that would help matters a great deal. I told you to do so before we departed, but you didn't heed my advice."

Raines was shocked to see the grown man cringe and blush at his mother's rebuke, and she knew who ruled that family. If Velma weren't so stiff-backed and proper, she'd actually feel sorry for the young woman. Imagine, being married to a thirty year old man who was cowed by his mother. She saw that this visit was going to be a trying one.

Adam asked about various relatives, more to make conversation, Raines thought, than out of interest. And, if all were like the three sitting in her parlor now, no wonder he had not bothered to invite any to their wedding. Why, they were as unbearable as Uncle Percival and his three daughters! The comparison brightened Raines's spirits and her nervousness vanished. She only prayed that her good manners and patience would stay with her.

Horace sat glancing around the room, and Raines thought he looked as though he was appraising the furniture. At last he turned to Adam and said, "Your marriage came as quite a shock to us."

Looking innocent Adam asked, "Oh, and why was that, cousin?"

188

Flustered by Adam's calmness, Horace glanced at Raines, as though reluctant to speak in front of her, and seeing her eyes on him intently awaiting his reply, he stammered, "You . . . uh . . . you know Adam, you had been sort of a rake. Why the talk around London was that you had vowed to never marry again . . . again, after . . ."

Adam finished for him, "After my first wife's death? I did make that statement, but it was before I met Raines. I might as well confess, she swept my heart away the first time I met her." He grinned affectionately at Raines, and patted her hand.

"Didn't you engage her as a secretary or something?" asked Velma making no effort to hid the implied sneer.

"I did indeed. Not only is she beautiful, but she is intelligent in the bargain. I can't think of any other family member who can boast of that combination, can you, Velma?"

Velma's face grew crimson and she floundered for a reply. "I can't think of anyone in our circle who had married a woman of the working class. Can you, Mother Langley?"

Raines resented being discussed as if she were not present. "I wasn't employed as a secretary, as you put it," she informed them. "Lord Kemp engaged me to catalogue his father's vast and expensive coin collection before it is presented to the museum."

"Presented to the museum? Adam, you can't be serious! You don't intend to give away the valuable Kemp coin collection, do you?" cried Horace, setting down his cup so hard Raines hoped it didn't break. "This is disgraceful!" Then his voice turned sarcastic and he said, "Really, Adam, when did you become a philanthropist?"

The attack did not ruffle Adam who replied calmly, "I'm sorry, but I can't take credit for this generous gift. Mother made this wish known before her death, and I hired Raines to carry out her request. However, I agreed with her that it was the logical thing to do with the collection. I had no interest in it, and since it is so extensive, it is of great importance to the British Museum."

"I should imagine so," retorted Mother Langley. Turning to Raines, she smiled sweetly and said, "So you came to catalogue the collection and fell in love. How romantic." Her voice did not sound as though she thought it was romantic at all.

"I think Raines and I had a story book courtship." Adam said. "We fell in love immediately, and after mother's death I saw no reason to postpone the marriage."

"Not even for a suitable period of mourning?" Ardis Langley sniffed.

"The solicitor's letter didn't have any bearing on your rush, did it?" asked Horace.

Raines held her breath, but Adam seemed undaunted. "I certainly intended to comply with the will's requirements, if that's what you're referring to."

"Yes, it would seem you did," snapped Horace. Raines was developing a dislike for this pompous boor. "I'll say this for you, Adam, you picked a beauty," said Horace, raking his eyes over Raines.

"Your name was Scott wasn't it, my dear? Are you related to the Scotts of Leeds?" asked Velma, who had remained silent until now.

"I'm afraid not."

The conversation died and they sat drinking their tea and staring at one another.

At last Horace said, "Mother and Velma want to go up and rest. I thought I'd ride over the estate with you. Has the hunting been good this year?"

Thankful to escape the Langleys, Raines showed the two women to their rooms and went off in search of the cook to see how the evening meal was progressing. Before lying down for her nap, Mother Langley had given Raines a long list of foods she could not eat and instructions on how her diet was to be prepared. Going briskly to the kitchen, Raines looked at the paper and muttered, "She'll be lucky if I don't poison her."

But even the Langleys couldn't dampen her delight in having passed the initial test. She and Adam had behaved like any young married couple. Now, all she dreaded was being alone with him. For a night in Adam's arms could weaken her resolve to never love him again.

Chapter 12

The evening meal was a remarkable success, thus Raines went to her room elated and in splendid spirits. Adam had played the attentive husband and she had enjoyed her role as the adoring wife. For once it had been possible to say and behave around him the way she truly desired.

She slipped out of her gown and into a dressing robe and comfortable mules, then humming softly, she moved to the dresser to remove her jewelry. There was a light tap on the adjoining door and she knew it was Adam. Happily she called out, "Come in, dear!"

She jumped up and ran to meet him. Throwing her arms around his neck, she said, laughing, "The visit is going gloriously well, don't you think? Oh, I've never enjoyed anything as much as shocking your stuffy old Cousin Velma and disappointing Horace. Did you see the pain in his eyes when you congratulated me on the fine meal and kissed me on the cheek?" She threw back her head and looked up into his eyes, merriment filling her own. "Oh, Adam, it's the most fun I've had in ages."

Putting his hands on her waist, he studied her a moment, grinning, before he said, "Why does it have to be play-acting?" He leaned down and kissed her softly on the lips. "I knew I'd married more than I bargained for almost before the ceremony was over. You would make a marvelous mistress." He kissed her again but she pulled away.

"Mistress? Adam, that's terrible. I don't want to be your mistress. I want to be your wife."

He raised one eyebrow in mock surprise, a grin rakishly turning up the corners of his lips. "All right, if you want to be my wife then come here and prove it. It's time to perform your wifely duties."

Raines moved farther away and sat back down at the dressing table to brush her hair. She didn't want him to see her hands trembling. With her back to him, she was able to speak more frankly. "Oh, Adam, you're deliberately trying to confuse me. Making love, without being in love, just seems so wrong to me."

"How else do you propose for us to beget the Kemp heir?"

She saw him studying her carefully in the mirror. "Or are you already expecting the heir?"

Slowly she shook her head. "No, I . . . I am not with child."

"Then don't you think we need to remedy that at the earliest possible opportunity? That is, unless you want Cousin Horace to win Balfour. If he suspects that our marriage is a merely legal arrangement, he may have grounds to contest its validity in terms of the will."

She laid down the hair brush and turned to face him. "No, Balfour is yours and you deserve to keep it.

I think Horace is hateful and mean to try to deprive you of it."

Grinning wickedly, he reached down and lifted her from the stool, carrying her to the large bed and placing her gently on the feather mattress. "Then I think we should get busy at preventing his claim, don't you?"

Without further argument, Raines nodded in agreement, although she did not smile. Quickly Adam blew out the last candle and slipped into bed beside her. As he slid his arms around her and drew her closer, she whispered, "Couldn't we at least pretend that we love each other?" she gave an involuntary shiver as his hands slipped possessively over her body in slow stroking motions.

Kissing her on the neck, he chuckled softly, "Do you want me to say that I love you?"

"Yes."

"All right, I love you." His lips came down hard on her mouth and he pressed her closer to him as he swiftly slid her gown from her shoulders.

When he finally broke away, he propped on one elbow and stared down at her. She could see him vaguely in the moonlight which streamed into the room. "Well, aren't you going to say anything?" he teased.

Blushing, she asked, "Like what?"

He sighed deeply, "Listen, you little minx, if I have to pretend that I love you, then you certainly have to do your part and say endearing things to me, also."

"Oh, Adam, I do love you!" she exclaimed, throwing her arms around his neck and drawing him close again. She hoped that her voice didn't betray that she wasn't play-acting. She knew it would be dangerous to allow Adam to have this powerful weapon to manipulate her at his will. She had heard how callous he became when a woman succumbed to his charm.

Where before their lovemaking had been exciting, tonight as they exchanged endearments and neither held back their emotions, they reached new plateaus of sensuality. Raines under the pretext of acting, cast off her inhibitions and responded with the warm and burning passion she was capable of. She matched his ardor and was swept up into the surging tide of desire until their need peaked and was spent.

Falling back upon her pillow Raines gasped for breath and said, "I never dreamed anything could be as wonderful as this."

Adam drew her back into his embrace and kissed her lightly on the cheek. "I always knew you had the ability to flame a man's desire to the limit, and now you've proven it."

Snuggling close in his arms and feeling warm and safe for the first time in her life, she said honestly, "Adam I do love you so much."

He kissed her again softly. "Hush, my dear, or you'll arouse my need for a repeat performance, and I must be up early in the morning to take Horace over to Squire Nelson's house." She ran her hand exploringly down his naked body, astonished at her own boldness.

Nibbling at her ear he chuckled and whispered, "I must admit, your idea of fantasizing did improve our performance."

She stopped and withdrew her hand as if she had burned it. He had only been pretending! It stung and tears came to her eyes. They lay in silence and in a few minutes she heard his soft breathing and knew he was alseep. She tried to ease out of his arms and turn away, but he held her too tightly.

When she finally fell asleep she dreamed of Adam and again heard him repeating the endearments he had so passionately whispered.

The next morning she wasn't surprised to discover that Adam had already left the castle before she awoke.

While she felt warm and happy and fulfilled as a woman, she also felt depressed that she was falling deeper and more passionately in love with Adam. After she delivered an heir, would he coldly ship her back to London and ignore her until time to produce another heir? Fear gripped at her and she felt angry that her body had betrayed her, and she had behaved so wantonly. Even this morning she still yearned for his touch and the stirring of desire began to swell within her.

Quickly she dressed and went down to join the visitors, who sat frowning silently as she entered the drawing room. "Have you had breakfast, Cousin Ardis?"

"Humph! At least two hours ago. Adam went off with Horace, and Velma and I had to breakfast alone."

"I apologize for sleeping so late. It was unforgivable of me. I don't usually oversleep, so I didn't instruct the maid to call me. It's just that I stayed . . ." faltered, a blush rushed up her neck, ". . . uh . . . I didn't go to bed as early as usual," she finished.

"I thought you and Adam went to your rooms at the

same time we did," said Mrs. Langley, eyeing her suspiciously.

Why the old snoop is trying to pry into what we did later, thought Raines, shocked. "You know how it is with newlyweds, don't you, Cousin Ardis?" replied Raines, trying to look coy when she really wanted to lash out at the woman.

Velma scanned Raines in the loose fitting morning dress which hung gracefully from her bosom, concealing her figure. "You aren't with child yet, are you?"

Taking the bait, Raines looked her in the eye and said, "If not now, then I most certainly will be soon."

She heard the older woman's intake of breath at such a bold statement. Raines continued, enjoying the sight of the two women squirming in embarrassment, "Adam and I want to start our family as quickly as possible. Children add so much to a marriage, don't you think?" She smiled innocently, glancing from one to the other.

Mother Langley dabbed at her face with her handkerchief. She turned to her daughter-in-law and said hastily, "Perhaps you should show Raines your needlepoint."

They spent the rest of the morning discussing needle work, fashions, and other boring topics, until Raines thought she might scream if someone didn't come to her rescue. At the moment she thought she could stand no more, she heard Adam's hearty laugh and knew the men had returned.

The rest of the visit was so uneventful that Raines was not surprised when Horace announced that they must be returning to their home since he had important business pending.

197

Standing arm in arm, Raines and Adam waved goodbye to the three disappointed relatives.

Once they were out of sight, Raines turned to Adam and cried delightedly, "I think we outfoxed them! Oh, if only you could have seen the look on Cousin Ardis's face when I told her we were working on producing an heir." She grinned mischievously as she imitated the older woman, patting her face with a make-believe handkerchief, "Oh dear, why don't we talk about needlepoint." Her mimic was perfect and Adam chuckled as he watched.

Taking her by the arm, he said, "Let's go in and practice some more. I think you enjoyed embarrassing poor Cousin Ardis."

Holding back, Raines argued, "Adam, we can't go to our bedroom in the middle of the afternoon. What will the servants think?"

"They'll think exactly what is going to happen."

Raines was surprised at how easy it was becoming to make love with Adam. She was happier than ever before and at that moment she felt sure nothing could destroy their happiness.

Chapter 13

But Raines's new-found happiness was short lived. When she and Adam walked arm in arm up the staircase, she was so happy she thought her heart would burst with joy. Their moment of closeness was interrupted by the resounding knock on the front door. "Who the devil can that be?" Adam asked, turning to listen to the urgent pounding.

"I haven't the slightest notion. You don't suppose Cousin Horace met with a carriage accident, do you?" Raines turned to watch in curiosity as Watson rushed to admit the visitor.

The moment the door swung open, a young crofter's boy dashed into the hall. Glancing up he spied Adam and waved. "Oh, Lord Kemp, thank heaven ye be home. I have a message for ye from Lady Ch . . ." he broke off in mid-sentence when he saw the slight movement of Adam's hand in warning. Catching his breath, the lad said, "I'm sorry to trouble ye, sir, but I do have an urgent message for you."

Adam turned to Raines and said, "Go on up, dear. I'll be only a minute."

Raines, curious to know what was so urgent, struggled with her desire to argue with Adam. Not wanting to spoil their new-found intimacy she replied, "I'll be in my sitting room when you're finished."

Adam moved back down the stairs and led the youth into his office, careful to close the door behind him. Raines lingered on the landing hoping to overhear some of the conversation. However, the two spoke in hushed tones, and within seconds Adam flung open the door and shouted for Watson to bring his cape and riding crop. Raines had to duck quickly behind a column to avoid being seen.

Quietly she moved on to her room where her window faced the front lawn. She watched as the stableboy led Adam's horse, and a second for the lad, to the front door. Both rode off with haste. Moments later there came a light tap on her door and she knew the message Watson carried for her. "Lord Kemp wished me to tell you that he had to leave on business and you are not to wait up for him tonight."

"Who was that lad?" Raines asked, trying to keep her voice light. "I thought I had seen him around before."

Watson shook his head. "I doubt, that, my lady. He is Farmer Gaiter's son, Marcus, and doesn't come often to the manor."

"Oh, so the farmer must be having some difficulty," said Raines hoping to pry more from Watson. It was possible he had heard more than she.

"That I couldn't say, madam."

She waved him aside. "Well, 'tis of no importance, anyhow." Her feelings were confused and she felt miffed at being left out of Adam's plans. She realized anew how little she knew about her husband. There was no denying that he maintained a secretive side which appeared dark and unapproachable.

Although she waited in her room until quite late that night, Adam did not return to the manor. Even more confused, her feelings of anger coupled with anxiety, she finally retired for the night, blowing out the candle with heightened resolve to learn more about Adam's past. Perhaps there was some connection between Alexandra and this secrecy.

The following morning after a restless night of fretful tossing and much turning, Raines rose determined to do some exploring on her own. She wondered what Adam had planned for the day.

Nettie knocked and entered to bring her a cup of chocolate. "Did my lady sleep well?" She moved over to the bed and began fussing with the covers.

"Has Adam returned?" Raines asked as she moved over to the dresser.

"That he did, Lady Raines. This morning he was up early and gone again, he was. He sent a message to say that he would be away most of the day on urgent business. He said that he could be away for a night as he might have to go to London town."

"London town! Whatever for?" Raines whirled and faced the trusted servant. "Nettie, why would he go there?"

A look of confusion crossed Nettie's brow. "That I can't say. Wasn't he planning to go today?"

"Not that I know. Did Watson give any hint of such?" Raines studied the woman closely. "You know something, don't you?"

Nettie bustled around the room avoiding Raines's

direct stare. "I be telling the truth, Miss Raines. Things don't seem exactly right but nobody says anything directly to me." She stopped her fidgeting and faced Raines. "If I may be so bold, I think there be a lot of secrets here at Balfour. It may be best if we don't know what's not to be our concern. Let the dead keep their secrets."

"A pox on you, Nettie, for being so superstitious! If there are secrets here, then I intend to find out what they are. Now you run back downstairs and send word for the groom to saddle a horse for me. I'm going riding and clear my head. The fresh air will help me think. There'll be no secrets for long, I can assure you of that."

"Lady Raines, please be careful. I don't like this idea of you going off by yerself one bit."

Raines waved her aside. "Such nonsense. I've been riding all my life and nothing is going to happen to me. Adam isn't an ogre." She smiled reassuringly to the servant. "Now run along while I slip into my riding habit. And tell the groom I want a spirited charge, not an old nag he'd saddle up for his grand-mother. Understand?"

Within the hour Raines was seated on her mount and ready to leave the stables. She had chosen the spirited stallion, Banshee, who tugged at the bit, anxious to be given free rein to race across the pasture. Raines guided the horse gracefully through its jump over the rock fence, and then gave it a gentle tap to urge it into a gallop. Sensing this new freedom, the stallion raced down the gravel path and into the woods. Once among the trees Raines pulled Banshee in and slowed his pace so that she could study the countryside.

The morning was perfect for riding with a crisp nip in the air which tingled on her cheeks and nose. A light frost still sparkled on the leaves but the mist had cleared and she could see for a long distance. Reining in at an overhang, she looked down into the valley where village cottages nestled out of the cold winter winds. Small curls of smoke drifted from several chimneys and Raines suddenly decided to go down and meet the villagers. Tugging at Banshee's bridle she guided the large black horse down the rocky path, reining in each time the stallion tried to quicken its pace. She, in her black riding habit atop the large black stallion, made an impressive picture as they worked their way down toward the valley. By the time they reached the foot of the mountain a group of village children had come out of their homes to watch her arrival.

"Have you come to see Darcy?" one towheaded lad called in greeting.

Smiling, Raines inched closer as she leaned down and patted the stallion's neck praising it for its steady footwork. Glancing over her shoulder she realized for the first time what a steep incline they had traveled. "Darcy? No, who's Darcy?" she said laughing. "I came to see all the children."

"Lord Kemp always comes to see Darcy," the youth replied.

Raines was about to ask another question when a woman rounded the cottage and called sharply to the boy. "Quinton, come here immediately! Haven't I told you to mind your manners when the manor folk be about?"

"But this lady didn't come to see Darcy," he explained.

The woman grabbed him by the shirt sleeve and boxed him on his head. "Enough! Hush your mouth!" she ordered.

"Don't hit him," Raines said pleadingly. "He isn't bothering me. I want to talk to all the children. Who is this Darcy he thinks I wish to visit?"

The woman shrugged her shoulders. "That I couldn't say, ma'am. You know how boys run on. Welcome to the village, Lady Kemp." She curtsied and smiled.

"Oh, so you already know my name. And what might yours be?" Raines prodded Banshee forward to try and keep pace with the woman who walked rapidly.

Suddenly the woman stopped and turned to face her. "I don't want to be disrespectful, ma'am, but I'm sure that Lord Kemp would be highly agitated with your being here. 'Tis best that you leave and we won't tell him you came."

Banshee pranced sideways and Raines patted him on the neck to calm him. "It seems my horse wants to gallop some more, so I'll be on my way today, but I will be back to visit again soon."

The woman reached out and grabbed the horse's reins. "Please forgive me, my lady, but ye've got to hear me out first. I beg of you." Her voice held a pleading note. "Me and my little'uns ain't got nowheres else to go should Lord Kemp turn us out. And if'n he learns you been about asking questions, we're sure to be sent packing."

A puzzled expression crossed Raines's smooth brow.

"I've never known Lord Kemp to be unkind to anyone. You must be mistaken. If there's any doubt, I'll tell him upon his return. There can't possibly be anything for you to be upset about."

"No, ma'am, I'm sure you're correct, all right. Please be on your way and have a good ride." An older man walked up to the village woman and took her by the arm. "My Betsy here has work to do, so if you'll excuse her, my lady."

"Certainly. Good day to all of you." Raines prodded the horse's sides and raced off in a gallop. She felt hurt and confused by the villagers' behavior. Of one thing she was positive, the instant Adam returned home, she intended to tell him of their strange conduct. Also she would question him about this Darcy whom he visited.

She rode toward the coast as she departed the village and gave Banshee his head, letting him twist and turn down the paths until he came to the cliffs. The thundering roar of the North Sea pounding on the rocky cliffs reminded her that she was a long way from Balfour, but Raines rode on. Still baffled by her encounter with the villagers, she wanted to ride and let her thoughts wander. The outdoors always seemed to clear the cobwebs from her mind.

Ahead she saw a young man walking along the path with his sheep dog. He entered her lane and glanced up, saw her, and started toward her. He waved in a friendly manner and she slowed Banshee to a walk. "Hello," she called in greeting.

"Good day to ye," he said in return. "Are you lost?"

"I don't think so," she replied, reining to a stop.

"I'm just out for a morning ride."

He nodded. "Aye, 'tis a fine morning for such. Where ye be from?"

"I'm Lady Kemp from Balfour Castle, and who might you be?"

He backed away from her as if she had struck him. "Oh, ma'am, I think ye best be turning back. Them from the castle will be upset at yer trespassing on their property."

Abashed by his words, Raines attempted to apologize. "I am most sorry. I had no idea that the owners would mind my using this path to the sea. It looks like a public road."

"That may be, my lady, but they would take offense to the likes of you being on it."

"Why ever would they mind? I don't even know to whom this estate belongs." She shook her head in disbelief.

For the first time she caught a glimpse of the huge gray castle in the distance. "It is a lovely place and we do appear to be neighbors."

The young man shook his head, and shading his eyes from the sun, he studied her intently. "This land belongs to Lady Alexandra's family and I don't think they, or Lord Kemp, would want you here." He added as if to soften his words, "You seem a fine sort and all, but the hate runs deep, if you please forgive my bluntness."

Raines felt the color rise in her cheeks. She had indeed blundered. Taking the reins up, she quickly began turning Banshee's head. "Oh, I'm terribly sorry." She glanced back at the lad and said, "Please, for my sake, don't mention to the family that I trespassed."

"Aye, 'tis a promise," the lad nodded. "Come along, Cher," he called to his dog.

Raines raced back to the main road and followed it without variation trying to remember which paths she had taken before. All the pleasure in her ride had been ruined by her uneasy encounters with the local people. She had learned one interesting thing today though: the feelings ran high between Lady Alexandra's family and the Kemps. Today's events only made her more determined to discover the root of the mystery.

She heard the pounding of a horse's hooves before she caught a glimpse of the lone rider who raced toward her. Slowing Banshee, she watched the rider's approach with curiosity until the distant figure became recognizable. The rider was Adam and she waved in friendly greeting. He acknowledged her wave with a frown and pushed his steed faster.

When he drew closer he slowed his horse and reined in beside her. "What in blazes are you doing out here?" he asked in a thunderous voice.

"Is that any way to greet me?" she asked, her temper rising. She had done nothing to deserve his wrath.

He sighed deeply and shook his head. "Raines, every time I let you out of my sight, must you always get into trouble?"

"I can't see where I'm in any trouble whatsoever. You appear to be the only one with your nose out of joint." She kicked her horse in the side and started off, but Adam whirled on his mount and soon caught up with her, catching her reins and pulling her horse to a halt. "Stop it, Raines! I've had about as much of your foolishness as I can take for one day."

She whirled on him now, her eyes blazing. "My foolishness! How dare you! I don't know what you're in such a dither about and I don't care!"

"Perhaps I'm being unfair," he yielded. "Come along, let's go home. There is a short cut through these crags."

"Perhaps?" she retorted. Anger rose in her again. "I think everyone around here is half-witted today and that includes you!" She nudged her horse ahead and refused to ride beside him. She knew that he was furious too, but at the moment she couldn't care less.

Once back at Balfour, Raines stormed into the castle leaving Adam at the stables with the horses. Slamming the door she took the stairs as if they were under attack. Just as she reached the landing she heard the front door open.

"Raines, come into the library!" Adam shouted up the stairway. She paused for a moment and then ignored him. "Either come down this moment or I'll come up and carry you down bodily!"

She leaned over the balcony and hissed, "You wouldn't dare! Have you gone completely mad yelling at me like a common chit?"

His face reddened under her obstinacy. "I'll do worse than that if you don't get down here immediately." He moved toward the stairs threateningly.

"Oh, all right, just calm down before you scandalize the household." With head held high she came down the stairs annoyingly slowly.

Adam turned and marched into the library to wait for her. "Shut the door," he ordered. He motioned for her to come over to his desk and sit down.

"I'll stand, thank you. Now for heaven's sake what did you wish to say to me?"

He slammed his hand down on the desk top with a loud bang and glared at her. "Stay out of the village and that which is of no concern to you. I warn you, Raines, I will not have a meddlesome wife prying into matters which are of no concern to her."

"Why I merely went for a ride today and stumbled on the village. This house is about to drive me to distraction and I thought a ride would be refreshing." Still angry, she hurled something she hoped would pierce him, "After all, I'm practically a prisoner here. Don't you have any friends? Nobody has been to call."

He studied her for a moment and then, his manner softened. He moved around the desk toward her but she backed out of reach. "I'll go riding with you and show you much prettier paths to travel and much safer ones." He dropped his hands to his sides in a gesture of surrender. "To be honest, when I learned where you had gone I feared highwaymen might set upon you. That is a favorite area of thieves."

"The villagers seemed nice enough," she countered stubbornly. She wondered if she dared ask about the person called Darcy.

"Of course the villagers are good people or I'd move them off my land. It's the roustabouts who lurk near the seacoast that I must warn you about. Promise that you won't go that way again and I will take you riding tomorrow. Agreed?"

It was difficult for Raines to remain angry with anyone—particularly Adam—for long, so she nodded.

"Agreed."

He cleared his throat and moved to pick up an envelope on his desk. "And about not having friends, I fear I'm to blame for that also. I have kept you out here away from the neighbors far too long. First we were in mourning and then I thought you preferred to work in privacy on the coin collection. However, this came by messenger today and you might wish to reply."

Curious to see the envelope she moved closer. "What is it?"

"The Duke and Duchess of Ramfield are having a weekend party at their country place and have invited us. Do you like to ride to the hounds?"

Now it was her turn to blush. "I'm sorry, Adam. I was deliberately nasty just now. I don't fox hunt . . . that is I never have but I'd love to go and meet some people."

"Then it is settled. Send our acceptance tomorrow and we shall attend." Frowning, he added. A large number of the London circle will be present and I trust you'll conduct yourself with behavior above reproach. Now don't get upset again," he said, quickly, anticipating her quick temper. "I merely wanted to warn you that if James MacBain should be there, I expect no repeat of the London fiasco." There was no mistaking the stern look he gave her.

Raines decided not to quarrel any more so she turned to leave but stopped to add, "I'm going to my room to change for dinner. I won't be late." Then mustering her courage she asked, "Adam, who is Darcy?"

At first he drew a blank so she continued, "In the

village they asked if I'd come to see Darcy. Who is he?"

"No one for you to concern your pretty little head about." He moved back to his desk and began reading a letter.

"Then you aren't going to tell me?" Anger crept into her voice again. When he still did not reply, she snapped, "Well, don't you fret, I'll find out."

In a voice as calm as a breeze he said, "Don't go meddling where you have no business. And never mention that name again. Do you understand?"

His soft voice frightened her more than the booming one of anger. "Do you understand?" he repeated.

"Yes," she replied meekly and moved to the door. But understanding and obeying were two entirely separate matters.

Chapter 14

Raines dined in silence, pushing her food around on her plate. All of Adam's attempts at conversation met with indifference. Once the meal was completed she excused herself to go to her room, pleading exhaustion from her long ride.

Nettie, sensing Raines's mood, had prepared a hot perfumed bath in the large copper tub and this did seem to lift her spirits. In truth she didn't know exactly why she felt so depressed. When she had accepted Adam's proposal she had expected loneliness but she had not been prepared for this inner turmoil with her emotions.

A cold rain lashed against the leaded windowpanes with such force that she told Nettie to check the latches. The weather, so bright in the morning, seemed to have followed her mood and now was a raging storm of anger.

"Please find my white nightgown," she said to Nettie. "The one with the high neck and long sleeves, and poke up the fire. It's getting damp and chilled in here. I tell you, Nettie, this place is almost as bad as

212

outdoors. I've never lived in such a cold place."

Knowing her mistress was just in a bad mood, Nettie clucked and said, "Lor' to be sure, 'tis better in this castle than out there in that frenzy. Now you just be in a bad mood tonight, Lady Raines." She brought over the soft muslin night gown and draped it over the young girl's shoulders, carefully straightening the seams. "Now, isn't that better? Don't you feel warmer already?"

Raines slipped her feet into soft mules and moved nearer the fire to sit on the chaise lounge. "I suppose it is somewhat better," she conceded. Sighing deeply, she picked up the romance novel which lay open on the table. "You may go when you're finished, Nettie. I don't feel like going to bed yet. But don't stay up and wait for me. I can take care of things for the rest of the evening."

Tidying up the room as fast as she could, Nettie said, "Thank you, Lady Raines. I do have something planned for tonight. Cook and Watson and I have got a little game of cards going and soon as they're finished, we'll be getting to it."

"Just don't you go losing your whole month's salary to the likes of them," laughed Raines.

"Don't you fret over that, ma'am. Nettie Ogg won't be no loser."

"Knowing you, Nettie, I feel sorry for Cook and Watson." Raines waved her away with her hand. "Now, off with you and good luck with the cards."

Raines picked up the book and thumbed through a few pages, scanning the paragraphs without much interest. Just as she tossed the book back on the table in disgust, there came a light tap on her door. With heart racing she moved to the door, knowing that Adam stood on the other side.

She opened the door and saw his eyes sweep over her and the quick intake of his breath. "May I come in?" His voice sounded low and husky. She also smelled the distinct odor of drink about him.

"Why?" she asked and then could have bitten off her tongue. She did not move from before him.

A scowl crossed his dark brow and he pushed her gently aside and strode into the room. "I see you weren't exhausted enough to retire for the night," he said, glancing around the room. He moved over to the fire and threw on a few more pieces of coal. "Aren't you afraid you'll catch cold running around the place in that light nightgown?" He continued to frown.

Raines had never seen him in such a surly mood and she decided it wisest not to cross him. So gently she said, "I was just getting my robe."

"No, wait," he said, moving close to her again. Reaching out, he ran his hand down the sleeve of her nightgown, his hands burning where they touched. "Isn't this better, my beautiful Raines?" he whispered softly.

"Really, Adam, I think you should go to your room. You seem much the worse for any conversation tonight." She tried to move from within his reach, but he stepped closer.

"What's the matter, my pet, don't you like to be near me?" He lifted her chin forcing her to stare into his dark, mysterious eyes.

With heart pounding so hard that she knew he must sense it, she said in a low voice, "This is something we should wait and discuss tomorrow, Adam. You've been near the bottle far too long tonight to talk rationally about anything."

"Who wants to talk," he whispered, tracing her cheekbone with his finger, barely grazing her skin, yet sending pulsing shivers down her body.

She opened her mouth to reply, but he was so near that nothing escaped her lips. The next instant his lips were pressed against hers and she tasted their sweetness. Raines felt the warmth rising in her body and she found herself returning his kisses. Like a shameless harlot her body betrayed her mind, and her hands slipped around his neck, burrowing into his thick hair. When he finally released her she sucked in breath and willed her knees not to go weak. And then she began to regain her senses and to realize that all he wanted was someone to warm his bed on a cold night. This was not what she intended to have from life and she tried to push him away without much success.

Drawing her nearer once more he found her lips and began claiming them a second time. Between kisses he whispered softly, "I want you, my stubborn little vixen."

Her eyes flew open and she struggled to be free, while at the same time forcing her body to calm its raging tides. "Adam, please don't," she cried when able to free her lips from his. "You remember our bargain. This . . ." she stammered, "Our being together was not to become an every night occurrence. You gave your word."

A quick flash of anger brought a glare to his expression but then he pushed her from him and stepped back. Raines steadied herself as if he had struck her and cringed from his look of wrath. "So be it, Lady Raines. Forgive my rude intrusion," he said in a low calm voice. "You will not be bothered by my affections again. There are plenty of others who would gladly warm my bed." With that he stalked out the door, slamming it with such force that Raines blushed. The entire household would be aware of their quarrelling.

Raines spent a restless night and the next few days she made an effort to stay out of Adam's way. To her relief he left in midweek for London town which gave her free access to the castle without danger of an embarrassing encounter. The few times they had met or dined together, their conversation had remained cool and impersonal.

There was plenty to keep Raines busy. Between the coin collection and choosing the right clothes to take to the duke's house party the days raced by without much time for her to brood over her troubles with Adam.

Finally one day when she felt she could not stand the castle another hour, she instructed the stableboy to saddle Banshee for her. The weather was cold but the fog seemed to be lifting so she dressed warmly and set out.

Adam had never brought up the ride he had promised so she really didn't have any route to take other than the one with which she was familiar already. And since the mist had not lifted as much as she had anticipated she decided the best route for her was to follow the paths which she knew. She wanted to avoid the village again, because she knew they would report her actions to Adam immediately. She had no intention of fueling his temper any more.

The horse seemed as delighted to be out in the countryside as she, and Raines let him set their pace. She rode briskly for a long distance and soon found herself nearing the overhang for the village. Out of curiosity she led Banshee to the cliffside for one quick look into the village. To her astonishment she saw the carriage with the Balfour crest pull into the village. Her curiosity piqued, she inched closer to see what transpired.

A lovely little girl with long black hair raced from the crofter's cottage and ran toward the carriage. The other village children, who had been playing nearby, stopped their game of soccer and watched silently. As the carriage door flew open and Adam stepped out, Raines sucked in her breath, for the little girl raced into his arms. He swung her into the air and twirled her around before hugging her closely to him. A moment later a second person emerged from the carriage and this time Raines gave a startled cry of pain then quickly placed her hand over her mouth to stifle the sound. The second passenger was a woman—Charlotte Brownlees. Some motion made by Raines, or Banshee caused the group to look up the mountain and Raines quickly drew her mount out of sight.

Turning in pain and anger, she moved rapidly back toward the castle. Now she knew who Darcy was. But if she was Adam's child, then why had he not married Lady Brownlees instead of her? Why had he made her fall in love with him if he wanted another woman? Raines arrived back at the castle before she was even aware of where she had ridden. quickly she turned Banshee over to the groom and raced into the house.

If only she had someone she could confide in. Adam had seen to it that she was banished to the country where no one would tell her of his secrets. Well, she would solve that problem. Her one confidant was James MacBain and the devil take Adam if he didn't like it. She would write James tonight and see if he planned to attend the duke's house party. It was very possible that he had already made plans to be there, but if not, perhaps he would come just for her. Now all she had to do was await the party.

It was after dinner that evening before Adam finally arrived at the manor. Raines had dined alone and sat in the parlor doing a cross-stitch sampler she planned to give Aunt Thea for her birthday, when she heard the carriage approach and the enthusiastic greeting Watson gave his master. Well, she would not dash out to meet the lord of the manor upon his arrival back from his mistress's arms. Neither would she flee to her room. This was her home and she would remain at her task.

Adam's voice grew closer and she heard him inquire as to her whereabouts. Then she heard the sound of his boots as he strode toward the parlor. Drawing in her breath to stop her pounding heart, she waited nervously. Had he seen her this afternoon, and if so, would he be furious?

"Good evening, my dear. Don't I even rate a welcoming smile?" Adam asked as he walked over to the fire which burned in the grate. "It's a devilish cold night out."

"Good evening, Adam," Raines said coolly, not glancing up from her needle work.

Adam studied Raines closely. "You look rather pale

tonight, are you feeling ill?"

"Oh, Adam, stop being such a bloody nuisance. I'm perfectly fine, but if you don't stop trying to chat while I do my needlework I shall soon have a headache."

He continued his scrutiny of her and Raines concentrated on her intricate rose pattern, trying to hide her nervousness. "I've never known you to be fond of needlework," he replied, watching her push the needle in and out.

"There is a lot you don't know about me." Then she sighed deeply and said more softly, "I have to find something to occupy the long nights."

He came over and stood by her chair and she thought her heart would surely give her away. "Are you truly that unhappy, Raines?" he asked in a voice so soft that it startled her. If he turned kind on her, she felt she would burst into tears and pour out her love and heartache to him.

"I have come to love Balfour, if that is what you are asking. To be honest, there are many hours when I'm lonely though. You are away so much of the time."

"When we have a child you will have someone to occupy your hours," he said.

Her eyes flew open wide and she felt the slow blush inch up her neck. "I'm sure a child would be a wonderful asset," she said, allowing only a hint of sarcasm to creep into her voice. Turning her face up to his, she shrugged. "But alas, that doesn't help my feelings on a day like today."

"Well, I have the perfect thing to cheer you, then." From the way he grinned, Raines grew suspicious.

"And what might that be?"

219

"A visit from your Aunt Thea and Cousin Glenda."
Moving over to the fire, he calmly held out his hands
and warmed them again. His eyes sparkled with
devilment as he watched her reaction.

Throwing down her needlepoint, Raines stared at
him with mouth agape. "What are you talking about?
I haven't heard from Aunt Thea in weeks and haven't
any notion of what you are referring to."

"Shame on you, Raines, dear, don't you miss your
closest kin and blood family?"

"Adam, you know that I respect Aunt Thea, but
you can't imagine what a bore that Cousin Glenda
can be." She gestured around her at the warm, rich
chocolate colors of the sofa and chairs. "If she and
Aunt Thea were to come for a visit they would be
rearranging my furniture and changing my draperies
within the week."

"Well, my dear, you'll just have to stand up to them
and show them you are the mistress of Balfour."

"When the time comes, I shall. But to share a small
confession with you, I hope their visit is months in the
offing."

Chuckling deeply, he walked over and tweaked her
upturned nose. "Ah, my lovely pet, but you are not to
get your wish. They are coming this next week."

Jumping to her feet, Raines rushed over to him and
looked up into his dark eyes. "What do you mean?
How can that be?" She fidgeted as she waited annoyingly long for him to answer. He was keeping her in
suspense.

"I saw your Aunt Thea and Uncle Percival in
London during my visit. They were at Swann's when I
went in for high tea. And while inquiring to your

220

health, your aunt hinted, not too subtly, that she wished to visit and see how you were managing as mistress of Balfour."

Nodding her head, Raines said, "Oh, I can just see her now. I'll bet she and the cousins have plotted this trip for weeks. Why didn't you tell her that I've been incapacitated these past few weeks and am too weak for guests for weeks hence . . ." Flailing the air hopelessly, she said, "Or even for years."

He tapped her lightly on her forehead. "But you aren't the least the worse for wear." Looking most innocent he added, "You couldn't honestly expect me to lie to your dear aunt, now could you?"

Conceding that he was right, she moved nearer the fire to warm her hands which felt cold already from nervousness. "You're right, Adam, I couldn't expect you to lie. But Aunt Thea . . ." The lout was actually enjoying her misery, she thought.

"All I've heard lately is how lonesome you are. Now I tell you that guests are coming and you seem even less pleased. Tsk, tsk, Raines, you are fickle."

She stamped her foot. "Adam Kemp, you know perfectly well that this upsets me. Why do you continue to torment me?"

Moving closer he embraced her with a hug, drawing her nearer. "I've teased you long enough. I knew that you would not be overly joyed at this news. And if it makes you feel any better, I did try to postpone the visit until the spring, but your aunt was adamant about next week."

Nervously Raines moved from within his embrace and paced the floor. "Well I suppose it ought to be nice to have ladies about to discuss certain things with, which tend to bore menfolk."

"I'm never bored with you, Raines," Adam said gently. Again his kindness startled her. What was he up to? Why was he being so nice? It would be easy to fall for his charm had she not seen him that very afternoon with Charlotte.

Grabbing up her needlework, Raines stuffed it in her knitting bag. "There's no time for this now. I've got to get this place spotless before their visit."

Adam groaned. "Not another cleaning like before Horace's visit. If so, I'm off to London until you send word that all is done and things are normal once again."

This time Raines paled. "You wouldn't dare leave me here alone to entertain Aunt Thea and Glenda, would you?"

He grinned. "We might be able to negotiate some type of settlement by which I'll stay around and help sweep the two off their feet. That is what you want, isn't it? To charm them until they think you the grandest hostess in all of fair England."

It was Raines's time to laugh. "And I'll bet you could just do it."

She moved to gather up her yarn bag and put it away for the night. All the while Adam watched quietly, which made her even more nervous.

Finally he spoke. "Won't you stay and have a glass of Maderia with me before you retire for the evening?"

How she wanted to do just that, but she was afraid that the Madeira would loosen her tongue and she would let slip about having seen him with Charlotte. "No, thank you, Adam. It's late and I have a lot to do tomorrow." Turning to smile at him, she added, "However, I promise to keep the cleaning to a minimum this time and the parlor maids out of your way. We'll clean your study while you're away from the manor."

"That's very thoughtful of you." Going over to the table he poured himself a drink. "One more thing I forgot to mention to you. My godson, Edwin Godfrey, may drop in for a few days on his way to the duke's houseparty. He has a break from Eton and said that he might pop in."

"That sounds splendid. Is he a nice chap?"

"I think you two will get along marvelously. He's very lively and quite a good sport." Shaking his head, he chuckled, "Sometimes he is more than his parents bargained for, but all in all, he's a fine lad."

Raines returned to her room feeling rather faint over having so much company to entertain on such short notice. Already she was curious to meet Edwin Godfrey. Perhaps the lad would drop a hint or two about Adam and Charlotte.

Chapter 15

Raines and Adam were in the sitting room when young Edwin Godfrey arrived amid much commotion and excitement. Always a favorite with the household, his arrival seemed to perk up everyone's feelings. Even Adam became happier with a jauntier step to his walk.

"Uncle Adam, I'm here!" called Edwin in greeting the moment Watson had admitted him into the hall.

Raines and Adam came out of the sitting room together to welcome the young, blond lad who stood dressed in his school coat and tie. His expression registered his delight at seeing Adam and he came forward to meet him. "Uncle Adam, you look great. Marriage agrees with you better than I had feared." He slapped the older man on the shoulder and grinned mischievously at Raines over Adam's shoulder. "And Lady Raines is just as I imagined her to be. I knew it would take a beauty to steal your heart and settle your wicked ways. May I kiss her, Uncle?" he asked politely.

"I would feel insulted if you did not," laughed

Adam, turning to Raines. "And this is my notorious godchild who will need your steady hand and influence, my dear. He is a scandalous tease but a decent sort underneath." They all laughed and Edwin gave Raines a quick peck on her cheek.

"May I call you Aunt Raines?" he asked as he glanced over at Adam.

"I would be honored. Now give your greatcoat to Watson and come by the fire. You must be chilled to the bone after your long trip. I'll also ring for Fannie to bring tea." They all moved into the parlor, choosing three damask chairs closest to the fire. A cold wind howled outside rattling the windows and causing the candles to flicker in their sconces. But the crackle of the fire gave a warm, homey feeling to the room, which was one of Raines's favorite.

"How is the semester going?" Adam asked when he had poked up the fire into a roaring blaze.

"That's one reason I've come to see you, Uncle Adam. Things are a bit of a bother at present. There was a bit of a scandal at school recently and a lot of us got sent down for the duration of the semester."

Adam frowned. "Does your father know about this, young man?" Nettie entered with the tea tray and set it on the table nearest Raines. Quietly listening, Raines poured tea and served them. Already she liked the jovial lad who was only a few years younger than she. He appeared very much at home and the twinkle in his eyes told her that he did not take life too seriously.

"Oh, Father knows all right. The headmaster had him down to the school before I was sent packing. Old

Henkleman didn't trust me to explain the situation to my father. Uncle Adam, he as good as accused me of masterminding the entire coverup."

"And did you? You're certainly capable, my lad."

Edwin looked to Raines for support. "My own blood and now my godfather both think the worst of me. Honestly, Uncle Adam, I expected more loyalty from you."

"Edwin," Adam drawled, "you have skipped all around the issue and I still haven't the foggiest idea what you were expelled for."

Reaching for another biscuit, Edwin popped it into his mouth and chewed rapidly. "Devilish good, my dear," he said to Raines between mouthfuls.

"I'll tell Cook that you enjoyed them. She'll be very pleased," said Raines, eyes twinkling.

After a drink of tea, Edwin held his cup for Raines to refill it. While she did so, he continued, "I don't know if I should discuss this in front of Aunt Raines, but Father did in Mother's presence, so I suppose it is decent enough." He set his refilled cup down and turned to give his full attention to Adam. "A few of the older boys in the upperclass decided to slip out of the dorm and go to King's Coachman for a mug or two and . . ." He glanced over to see how closely Raines was listening. She sat quietly, not willing to miss a word. Clearing his throat, Edwin continued, "And to talk with the new barmaid. She's a bit on the cheeky side, but not bad when all's considered."

"And did you go with them?"

"That I did not, Uncle Adam. I knew Father would horsewhip me if I dallied with the barmaid." Catching Raines's eye, he grinned and added, "And besides she isn't nearly as pretty as Henrietta Highsmith, who would have dropped me like a hot scone had word drifted back to her."

"Then quit stalling and tell us what part you played in this deviltry."

"Well, the lads had no way to get back into the dorm when they returned in the wee hours." Turning to explain for Raines's benefit, "You see the nightwatchman locks up at half past ten. That's when lights out sounds for us. And, of course, he had no idea some of the lot were not where they should have been."

"Go on, and quit hedging. You've not gotten to your part yet, although I'm beginning to suspect what it might be." Adam looked at Raines and shook his head.

"Aye, Uncle Adam, I did exactly what you suspect. When the fellows returned, they threw rocks at my window." At this he grinned wickedly and added, "It took them a devil of a time to rouse me, so their account goes. I sleep like the dead. At any rate, they finally did and I tiptoed downstairs, got the key from its nail in the hallway and unlocked the door. We almost made it, and would have, had not the barmaid come up a bit late and hollered foul on the poor chaps." Now he looked to Adam for sympathy. "I tell you, the bloke who owns the King's Coachman is her father and he came up to the school weeks after the event and you've never heard such hollering and raging as he did." He reached for another biscuit and popped it into his mouth. "Never laid the blame on a one of the lads, though. I'll give old Henkleman credit for that one. Henkleman said that no young gentleman from his school would be saddled with the likes of that filly. They must have gone round a good two hours, and not a boy was found out of his room, for we knew Henkleman might have stood up to the tavernkeeper, but heads would roll before he was finished with it."

"And the lot of you got sent down?" Grinning, Adam shook his head in disbelief. "How could you get involved in such a mess?"

"Honest, Uncle Adam, it's like I told Father, I was really the innocent scapegoat. No honorable Englishman would let his friends down in their moment of need. Now be truthful with me, Uncle Adam. You and Father would have done the same."

Shaking his head, Adam laughed, waved the lad to silence. "I'm not about to let you go home and quote me to your parents. They've faced the problem and handled it, I'm sure. So you'll not go upsetting them by saying that I side with you." His words were spoken with warm affection and Edwin smiled.

Turning to Raines for support, Edwin continued, "Father said that he ought to horsewhip me, but Mother said that expulsion, and the disgrace it carried, were probably enough punishment. And that the best thing they could do was get me out of town before matters were made worse than they appeared when the gossips got hold of it. So she suggested that Father go see Uncle Adam, and get his consent for me to stay down here for a few days, until Father can make arrangements for me to go to Bath and work in one of his offices until the second semester begins." Grinning sheepishly, he shrugged. "So now you see why I've come to visit on such short notice." Quickly, he added, "I hope you don't mind, Aunt Raines. Uncle Adam has always been so glad to see me visit that I don't suppose Mother thought of how it might inconvenience you."

Smiling and laughing for him to stop, Raines said, "I'm delighted to meet you and you are welcome to stay as long as your parents desire. It's very quiet here at Balfour and I think a visit from you is just what we need to brighten the winter months for everyone."

Adam rose and set his cup on the table. "I'm delighted to see you two are getting along so well. There are several pressing problems that I need to discuss with my farm overseer, so I'm putting you in charge of Edwin." He nodded to Edwin and grinned, "I'm sure you prefer entertaining Raines with your tales of boyish pranks and adventures to trailing along behind me as I ride around Balfour."

Seeing Edwin's wide grin of approval, he continued, "I will work in a few days trout fishing for us, my boy. We'll get together later to discuss the time. For the present, help Raines with anything she asks, and stay as long as you like." To Raines's surprise, he walked over and kissed her affectionately on the cheek. "I'll be home in time for dinner." And with that he left the two alone to get better acquainted.

Within a few days all the household seemed in brighter spirits and all attributed their good moods to Edwin's presence. Raines even passed through the kitchen to find Cook singing as she prepared dinner, and Edwin sitting at the table devouring a plate of hot shortbread made especially for him. Smiling to herself, Raines wondered if a young heir would also bring the same joy to the staff. Secretly she felt assured that a baby was exactly what Balfour needed to pull it forever out of the doldrums.

The latter part of the week Raines was busy sorting her embroidery yarns when Edwin came into the sitting room and plopped down on the footstool beside her chair.

He watched her carefully for a few minutes before speaking. Finally he sighed and said, "Aunt Raines, I'm beginning to miss all the boys from school. Old Henkleman would love to hear this confession, but I'm even beginning to miss the books a bit. Do you think you might put aside your work and go riding with me? I can't find Uncle Adam this morning."

"He left early to go over to the adjoining village. It seems Crofter Jenkins found a bull over there which he wishes Adam to buy to improve Balfour's stock. I'm afraid he won't be home before night."

"Then do you think it possible that you could spare a poor miserably boy a little sweet company?" He looked pleadingly like an urchin.

Laughing, she laid aside the yarn and nodded. "I think a ride sounds wonderful." Then looking outside, she hesitated. "Doesn't it look like snow is in the making? Are you certain that it is wise for us to go out?"

"Oh, pooh on this weather. You know that it looks like snow most of the time. If we depended on a sunny day to venture forth, we'd be home most of the time."

She conceded that he was correct. "Well, wear your warmest riding habit then, and a thick sweater underneath would not be a bad idea." Moving to the door, she asked, "How long will it take you to get ready? I'll go and have Cook prepare us a lunch. We can stop and picnic by the stream in the high pasture. I'll send Watson ahead in the carriage to carry the necessary things for us."

"Splendid. I knew we'd be the best of friends, Aunt Raines, the second that I laid eyes on you."

Tweaking his ear affectionately, she said, in a cockney voice. "And I knew you were a magnificent con man the instant I laid eyes on the likes of ye." She laughed and moved to the door. "Now off with you and don't be late. Tell the groom to saddle you a horse that can keep up with Banshee because I intend to race you to the Glencoe Abbey."

"Shall we put a little wager on the race, Aunt Raines?" He followed her into the hall, his excitement twinkling in his eyes.

"What kind of race would it be, if we didn't place a small wager on it?" She paused and thought of a price. "If I win, you must do an additional four pages in those books your father sent over this week." Seeing his frown, she said, "Ah, ha! You didn't think that I knew about them, did you? Your mother is concerned that you will fall too far behind to pass this term, so she wants you studying at least three hours each day. Is it a deal?"

"And if I win?"

"I'll have Cook bake your favorite cake with lots of mincemeat and raisins."

Holding out his hand, he shook hers enthusiastically. "You drive a tight bargain, but it's a wager."

Within an hour they were off, racing across the pasture, scaring the sheep and cattle. Even farm boys stopped their tasks to watch the two race down lanes and around markers, for Raines and Edwin were skilled equestrians. Raines came to the rock fence at the pasture's north end and Banshee lifted over without touching a stone. Glancing back she saw Edwin follow without a second's hesitation, for the groom had given him a magnificent gelding who was in top form this morning. Deciding to try to out-maneuver him, Raines steered Banshee into the woods and up into the mountains, planning to cut off on her secret shortcut, shortening her route by several hundred yards, which would give her a large lead.

But a farmer on a cart loaded with hay suddenly appeared before her on the narrow path and there was nothing for her to do but slow down. Soon Edwin came up beside her laughing, "You were outfoxed by your own cunning, weren't you, Aunt Raines? I know the short cut you planned to take."

Catching her breath, Raines looked innocently over at him. "Do you really think I'd resort to chicanery to beat you?"

"Yes, I do. But I must admit that you and Banshee were racing so well that I feared you'd get thrown."

"Nonsense. I've been racing since I was a child."

"That may be true, but there are a lot of dangers around here and I don't want you to get hurt. Uncle Adam would never forgive me if I caused you to have an accident."

She realized that the boy was being sensible, so she said, "Perhaps we should save our racing for the open pastures. Shall we just ride and talk?"

The worried look left his eyes and he nodded in agreement. "That sounds like a splendid idea. Tell me something about your home and how you met Uncle Adam. I don't want to sound presumptuous but your marriage did come as somewhat of a shock to us."

With merriment in her eyes she nodded. "We had a very short betrothal. I suppose you could say your uncle is an impulsive person."

"All in all, I think he made a wise choice. A lot better than . . ." Suddenly his face turned scarlet and he stammered, "I beg your pardon, Aunt Raines. That was a terribly rude thing for me to say." Shaking his head, he said, "My mother says that I'm too outspoken and too much of an upstart most of the time." Looking his most appealing he said, "And I fear she is correct as always."

"To the contrary, Edwin, you're a refreshing respite from all the dullards that surround me most of the time. Like my boring cousins and cold fish of an aunt." Glancing over to see how he was taking this bit of news, she continued, "There, you see, after only a few days I'm confiding secret thoughts to you that I haven't shared with anyone but Adam. Tell me something about yourself now."

"Well, there isn't a lot to tell. I've been coming to visit Uncle Adam since I was a little boy. And while we're sharing confidences, I like you a whole lot better than Lady Alexandra."

"Oh, do you remember her?" This was the type of

information Raines had hoped to learn from the boy.

"I remember she was breathtakingly beautiful. She would come and talk to me, but she never seemed really interested in what I had to say." He squinted as he tried to remember. "Then I was off at boarding school and I don't know much about what happened. Just one holiday I came home and Mother said that we must go visit Uncle Adam because he was very sad. When we arrived I remember being shocked at his appearance. He had lost weight and needed a shave. I was frightened of him but I tried not to show it. And when we left, I asked my Mother if he were going to die. She laughed and asked whatever gave me that silly notion. The next time I came to visit he was himself again." He thought for a moment. "Except for his eyes. He never looked happy again. That is until this visit. He must love you a lot, Aunt Raines."

She was glad the boy did not know the secrets of their strained marriage because she wanted it to be like Edwin thought. If only Adam could learn to love her as he must have loved Alexandra.

When they arrived at their picnic spot Watson sat waiting for them with the tablecloth spread on the dry grass and the hamper of food nearby. They ate quickly and hungrily and then went to the stream to wash their hands in the ice cold water while Watson folded and replaced everything in the hamper. Once they had rested in the warm sunshine, they waved Watson off back to the manor and proceeded on their ride with Edwin leading the way since they were farther from home than Raines had ever been.

Growing weary of their slow pace, Raines pulled

alongside and said, "Follow me!" Digging her heels into Banshee's sides, she leapt forward and was off. She could hear Edwin calling to her but she did not stop.

Rounding a curve she saw the thick woods ahead, but slowed only the slightest before giving Banshee his head. The horse raced down the leaf covered path and into the thickest grove. The path was shaded from the sun's rays by thick overlapping oak limbs and the air became colder instantly. Glancing around, Raines thought the place had an eerie feeling and she grew anxious to exit into a field once more.

Suddenly, a man stepped from behind a rock, waving a cape and trying to stop them. Banshee, startled by his sudden appearance and the flapping garment reared, pawing the air as the man grabbed for the reins. Raines's scream of terror pierced the countryside as she was hurled from the saddle.

Edwin rounded the curve just in time to see the man grab Raines's hand and snatch the ring from it. "What the devil is going on here?" he yelled, racing to where Raines lay quietly, not moving.

The man dropped Banshee's reins in surprise at seeing the lad racing toward him and when he tried to regain them, Banshee shied away and galloped down the path and out of sight. The man fled into the thicket. When Edwin attempted to go after him, a loud gunshot filled the air. Stopping abruptly, Edwin turned and raced back to Raines.

Jumping off his horse, he ran and knelt by Raines's still body. She appeared very pale, but feeling her pulse, he sighed with relief, for her heartbeat was strong. It was then that he noticed the blood trickling from her forehead. A quick investigation proved his worst fears. She had a large knot on her head and the blood came from there. Quickly pulling his handkerchief from his pocket he tied it around the wound. "Oh, Raines, what will I do?" he half sobbed in his fright. He had to get her to a doctor but he didn't know how he could manage it. He gathered her up in his arms and tried to mount his horse, but he was not strong enough to do so. Finally in frustration he realized there was nothing he could do but leave her well hidden and go for help. Quickly he searched until he found a place behind some rocks where he lay her gently. Pulling off his top coat he used it as a second cover and then dragged branches from a nearby pine tree and covered her. Stepping back he studied her hiding place. Once he was satisfied that she was well hidden, he mounted his horse and raced back down the path to the village which was closer than the manor.

When he reached the village he gathered several men and a farm wagon and ordered a youth to run to the manor and bring Adam. Edwin had never been so frightened before. He was afraid the thief would return to find Raines and harm her. What if she died? He would not let himself dwell on that possibility. He knew she was strong and healthy if he could just get back in time to help her.

The sun had dropped low in the sky when he and the village men finally returned to his hiding place. To everyone's relief Raines lay as he had left her. Gently the men placed her on the bed of straw in the back of

236

the wagon and Edwin rode beside her, cursing the men when they went too slowly or hit a hole in the road too soundly. It was decided that they would take her to the village, which was nearer, and wait for the doctor who had been sent for as they left.

It was night when they arrived back in the village and to Edwin's dismay Adam's horse was not tied to the hitching post. Where was he?

The doctor heard them approaching and came from within the cottage where he had been waiting impatiently. Before he would allow her to be moved, he examined her in the back of the wagon and frowned. "Take her inside and place her gently on the bed. She's alive but too gravely injured to risk going on to the manor tonight." Looking around he asked, "Has anyone gotten word to Lord Kemp yet?"

A youth ran up and said, "I went to the castle but Lord Kemp was not there. He has gone to London. I left word for him to come immediately. Watson sent the groom to bring him home." Curious to see her, the lad moved closer but the doctor swatted at him with the back of his hand. "Be off with you and don't be milling around the cottage where your loud talking might disturb the lady. You there," he motioned to a tall boy to come closer, "go fetch me three buckets of water for Mrs. Murdock to heat. I want to cleanse the wound. Now be quick about it or I'll take my belt to you!"

Some time during the night Raines finally opened her eyes to see the doctor smiling at her. "That's a good girl. Had a nice rest, did you?"

"Where am I?" She tried to move her head to look

237

around the cottage, but winced in pain.

"You are in Mrs. Murdock's cottage. You had a little fall from your horse and we brought you here."

"Adam?" Raines glanced around her in panic. She realized that she must be in the village and Adam would be angry.

Misunderstanding her anxiety the doctor patted her shoulder gently. "Now, now little lady, you're fine. We've sent for Lord Kemp but he is in London and it will take a while for him to get home. I'll stay with you until I'm sure you're out of danger and then Mrs. Murdock will see to you." He motioned for a woman who had been hovering in the shadows to step forward. "I'd like you to meet your nurse. This is Mrs. Murdock and she is one of the finest in these parts, so don't you fret. Now just go back to sleep and rest."

"What about Edwin? Where's he?" Suddenly Raines found herself crying and she couldn't stop.

Hearing his name, the youth jumped up from the chair where he had been dozing and ran to the bed. "Aunt Raines, I'm here. I'm all right. You were set upon by a highwayman but I rescued you."

For a few seconds Raines had difficulty understanding what he was talking about, and then the frightening events began to return to her memory. "What did he want?"

Edwin looked to the doctor waiting for his permission before he answered. "You might as well tell her, young man, she's a strong little lady. There's no need to keep secrets from her."

"I think the robber was looking for jewels and money. At any rate you didn't have a purse. All I've discovered missing is the wedding ring Uncle Adam gave you." Seeing Raines tear up again, he added quickly, "Now don't you worry. Uncle Adam will buy you a new one immediately. The main thing is that you're going to be all right."

"I think you've talked to her enough, young man. Let her rest tonight and you can be here bright and early in the morning. Next time I'll let her talk to you until she gets tired." The doctor motioned for Edwin to move out of Raines's hearing. "She has a concussion and I must stay to see that she doesn't fall into a deep coma. I'll wake her every few minutes and talk with her. But there is no need for you to stay. Why don't you go back to Balfour and get a good night's sleep. Whatever is left of it."

"Thank you, sir, but I think someone from the family should stay with her, so I'll stay until Uncle Adam arrives."

"Suit yourself, lad," said the doctor. "I don't think Mrs. Murdock has an extra bed. The girl is sleeping in the small bed in the corner. There is a comfortable chair near the fire and I'm sure Mrs. Murdock will get you a warm blanket." Squinting in the dim light, he added, "You don't look so well yourself. Get Mrs. Murdock to fix you a bowl of stew. That should put a little color back in your cheeks."

Mrs. Murdock heard the conversation and immediately brought Edwin a heaping bowl of hot soup which he ate with surprisingly good appetite. Once the bowl was cleaned, he placed it on the table and went to sit by the fire. Suddenly he found himself trembling from fatigue. He dozed off and when he awoke he found a heavy wool blanket had been draped around his shoulders. The next time he awoke the sun was beginning to stream into the cottage. Glancing around, he saw the doctor and Mrs. Murdock whispering quietly in the corner. Fearing that something had happened to Raines, he jumped up from his chair and rushed over to where they huddled. "Is Aunt Raines all right?" he cried.

Frowning, the doctor looked at him through red streaked eyes. His eyelids were puffy from lack of sleep and the lines on his face seemed etched deeper into his skin. But he smiled and said, "Don't go getting yourself all upset. And come away from that bed before you go and wake Lady Kemp. Mrs. Murdock and I were just talking about a little oatmeal for breakfast. Will you join us?"

They were finishing their bowls of hot cereal when the little girl stirred in her bed and sat up, rubbing her eyes. She looked around and seeing all eyes on her, she grinned. Climbing out of bed, she came to the table and crawled up on Mrs. Murdock's lap.

Before Edwin could speak to her, Raines called out in her sleep. Jumping up from the table he and the doctor rushed back to her side.

"Lady Raines," called the doctor softly, "can you hear me?"

Raines opened her eyes and seeing Edwin, smiled weakly. "I'm a sorry lot today," she joked in a hoarse voice. Clearing it she tried again, "Where's Adam?"

"I'm so happy to see you awake and talking," cried Edwin. He reached for her hand and patted it gently. "You gave me a horrible scare yesterday, but I came and got help." He quickly told her all that had happened.

"Did they catch the robber?" she asked looking from the doctor to Edwin.

"I'm afraid not, Aunt Raines. But I'm sure that when Adam gets here, he'll have a talk with the constable. I'll bet Uncle Adam has the louse brought to justice. You just wait and see."

The little girl moved closer and squeezed herself between the doctor and the bed. "Hello," she said in a bright little voice.

Smiling down at her, Raines said, "And who might you be?"

"Darcy," replied the child.

Raines glanced up at Edwin and the doctor with fear in her eyes. What would Adam say about her being in Darcy's home?

Chapter 16

"Now don't go bothering Lady Raines, young lady," said the doctor taking Darcy by the shoulders and gently moving her away from the bed. "Go back to Mrs. Murdock and she'll fix your breakfast."

Holding up her hand to stop him, Raines said, "She isn't bothering me. Let her stay."

"No, my dear, you need rest. Do you feel up to some breakfast now? Mrs. Murdock has some delicious oatmeal this morning."

Trying to be a good patient Raines ate the cereal although she was not the least bit hungry. While she ate she glanced around the room inquisitively. It was a very neat and attractive cottage. The large room was partitioned off into a sitting area, the kitchen and the bedroom nook. The walls had been recently white-washed and the cobblestone floor glistened from many waxings. One thing which caught Raines's attention was the number of toys the child Darcy had. There were stuffed bears in her bed and a wooden rocking horse with real horse hair beside the wall. This child was definitely not a mere village urchin. In the background she heard Mrs. Murdock talking softly to the little girl. "I'm going to send you to play with Priscilla today," she explained to the child.

"But, Nana, you promised we would make doll clothes today," protested the child.

"We'll make lots of clothes when Lady Kemp is well," explained the woman patiently. "Now you gather up your toys and I'll walk you over to Priscilla's. Run along and don't take long selecting a few dolls for you and Priscilla to play with."

Raines felt instinctively that the woman was getting the little girl out of the cottage, so she could not ask too many prying questions. Having finished the oatmeal, Raines felt exhausted again and dozed off once more. When she awoke the next time it was late afternoon and the cottage was quiet. Darcy was nowhere to be seen. Mrs. Murdock sat at the table quietly peeling vegetables, the doctor dozed in a chair near the fire and Edwin was gone. Raines was about to ask where he was when she heard the loud noise of running horses and the sound of a carriage pulling up outside. There were men's voices and rapid footsteps, and the next moment the door flew open and Adam entered the cottage.

"How is she, Doctor?" he asked in greeting, walking past the older man and over to where Raines lay, before the doctor could answer.

"She's fine but she needs bed rest for a few days. It was a close call. That was a nasty lick she got on her head, but if you make her rest, she's young and healthy and should pull through without any complications." The doctor moved over to stand beside the bed, checking Raines's pulse.

Seeing that she was awake, Adam grabbed her other hand and squeezed it tightly. "Dear Raines, I'm so happy to see you well and smiling. All the way from London I've had the worst nightmares of what might be happening. Thank God you're alive."

"I'm fine, Adam. Just a little weak and I seem to have an awful headache, but other than that, I'm not the least incapacitated."

Turning to the doctor, Adam asked, "Can she be moved now? I'd like to take her back so Nettie can nurse her." He quickly added, "I'm sure Mrs. Murdock is doing a splendid job, but I'd like to get her back to Balfour."

Nodding the doctor said, "I think it will be safe for you to move her, if you do so gently. And tell the driver to avoid jolts and rough driving."

Adam came back to Raines and swooped her into his arms. She was forced to put her arms around his neck to steady herself. Up close she saw his reddened eyes from loss of sleep and the growth of unshaved beard. Smiling weakly at him, she teased, "You look a wreck and much worse off than I."

"If you don't hush being so sassy, I shall drop you right here on the hard floor," he snapped, but he smiled down at her in a way which made her heart quicken. "Raines, you scared the life out of me. Don't you realize how dangerous it was to go riding in the north country?"

"That was partly my fault, Uncle Adam," said Edwin arriving at that moment. "We went riding and I should have insisted that we turn back sooner, but I

244

didn't. I feel terrible about it."

"That's foolishness," argued Raines. "It's as much my fault as anyone's. I'm the one who raced ahead into that dark section of woods. So Adam, if you must be angry with anyone, be so with me."

He looked down at her with a warm and tender expression. "Darling, I'm not angry with either of you. I'm just so thankful that you are both alive and not in worse condition." They had reached the carriage. "Now, here we go. Just relax on the seat until we get to the castle. It won't be the most comfortable trip, but I'll ride up front with the driver and try to help him avoid potholes and the like." Turning, he instructed Edwin, "You ride in the carriage with her and see that she doesn't fall off the seat. Keep her covered. I don't want her catching pneumonia."

"Yes, sir," said Edwin, quickly climbing into the carriage.

Before they left Raines overheard Adam talking quietly with Mrs. Murdock. She heard him inquire as to Darcy's whereabouts. And then she heard him ask, "What did you tell Lady Kemp about Darcy?"

"Nothing, my lord. She never asked and the situation was avoided when I sent the child away for the day."

"Good thinking," he murmured.

Raines felt the anger rising within her. How could Adam treat his own child this way? And she such a lovely little thing at that? She wondered when, if ever, he intended to tell her about the baby's presence.

"Aunt Raines, are you all right?" asked Edwin anxiously. "You are frowning so fiercely."

Waving him away, she said, "I'm fine, Edwin. Now don't fret over me. I'll be glad to get to Balfour and into my own bed, however. I felt like I was intruding and in the way at Mrs. Murdock's."

"Well, you'll get your wish soon enough, I see the castle in the distance now."

When the carriage pulled into the drive, Nettie and Watson were standing there waiting to greet her and to offer their assistance. Adam waved them aside and opened the carriage door. "I can carry her up to her room. It's best that I do it, so I can drop her over the banister if she gives me any trouble."

"Sir!" said Watson, shocked.

Nettie laughed and said, "'Tis exactly the way to handle the likes of Lady Raines, sir. I know how obstinate she can be when one tries to confine her to the bed."

"This time you two are plotting unnecessarily," laughed Raines. "I don't think I'm up to defying either of you just yet."

"'Tis good to have you home, madam," said Watson. And to Raines's surprise, she thought he really meant it. What a good feeling to realize that she was becoming part of the household and a true Kemp of Balfour.

Adam carried her up the stairs as easily as if she had been a bundle of clothing. Once in the room he lay her gently on her bed. "I'll leave you and let Nettie get you undressed and to bed, for you still look a bit peaked."

Nettie had followed them into the room and began fussing over Raines immediately. "Call me when Lady

246

Raines is comfortably abed, Nettie," he instructed.

"Aye, Lord Kemp. I'll have her comfy in no time, sir."

"Oh, Nettie, it is wonderful to be home again. And Balfour is truly beginning to feel like home."

"That pleases me mightily, Lady Raines. Now slip into this nightgown and then into this nice soft bed." Nettie gathered up the soiled riding habit and took it out with her. "I'll give this to one of the maids for cleaning. I don't know if it can be saved or not, though ma'am."

"Please tell Adam to come in now. There are several things I'd like to discuss with him." Raines viewed her reflection in her silver hand mirror and was stunned at how pale she appeared. The bandage on her forehead looked neat but awesome and her eyes seemed sunk back in their sockets. For the first time she admitted to herself how lucky she was to be alive.

There was a light tap on her door and Adam stuck his head in to check on her. "May I come in?"

Fluffing up the plump down-filled pillows, she smiled in greeting. "I'll be delighted to have some company. Now that I'm home I've had a chance to realize how lucky I am to be in one piece. The alternative is rather frightening." She patted a place on the bed beside her. "Come over and tell me what the constable has learned. Does he have any leads on my attacker?"

Adam shook his head and sat next to her. Taking her hand in his, he stroked it gently. "That trip back from London was the longest of my life. I kept thinking of the worst possible things." Staring into her

247

eyes, he said softly, "I can't imagine my life without you. You have brought such joy to Balfour. If anything terrible had happened to you . . ." He let his voice drift off. Leaning forward he kissed her gently on the lips. It was a sweet, lingering kiss softly capturing her lips and tasting their sweetness. Raines held her breath and felt the world spinning around her and it was not caused by her head injury. When he finally pulled away she wanted to beg him to kiss her again, but instead she remained silent, gazing only into his dark eyes. "I could crush you in my arms, my darling, but I might injure you. Now get well and I promise to show you how much I care for you." He leaned close again but a knock on the door prevented his kiss. Turning they saw Edwin pop into the room.

"Hello, I came to see how our patient is doing," he called cheerfully.

"Oh, Edwin, I haven't thanked you yet for being such a brave fellow. Come here and let me give you a kiss for everything."

Swelling with pride, he walked over to the bed and leaned over to be pecked on the cheek. "You are such a darling boy that I may write to your mother and offer to keep you forever."

"That would be wonderful, Aunt Raines, but I'm getting a bit homesick to return to my classmates." Grinning sheepishly, he turned to Adam. "Did you ever think you'd live to hear me admit that?" They all laughed good-humoredly.

The three chatted for several hours and had tea late in the afternoon. Their visit was interrupted by the sound of an approaching carriage. Looking at Edwin and Adam, Raines asked, "Who could be coming to call?"

Shaking his head, Adam moved to the window and glanced out onto the courtyard. Suddenly he uttered a sharp oath under his breath, but returned without further comment.

Curious to see what was happening, Edwin moved over to the window and announced, "It seems a lady is coming to visit. Probably one of your neighbors has heard of your mishap and is paying her respects."

Raines watched Adam quietly but he made no further comment. In a few minutes there was a tap on the door and Watson entered. "There is a lady here who insists on speaking to you now, sir." He bowed. "I tried to explain that your wife was ill, but she would not be put off."

Standing, Adam sighed and moved toward the door. "I'll be back as quickly as possible, dear."

When he had left, Raines called Edwin away from the window. "Do you have any idea who our visitor is?" She watched him closely because she was certain he had recognized the caller.

"I . . . I can't say for sure." Glancing around for something to do, he said, "Let's play a game of cards, shall we?"

"Edwin, you come here this minute and answer me. You know who our visitor is, don't you?"

Dropping his head he blushed slightly. "Yes, I do. But I don't think her visit is of any importance."

Completely confused by his reluctance to name the person, Raines pursued the issue. "Young man you tell me at once or I'll not be your friend another instant. What are trying to hide. Who is she?"

"It's devil if I do and devil if I don't." Shrugging he said, "It's Charlotte Brownlees."

An involuntary gasp escaped her lips and she gave a cry that sounded like a wounded animal. "What? The nerve! And here in my very own house." She struggled to get out of bed and a searing pain shot through her head. Clutching her forehead she fell back on the pillow.

Terrified, Edwin ran to her. "Shall I call Nettie or Uncle Adam? Are you all right? Answer me, please."

"I'll be fine in a minute. I just moved too quickly. Please bring me a damp cloth and I'll be fine. I just feel a bit nauseous."

Following her instructions he was back in an instant holding a very wet cloth. Wringing some of the water out, Raines placed it on her face. Once the coolness calmed her flaming cheeks, she looked up at Edwin and said, "You've got to do a favor for me, and pledge never to tell Adam."

"Of course, you have my word." He held up his hand and grinned. "Just don't try to get out of that bed."

"If I could get downstairs I'd ask that woman to leave. But since I can't, I want you to go downstairs and eavesdrop on their conversation. I want to know why she's here."

Poor Edwin gasped in shock. "You know Uncle Adam would skin me alive if he should catch me."

"Well, I'll be in a pretty plight too, so you'd better not get caught. Understand? And you must vow on your grandfather's grave to never tell a soul what we are doing."

"My grandfather isn't dead," Edwin whispered.

"That makes no matter. You know exactly what I mean. I want to know why she is here. What could possibly be so important that she has the audacity to come into my home?" Her voice began to tremble and she closed her eyes tightly to keep the tears from stealing out and down her cheeks. "You know that she was Adam's mistress. Oh, Edwin, do you think she still is?"

Patting her arm reassuringly, he said, "Please, Aunt Raines, don't upset yourself. I'm sure there's some logical explanation for her visit."

"Are you going to do what I ask?"

Sighing deeply he rose from his chair and said, "I'll try, but if I get caught what he does to me will be far worse than what happened in Henkleman's office. He'll horsewhip me for sure."

"Edwin, I swear that I wouldn't ask this of you if my life didn't depend on it. I must know why she came here."

"Then I'll do my best to find the answer. Now you rest until I return. And if Uncle Adam catches me, may God have mercy on me."

After he left the room Raines fidgeted with her needlework, tried to read and even tried to sleep, but nothing could take her mind off the events taking place downstairs. What if Edwin got caught? She trembled to think of the consequences.

Finally when she could think of nothing else to do, she rang for Nettie to come and punch up the fire. Once Nettie arrived she said, "Don't go back to the

251

kitchen just now, stay and talk to me. Does Adam still have company?"

Giving her a sharp look Nettie answered cautiously, "Aye, that he does, ma'am."

"What did Lady Charlotte say her business was? Did you hear Watson say?"

The maid shook her head. "That Watson be as close mouthed as the master, ma'am. You don't get a slip from him."

Sighing, Raines frowned. "Well, I'm sure Adam will explain it to me later so I'll just have to wait until the meeting is over." Motioning the maid away, she said, "Go back to your chores. I'll be all right until dinner this evening. Now run along and don't worry about me."

As Nettie closed the door, Raines heard the carriage pull away from the front drive. She glanced at the clock on the mantel and noticed that the visit had not, in fact, taken but a short while. It had merely seemed long to her.

But when Edwin didn't return right away, she began to panic. Had he gotten caught? A good thirty minutes passed before he came dashing back into the room. Plopping down in the nearest chair he sighed deeply and gasped, "Lord, Aunt Raines, that was too close to describe."

Raines blanched and her hands began to tremble. "You didn't get caught, did you?"

Shaking his head, he motioned with his hand. "No, but I came so close. I had just positioned myself outside the door when I heard footsteps coming toward the door. To be sure, I thought my heart would fail. Glancing around the only place I could find to hide was the coat closet under the staircase. Would you believe that Uncle Adam came there to get his coat. Where the devil was Watson?"

Giggling, she said, "I can't imagine. How did you keep Adam from seeing you?"

"I hid behind some old coats and a stack of lap robes." Running his hand across his face, he removed spider webbing. "You don't know how terrified I am of spiders. If one had crawled across me, we'd both be dead pigeons tonight."

"Enough of your adventure. What did you hear?"

"Well, for all the trouble I went to, not a lot. When I got to the study they were having a heated argument because both were raising their voices. It had something to do with someone called Darcy. Lady Charlotte wanted to do one thing with her and Uncle Adam another."

"That's all you heard?" She couldn't keep the disappointment out of her voice.

Shrugging and looking helpless, he said, "That's about it. When they came out I did hear Uncle Adam say, 'I'll agree to it but I don't approve.'" Then Edwin blushed and glanced at the floor.

"You heard something else, young man. I want every detail."

"Are you sure?"

"Absolutely! Now quit stalling."

"Lady Charlotte said, 'None of this would be a problem if you hadn't married her!'" Glancing up, he added, "I'm sorry, but that's what she said."

In a cold voice, Raines asked, "And what did

Adam reply?"

"I really didn't hear. He was opening the door and I was so busy holding my breath, and staying perfectly still, that I missed his answer."

"No matter. I can imagine what he said." Suddenly it struck her that Adam had been getting his coat. "Did he leave with Lady Charlotte?"

He brightened at this. "That I can answer. No. She left in the carriage and I heard him tell Watson to send for his horse. He had to ride to the village." Looking like an anxious child, he asked, "Did I get anything of use to you?"

"Indeed you did." Turning to face him, she said in her most serious tone. "Promise me one thing. Promise that you will never tell what you heard."

"Oh, you have my word of honor on that."

They sat in silence while the fire crackled in the grate and the only other sound was the wind blowing against the windows. Each sat lost in his own thoughts. The clock ticked rhythmically as the sun faded into evening.

Finally Edwin broke the silence. "Who do you think Darcy is?"

"The little girl Mrs. Murdock is caring for."

"That's exactly who I thought, too." Realizing the implication of the matter, he hastened to add, "You have nothing to worry about. I'm sure there is some logical explanation for this."

"No, Edwin, I don't think there is any excuse for Adam bringing his mistress into our home."

"That's really not fair, you know. He didn't invite her. From the expression on his face she showed up unexpectedly." He thought about the matter a few more seconds. "And as I recall he did not sound pleased with her visit. In fact, I'd describe his tone as short, curt, and angry."

"Not half as angry as I am, Edwin. Not half so angry."

Chapter 17

Raines waited up for Adam's return that night, but to her dismay she never heard his approaching footsteps. Finally in the early morning hours she dropped off to sleep. When Nettie came in to bring the breakfast tray, she inquired about him. "Did Adam come in last night?" she asked.

"That he didn't, ma'am. A farmer's boy delivered a message that he was up with the veterinarian. They's having some lambing troubles in the east section. The boy instructed Cook to send over some soup for Lord Kemp and the doctor."

Ordinarily, Raines would have been reasonable about this matter, but the fact she already felt at the breaking point, caused her to explode. "That's it, Nettie! If Lord Kemp comes home and wishes to see me, tell him that I'm indisposed and do not wish to be disturbed."

Nettie raised an eyebrow and fretted with the covers. "Now, Lady Raines, don't go getting all worked up about whatever is troubling you."

"I'm not overwrought and I'm not having hysterics.

I just never want to speak to Lord Kemp again for as long as I live. I hate him!" Tears began streaming down her cheeks as she visualized Adam with Charlotte.

Picking up her breakfast tray, Nettie said, "I don't know what has gotten you so agitated, but when you're up and around again, I think you'll feel differently." Then taking a chance and knowing she stepped far out of line, she added, "Lord Kemp seems to be a fair man to me, ma'am. He was certainly upset when he thought you'd been hurt."

"Oh, fudge, Nettie! He was just afraid something would happen to me and he wouldn't get his precious heir to Balfour." The instant spoken, Raines realized she had said too much. Putting her hand to her forehead she said, "I don't know what has gotten into me lately. I just have these weepy spells and feel so depressed."

"What you need is rest and I'll tell Edwin not to disturb you this morning. He's already been asking if you're awake."

"Bring my gown, Nettie. I'm getting up. I've had all this staying in bed I can stand."

Alarmed, Nettie rushed over and helped Raines, who seemed a bit wobbly. "Lor, and to be sure you'll kill yourself yet," cried Nettie.

"I'm perfectly fit today and I don't want any more coddling. Now get my gown and hurry about it," snapped Raines who was rarely ever curt with Nettie.

Within the hour Raines had dressed and moved downstairs into the front drawing room so she could hear Adam when he entered the hall. There were a few things she wished to discuss with him and the sooner they settled the matters, the sooner she would begin to feel better.

She had not been in the room more than an hour when she heard his footsteps approaching and his deep voice. Her heart quickened as she prepared herself for their encounter.

"How delightful to see you downstairs today, my dear," Adam said as he entered and moved toward her. Reaching out he put his hands on her shoulders and leaned over to kiss her cheek.

Pushing him away, she said, "Really, Adam, I prefer that you not do that."

Stunned, his eyes searched her face trying to discern her curtness. "Aren't you feeling well? If not, we'll send for the doctor right away."

"I'm perfectly fit this morning. There are just a few things I've wanted to talk to you about and I think now is as good a time as any."

Perplexed, he watched her carefully. "All right. Do you wish to sit by the fire or stand?"

"Oh, what does it matter?" She glanced around frantically mustering the courage to say what she wished next. "Stand I suppose. The truth of the matter is that I don't think this marriage is working and I think we should call off the whole farce."

Now Adam's face reddened and he moved closer. "What ever are you in the sulks about today? You seem to have worked yourself into a regular frenzy."

"I wish you would take this matter seriously and not make light of me."

"It certainly isn't my intention to make light of you.

But for the life of me, I can't deduce what is troubling you so greatly." Again he tried to move closer and she turned away.

With her back to him, she said, "I . . . I don't think our sharing a bed from time to time is working." There she had finally gotten it out.

Raising an eyebrow, he studied her for a moment. "I wasn't aware that you found me so revolting."

She turned to face him with cheeks aflame as she remembered how agreeable she had been. "That's odious! It's just the sort of thing I'd expect from a rake like you."

This time he could not suppress the grin which crept to his lips. "Oh, so now I'm an abominable rake, am I? Well, my dear, I own up to the fact my reputation wasn't spotless when we married, but it does seem a bit late to be holding it against me."

Realizing that she was losing this argument because he refused to understand, she lashed out in anger. "Don't you understand what I'm trying to tell you. I can't stand for you to touch me!" she lied.

Stunned this time, Adam's brows met in a frown and his face reddened in anger as he said, "Then, dear Raines, you will not be bothered by my attentions again!" he snapped. Turning on his heel abruptly he stalked to the door, then stopped. As an afterthought he hurled, "The next time we share a bed, it will be you who come to mine."

"I'd freeze in the worst blizzard before I'd ever share your blanket," she retaliated, warming to her fury now.

"Then good day, Lady Raines!" he pronounced

coldly. The steely calm of his voice belied the rage which flamed within him.

Once he had closed the door Raines stalked around the room trying to control her frustration and anger. He had not even been sensitive enough to see how she was hurting. Didn't he even care enough to feel he owed her an explanation for Lady Charlotte's visit and his staying out all night. To her amazement, she realized she was behaving like a jealous wife. She prayed that he never realized how much she loved him, and wanted him to love her in return.

In the days which followed Raines and Adam existed in an atmosphere of silence, speaking only the polite words of civil coexistence. Each day as her frustration grew, so did her anger. His indifference she found more intolerable than she had imagined. He still seemed concerned over her health and politely inquired as to her improvement. But he did not make any gesture which she could interpret as affectionate. If her mood was cool, his could only be described as icy. She even found herself deliberately crossing his path at times just to see how he would react.

Then one day before Aunt Thea and Cousin Glenda were scheduled to arrive a coachman arrived at Balfour with a message from Rosewood.

Raines, now fully recovered from her fall, was busy cataloguing gold coins from Spain while Adam and Edwin played a quiet game of chess. The outward impression of the scene was one of family harmony. Only Adam and Raines knew of the strife and turmoil boiling underneath.

Watson knocked on the door and entered with the

young coachman. "A message for Lady Raines, sir."

With a puzzled expression Raines lay down her coin and stared at the visitor in amazement. "You're from Rosewood. Whatever is the matter?" Quickly she rose and came to accept the outstretched envelope. Adam and Edwin stopped their game awaiting her next words.

"Oh, my! Uncle Percival has had a stroke. This is from Aunt Thea urging me to come at once." Remembering the messenger's long ride, she turned to Watson. "Please take the man to the kitchen and find him some food. He must be tired from his long journey." Turning to the man, she asked, "How serious is it? Do you know?"

"That I can't say for sure, ma'am. But when last I heard, the doctor was with him and told your ladyship to call all the family."

"'Tis as I feared. Go along with Watson."

Adam came to stand beside Raines. "This is dreadful news but you aren't thinking of going, are you? After your serious head injury last week, it doesn't seem wise. I don't think you are well enough for the trip. Can't you explain your accident and ask them to understand?"

"Nonsense, I'm perfectly healthy again." Then facing him she appealed to his understanding. "I really should go. Uncle Percival was decent to me after Father's passing. I owe it to him to go. After all, he is the only family I have left. It would be unforgivable of me not to do so." Shaking her head, already knowing how much she dreaded the visit, she felt she had no alternative. "If it were Aunt Thea I could justify not going, but in this case I really must, Adam."

He nodded in understanding. "Do you wish me to go with you?" It was his first move toward a reconciliation.

"No!" replied Raines a little too quickly. She felt ashamed of rejecting his offer so abruptly, but she did not think she could survive riding two days in the carriage with him so close and yet so distant. "I don't want to disturb your plans since I know how busy you stay with the estate matters. No, Nettie and I can make the trip with no problem."

A scowl crossed his handsome features, but he made no further argument concerning his accompanying her. Instead he suggested Edwin ride with them. "There are many things it is best to have a male along to supervise," he argued. "I don't like the idea of you and Nettie traveling alone."

Struggling to hide her disappointment, for she had perversely hoped that he would insist upon accompanying them, she said, "That all depends on how Edwin feels about the matter." They both turned to the youth who jumped to his feet immediately.

"Of course, I'm at your service, Aunt Raines. It will be an honor to accompany you." Glancing at his godfather, he beamed with pride. "I'm just delighted that Uncle Adam feels I'm mature enough to fulfill such a task."

Adam nodded. "Good, then it is settled. I suggest you get packed as quickly as possible. I'd like to see you get an early start for London. I'll send two of my best coachmen to drive and perhaps they will ward off any thoughts of highway robbery by rogues."

"I think we'll manage without any problem. Now let me ring for Nettie so she can commence packing and we can be on our way."

Early dawn the following morning, all was packed and the party was ready to set off for Rosewood Manor as the sun began to lighten the sky. It was a cold day and the three travelers set in the carriage huddled under thick wool lap robes. Adam reached into the carriage and tucked the edges of Raines's robe securely around her. He made no effort to bid her a private or personal farewell which forced her to struggle to hide her tears. Studying her closely, he mistook her paleness to be anxiety rather than grief.

"You still look a little peaked my dear. Are you certain you are up to this journey?" Raines nodded, not trusting herself to speak with him so close. "Then do take care. If I'm needed, send one of the footmen and I'll come immediately." She nodded again and he closed the door. The next instant they were off and she gave way to the tears which had been threatening to overflow.

"Aunt Raines," cried Edwin in alarm, "don't fret yourself. We'll be safe."

Shaking her head, she said, "How silly of me. Of course we'll be in good hands with you along. I just hate the thoughts of leaving my new home." She didn't understand why she cried so easily of late.

Nettie gave her a strange look but didn't comment. She brushed away her tears and suggested that everyone try to get a few hours rest as the journey was long. With her eyes shut and the other two napping, Raines let her mind wander over the events of the past few

263

months. She wondered if Adam really cared what happened to her. He behaved so strangely at times. Outwardly he showed great concern and interest in her well being, but their relationship had remained so cool since Lady Charlotte's visit. True she had been emphatic with him about their relationship, but it would have been comforting had he held her in his arms after the disturbing news about Uncle Percival.

Their trip proved uneventful and after a night spent in the London townhouse they arrived midmorning of the following day at Rosewood.

"Oh, Raines, it is so grand of you to come," cried Aunt Thea upon their arrival. "Percival is somewhat better today, but far from himself yet. Do come in and warm by the fire. You must be chilled to the bone."

This gracious welcome surprised Raines who had never seen her aunt exhibit much warmth. Immediately her suspicions were aroused. Just entering the hall of the manor where she had suffered so much unhappiness had caused her spirits to plummet. Glancing around the library once more she noticed how cold and impersonal everything was. Cousin Glenda put down her needlework and came forward to kiss Raines in greeting. Raines pretended to be happy to see her but in truth she only longed to be back home at Balfour.

Quickly she introduced Edwin, who began immediately to charm the women with his friendly wit. Raines moved to the sofa nearest the fire and sat down, removing her gloves. Nettie had been instructed to take her bags up to her old room.

"The doctor said Percival suffered a light stroke,

but sometimes patients recover completely if there are no additional ones. So far he doesn't appear to have had a second stroke and we are all very hopeful," explained Glenda.

"He's resting comfortably at the moment," continued the cousin smiling and letting out a sigh of relief. "We were so frightened the day he had the stroke. I tell you, Raines, it was a close call."

"I'm sure it was." Looking around, Raines inquired, "Where are the other cousins?"

"Margaret is on the continent and we haven't been able to get word to her. But we have good news about Ellen. She is expecting her first grandchild and has been advised by her physician not to travel." Glancing down at Raines, Thea Scott continued, "I don't see any signs of a new edition on the way in the Kemp family." Raines did not miss the glance her aunt gave to Glenda, nor the latter's smug smirk.

"I didn't know there was a race," retorted Raines. "It was my intent to let nature take care of such matters. Lord Kemp and I certainly plan a large family." Standing she said, "Now if you'll excuse me, I'll go up to my room and freshen up a bit before lunch. It has been a tiring trip." Turning to Edwin she smiled and said, "If you're ready to go up, I'll show you to your room."

Once out of the family's hearing, she whispered to Edwin between clenched teeth, "I don't know if I'll be able to stand those two for three days or not. If Uncle Percival continues to improve we will be on our way early on the fourth morn."

Patting her arm he whispered in reply, "Don't fret,

Aunt Raines, we can find enough here to keep us occupied for that short length of time." Glancing around the manor, he inquired, "Is there anything to do here to amuse oneself?"

"We can go for a walk if the sun comes out tomorrow. There is a fascinating old abbey just down the road. However, today is so overcast that who knows what tomorrow may bring." Clutching his hand, she said, "I wish Adam had come with us. He would have known how to handle the likes of Aunt Thea and Glenda."

"You just let them bother you too much. Remember you aren't here to stay. This is just an inconvenient visit."

Laughing she squeezed his hand. "You are such a dear boy. I'll try to remember that. Now, we're almost to your room. Have a quick rest and I'll have Nettie call you for luncheon."

That afternoon Raines visited her uncle and found him to be a very strongwilled man. Only three days after his stroke and he was beginning to regain his speech. If he continued, at his present rate, she felt good about his recovery. At least this was something to brighten her spirits. His condition appeared so promising that she secretly wondered if Aunt Thea had been hasty in summoning her this great distance. Sighing deeply, she reasoned that since she was here, it was best to set about making a pleasant visit.

Although time seemed to drag, on the third day, the sun did peek from behind a cloud and warm the garden enough for she and Edwin to go out for a stroll. Wearing her warmest cloak and carrying her muff, they strolled through the mazes of well kept hedge.

They had walked in silence for some distance when they heard voices and a heated conversation taking place on the opposite side of the hedge. Raines was about to make their presence known when she overheard her name mentioned. Putting her fingers to her lips she motioned for Edwin to be silent.

"Raines doesn't appear very happy as Lord Kemp's bride, does she?" said the first voice which she recognized as Glenda's.

"Can you blame her? I've always told you there is something odd about that rushed affair." This from Aunt Thea.

"Well, she certainly isn't pregnant as we once suspected."

Raines felt her cheeks burning. She started to step through the hedge but Edwin caught her by the arm to stop her. He tried to lead her away from the voices, but she shook her head.

"All I can say is that things aren't as they should be at Balfour or Adam Kemp would not have resumed his affair with Lady Charlotte so quickly."

"Glenda, how can you say such a thing?" gasped her mother.

"Mother, dear, it's the talk of every drawingroom in London these days. Charlotte has confided to her closest acquaintances that a divorce is imminent and she will yet live to be the Marchioness of Balfour."

At that Raines whirled and raced back up the pathway with Edwin following close behind. Tears were biting at her eyelids as she blinked to hold them back. Edwin steered her around the house and to an entrance away from the garden.

"Please, Aunt Raines, don't pay any attention to those malicious wags. They don't know what they are talking about."

Straightening, Raines blinked back the tears and resumed her stoic expression. "Whether they are right or not, I shall put a stop to this talk once and for all when we get back to Balfour. I will not be made the laughing stock of London, Edwin!"

Chapter 18

But after Raines arrived home there was no opportunity for her to confront Adam. Upon arrival he greeted her coolly and then left immediately for Squire Norwalk's farm to discuss some farm matters. She wondered if he were deliberately finding excuses to avoid her, since he seemed to spend more and more time away from Balfour. Had it not been for Edwin, who kept her constant company and did his best to cheer her, she feared that she would have a fit of the vapors, an appalling thing which she had never succumbed to in her life. To add to her melancholy, Edwin's father summoned him to report to Bath to commence his apprenticeship.

On his departure day Raines was so wracked with sadness she cried, "Oh, Edwin, how will I ever survive without your dear presence? You've been such a marvelous friend and companion." She bit back tears as she thought of the lonely hours ahead. Hugging him affectionately she said, "Do come back next vacation if your parents will allow." Grinning broadly, he shifted from foot to foot, beaming from her attention.

"Now, Raines, if you don't stop fussing over the lad, he's likely to go back to Eton and get expelled just so he can return here," laughed Adam.

"Much as I enjoyed my visit, Uncle Adam, when I get back to school this time, I intend to live the life of a paragon until I complete this term." His eyes twinkled with mischief as he shook Adam's hand and kissed Raines's cheek. Stepping into the coach he called, "But I'll be back next summer during my holiday, I promise." They stood in the courtyard until his carriage had rounded the drive and exited the iron gates.

To Raines's surprise the days sped by rapidly until the hour of their departure for the Duke and Duchess of Ramfield's house party. It was a gray overcast day when the two carriages pulled away from Balfour headed for the north country of York. Adam and Raines rode in the first coach followed by Nettie, Adam's manservant and their mountains of luggage in the second carriage.

"It's a long and tiring ride to Ram's Castle and I suggest you make yourself comfortable," said Adam after they had ridden several miles in silence.

"I'm quite well stationed," replied Raines primly, resigned to being civil to him, but still not reconciled.

With a slight quirk of his lip he glanced out the window ignoring her prudish air. "There are some lovely sights in these parts if you'd care to get over your sulks and enjoy them."

"I am most definitely not sulking." she replied

primly.

Unable to conceal a grin, he said, "Well, you could certainly fool me. You haven't been yourself in weeks."

"Pray, and what sort of person did you imagine me to be then? Am I so different today?" she asked, watching him cautiously. By now she knew him well enough to know when he wanted to tease.

"The young woman I married was full of energy, confident of her place in the world, and laughed a great deal. I don't see her anymore."

"Then pray tell me what you do see, for I am one and the same."

"Well, if you haven't changed, then something of great magnitude is bothering you."

"Honestly, Adam, I'm not up to your teasing this morning. I'm a bit nervous over visiting the duke and duchess since I know neither. 'Tis enough to ruffle the best, I'm sure." She turned to face him for the first time.

Reaching over he patted her hands. "Don't fret over that. You'll find them both decent sorts." Picking up her hand, he said, "Why your hands are like ice!"

Snatching back her hands, she buried them in her fur muff. "I'll just warm them a bit and all will be fine." He must never know she was nervous over being alone with him.

"That's a most lovely cottage there," said Adam, leaning close to the window and studying the thatched dwelling on his left.

"The cottage or the milk maiden?" inquired Raines before she could stop herself. A young girl with golden plaits and rosy cheeks walked toward the cottage with

271

two pails of milk.

"Why Lady Kemp, I'm shocked at you. I never even noticed that young maiden." His expression was one of total innocence.

"Humph!" retorted Raines giving her full attention to the row of cottages they were passing. "This is a lovely little village," she replied.

"Why, madam, did I see you wink at that young lad?" gasped Adam in mock shock.

"You did not!" she added a bit too sagely. In truth, on impulse she had winked at the boy of about eight who had waved as the coach passed by. They both burst out laughing and the tension between them lifted.

The rest of the trip proved long but pleasant and when Ram's Castle came into view with its lighted torches heralding their arrival, Raines felt a moment of sadness that the intimacy they had shared was to be shattered.

The coach halted at the huge oak doors with their royal crests hammered in gold, and the door flew open immediately. Several servants came down the stone steps to escort their guests into the castle, and to see to the luggage.

Raines took Adam's warm hands as he helped her from the coach. She quickly straightened her traveling outfit and whispered to him, "Do I look presentable?"

"As lovely as a winter's rose," he whispered back.

Beaming under his praise she moved confidently toward the door; she looked forward to this party with renewed good spirits. It seemed Adam's attentions brought happiness into her life when nothing else could. If only he loved her as she did him, she thought sadly.

"Welcome to Ram's Castle, Lady Raines," said the duke in greeting, taking Raines's hand in his. "You are as lovely as the gossips have indicated, my dear." Glancing at Adam he nodded, "A beautiful choice, Lord Kemp."

"Thank you, sir, I think so myself," replied Adam.

"It is an honor to have such an attractive young visitor," her host added.

"The pleasure is mine, my lord," Raines replied, glancing around her. She smiled at the stunning woman who stood quietly by the duke's side. "Good evening, my lady."

"We are delighted to have you with us. Lord Kemp has kept you to himself far too long. We've all been beseeching him to bring you to London to enjoy the *ton*," the duchess added. Turning to Adam, she chided, "Shame on you for harboring this sweet thing out in the country where we couldn't get to know her."

"Next season we'll have to change that," laughed Adam taking his hostess's hand and following her into the main hall.

The four moved into the great marble hall which was brilliantly lighted by candles and sconces. A chandelier with hundreds of candles glowing gave the room a twinkling, soft, warm feeling. Even the wealth of Balfour paled by comparison to the gold ornate moldings and English hunt scenes which graced the walls. At various focal points Italian marble sculptures stood on tall mahogany pedestals.

"I have prepared your rooms feeling that you would desire to retire early since the activities will begin quite early in the morn," explained the duchess. "Zelda will show you to your rooms and I will see you at breakfast, Lady Raines."

Zelda led the couple up the winding stairs and down a long hall to two connecting rooms at the far end of the corridor. Once inside Raines said, "Thank you, Zelda. This is lovely. Please tell Nettie that I'll ring when I'm ready for bed."

"If that be all, m'am, good night." Zelda curtsied and left, closing the door softly behind her.

Raines turned to Adam and said, "This is truly a beautiful suite, isn't it?" She glanced around the room with its soft apricot tinted walls and ornate green velvet draperies. On the floor was an oriental rug in shades of apricot, gold and green. The large bed stood against one wall beside a washstand and oval mirror, while in the opposite corner of the area a cozy chaise lounge and several thick cushioned chairs faced the small grate where a vigorous fire burned.

Taking off her mink lined cloak she draped it across a chair and moved toward the fire. "Won't you come nearer the fire and warm a bit before going on to your room?" she invited.

Until now Adam had stood silently and Raines had found the atmosphere a bit strained. But he grinned and moved toward the heat, holding out his hands to warm them. "From the sound of the wind which seems to be building outside, we may have a gale before morning." He unbuttoned his greatcoat and dropped it beside Raines's cloak.

"I hope bad weather doesn't spoil this party, I've looked forward to it for so long." Adam was watching her so intently that she nervously moved away from the warmth of the grate and over to the window. "It's so dark out that I can't see anything," she said pulling back the drape and peering into the blackness.

"Raines, come back over here and quit running from me," said Adam softly. "I think we have more important things to discuss than the weather."

A rush of color surfaced in her cheeks as she moved back toward the fireplace. "Whatever you say, Adam. I didn't realize there was anything of great importance to talk about." Trying to sound flippant she added, "I mean, we have been together in the coach for the entire day. What more can we have to discuss which hasn't already been covered?"

Putting his finger over her lips, he smiled down at her and said, "Has anyone ever told you that you chatter like a magpie when you're nervous?" His eyes met hers and she thought she read affection in them. Not trusting her voice, she merely shook her head.

"Well, you do," he laughed. "Raines, when you look up at me with that adorable innocence I could hug you like an affectionate puppy."

"I'm not a puppy," she said in a voice barely a whisper.

"I know," he said softly, staring into her eyes. Clearing his throat, he stepped back a few inches and reached into his pocket. "I've been meaning to give this to you," he said, holding out his hand.

Filled with curiosity, she moved closer. "Whatever can it be?" Then seeing, she cried, "Adam! My ring! You found my wedding ring! How did you get it back?"

Taking her hand he gently slid the gold ring on her slender finger. "The constable found your attacker

275

and the thief still had the ring in his possession. The constable returned it to me several days ago."

Surprised she asked, "Why haven't you given it to me before now?"

"I wanted the moment to be right. We've seemed to drift apart lately and I wanted to wait until you had changed from that cool aloof attitude you've had toward me."

She was touched by his kindness and she wanted so much to tell him how she loved him, but he had not mentioned love to her and she could not bear to be humiliated. Instead she said, "Thank you, Adam. I'm happy to have it back."

Moving a step closer he said, "Raines, there was more that went with our bargain. I want heirs. And I want them soon." Seeing her frown, he added, "I won't force my attentions on you but it is fair to warn you that I am not a patient man. Do you understand me?" He put his finger under her chin and lifted her face to his. "Answer me, Raines," he ordered in a low, firm voice.

Thinking her heart would explode from his nearness, and wanting him, she whispered softly, "I understand."

"When you want to return to my bed, the move will be yours to make. I will not bother you again." He dropped his hand and strode to the door. Raines stood watching, not moving until he had vanished through the connecting doorway. Why hadn't she told him that she could never come to his bed as long as he had Charlotte Brownlees as his mistress? Where had her tongue been? Still angry with herself for being so hesitant, she rang for Nettie and prepared for bed.

Once the candle had been snuffed she lay in the darkness and thought of Adam in the adjoining room. How wonderful it would be to have him here to snuggle close to under the down coverlet with the wind howling outside. She could hear the first drops of rain pinging on the window panes. Soon she drifted off to sleep determined to work harder at making Adam fall in love with her.

It was after midnight when the wet glob hit her forehead and rolled down her cheek. Raines's eyes flew open and she wiped her hand across her face keeping the rest of her body well under the covers for the fire had died down in the grate and the room was cold. What on earth had hit her head? Lying perfectly still she waited. Pong! A second wet blob landed on her cheek. What in heaven's name, she thought panicked. And then the water began falling rapidly as the storm outside increased its intensity. "My room leaks!" she cried sitting up in bed as the realization hit her. Quickly she bolted from the bed and ran barefoot across the icy floor to light a candle by the last embers of the fire. Shivering she moved back toward her bed noticing that her breath made smoke puffs as she walked. Setting her candle down on the night table, she tried to shove her bed out of the flow of the water which was now puddling in her warm bed. The heavy ornate bed would not budge from where it had probably stood for a hundred years. Her mind raced ahead to think of what she should do. Tiptoeing, for no sensible reason, back toward the fireplace she checked the clock on the mantel. It read half past one. What was she to do? All the servants would be asleep by now, and she didn't want to disturb her hosts. Besides, her toes were beginning to feel like frozen sticks and she couldn't find her slippers in the darkened room. Running back across the room she went around to the opposite side of the bed and slid under the cover. But the indention she made in the feather mattress caused the puddle of water to run to her side and she gasped as the cold water hit her skin. Now soaked, she jumped out of bed, grabbed the candle and headed toward Adam's room. He would know what to do.

As she entered his room she heard his rhythmic breathing even above the wind which sang its way mournfully through the cracks in the windowsills.

"Adam," she called softly, moving to his side of the bed and holding her candle so she could study his face. By now she was so cold that the candle wavered in her trembling hand. "Adam!" she called louder, and reached over to touch his shoulder. Instantly his eyes flew open and he sat up in bed. And then he grinned rakishly. "Well, my dear, it didn't take you long to decide that this is where you belong, did it?" He patted the place beside him and said, "Come to bed."

"Don't be ridiculous!" she snapped. "Adam, listen to me. My room leaks and my bed is soaked. What must I do?"

He grinned such a devilish smile that Raines wanted to shake him. "Raines, come on and get in this bed with me before you catch your death."

"I will not!" she snapped, shaking her head indignantly. The force of her breath caused her weak candle to flicker and go out. "Adam, you've got to get me a light," she cried. I'll never find my way back to my room. I'm freezing to death!"

Laughing heartily, he slid out of bed and came to her. "Give me your candle and I'll light it with this flint," he said between chuckles. Touching her hand he added, "My God, you are like ice."

By now her teeth were chattering and she was furious with him for laughing at her. "Just get that candle lit, so I can see where I'm going," she snapped.

He lit the candle and she gasped. "Adam, you don't have any clothes on. For God's sake cover yourself."

"All right," he said and handing her the candle, he slid back in bed, drawing the covers to his chin.

"Adam! You can't leave me out here in the cold! What are you going to do?"

"I, my lovely, am going back to sleep. Good night."

"I don't believe this! My own husband!" She was now dancing from foot to foot trying to bring some circulation back to her cold toes. "Adam! Don't you dare go to sleep. What am I going to do?"

Sighing, he opened his eyes and grinned at her. It was clear that he was enjoying her misery. "I have this perfectly warm side of the bed which you may share, my wife. If you don't wish to, then snuff out that candle so I can get some sleep."

"I'll die before I get in that bed with you," she said heatedly.

"That you probably shall before morning," he said matter-of-factly, snuggling further under the covers and closing his eyes once more.

"You're enjoying my plight!" she hissed, moving closer so she could study his expression.

"If you drip that candle wax on me, I shall take you

over my knee and give you a good thrashing, even if it wakes the whole household," he warned.

When she backed away quickly, her candle went out again. "Oh, I can't see where I'm going."

"Well, I shan't get cold again lighting it for you, so just do the best you can making your way back to your room." His voice sounded muffled like he had pulled the warm comforter over his head.

Setting the candle on the floor, Raines felt her way toward the bed. "Beast!" she hissed as his muffled laughter filled the room. Feeling her way around the bed, she finally reached the opposite side away from him. There was simply nothing to do but get into the bed and get warm. She lay down as near the edge as possible without rolling off, expecting him to make some comment, but there was complete silence from his side of the bed. Her teeth began chattering and she began to sniffle.

"Raines, move closer and let me warm you," Adam whispered kindly. Sliding over reluctantly, she moved within his reach.

"Woman! What the devil?" he shouted. "Your nightgown is soaking wet and like ice! Get that thing off now!"

This time it was her turn to giggle. "Serves you right if I soak you too," she whispered. "And lower your voice or you'll wake everybody."

"Get that wet nightgown off or I'll throw you out of my bed." He moved away from her. "You'll soak the sheets."

"I told you it was leaking on my bed." She giggled again. "And you wouldn't dare kick me out." She felt his hands on her shoulder and the curve of her back.

"All right, I'll take it off," she promised, unbuttoning the tiny row of satin buttons down the front of her gown. With his help she wiggled out of the wet garment without getting out from under the covers. "What'll I do with it?" she asked, once it was in her hands.

"Here," he growled, "I'll take care of it." She heard the thump when it landed on the floor.

She had to admit snuggling close to him was better than freezing. Fitting her body into the curve of his she began to feel warmth coursing back through her veins. Slowly he stroked her body, warming it with his touch. Turning to whisper something to him, she felt his lips touch hers. At first startled and then relaxing, she let his lips consume hers. Gently he kissed her, almost teasingly until she locked her arms around his neck and drew him closer. Her once cold body now felt aflame with desire as she pressed ever closer. His hand trailed down her neck and gently caressed her breast, cupping it in his palm. Drawing in her breath she thought that she would die from the sheer longing for him to enter her. And when he did, she gave a small cry of joy. This time she accepted him and knowing what was expected, she rode the crest of passion with him until both bodies were satisfied, and they lay spent. Afterwards she cuddled in his arms, falling into the most peaceful sleep she had known. If only they could be like this forever, she thought, just before sleep claimed her.

The early dawn light filtered into the room and Raines rolled over to get away from it, snuggling closer to Adam. Suddenly, remembering what had happened in the night, she opened her eyes and glanced around.

"Good morning," said Adam, kissing her lightly on the tip of her nose.

Not being abashed by his actions, she grinned up at him and snuggled closer. Within a short period of time she succumbed to his passion once again. Each time left her more fulfilled and content than the previous. Adam must love her. How else could he be so gentle and patient, she reasoned.

Shortly afterward there was a soft knock on the door and Adam's manservant entered with his breakfast tray. Without a flick of an eyebrow he stepped around Raine's nightgown and placed the tray on the bed. "Your morning tea, sir," he said.

"Lady Raines's room sprang a leak last night, Jacob. Please take care of it today, and send Nettie to assist her, please. She needs a warm robe and slippers."

"Yes, sir," said Jacob. "Will that be all?"

"Thank you, Jacob."

Raines had buried down in the covers, her cheeks scarlet with shame. Pulling the covers away, Adam teased, "You can come out now, my lady. Your reputation is tarnished forever."

"Really, Adam, I don't think it wise to make jokes at this time. What must Jacob think of me?"

"That you are an obedient wife, my pet. Now finish your nap, but I must dress for the hunt. The men are to leave quite early." Leaning over he kissed her affectionately before he slid out of bed.

Reaching for his trousers he dressed swiftly and moved over to throw more coals on the smoldering ashes. Laughing he said, "We must have shocked poor Jacob, because he left without stirring up the fire." He continued to chuckle.

"I still don't think it's funny," Raines hissed. And then she broke into peals of giggling. "Oh, it's such a lovely day that I hope Nettie hurries. I'm ready to go meet all the guests. Do you know who has been invited?"

"Oh, just the usual group, I should imagine. You'll probably know most from the ball in London."

This was the first time Raines had thought about the note she had sent to James MacBain. She would have to do something to discourage him. No matter, she thought, she could handle him without any embarrassing consequences. This time she would not go anywhere alone with him.

Glancing at the clock on the mantel, Adam moved over to the bed and kissed Raines one last time. "I'm off to the hunt. I'll see you this evening."

"Do you think they'll have the hunt after all that rain last night?"

"It will only make the fox friskier," he said laughing.

Nettie, who had been waiting in the hall for her master to leave, came bustling in and warmed Raines's robe by the fire before holding it for her to slip into.

"Oh, Nettie, I'm telling you, the rain poured in my room last night."

"That right, ma'am?" said Nettie with a straight face.

Dressing in her new light pink morning gown, Raines checked her appearance in the mirror as

Nettie helped her put her hair up in a becoming fashion. She saw the added sparkle in her eyes, and the heightened color in her cheeks that her new-found happiness created. Today the world seemed a splendid place to live.

Raines walked down to the dining room with a lively step and a heart so happy that it felt near bursting with joy. The duchess saw her enter and called, "Come, my dear, and join our table." The guests stopped eating to greet her. Helping herself to kidneys, eggs, sausages, and hot yeast breads, Raines turned from the buffet and moved to an empty chair near the duchess. Suddenly her happiness was shattered. Looking up, she saw Charlotte Brownlees enter the dining room and heard her greet several ladies in a cheerful voice.

Glancing down at her plate Raines tried to hide her indignation at this woman's gall. The nerve of Charlotte to come when she had to know that Adam and Raines were invited. She could have had the decency to stay in London, Raines thought angrily.

Finishing her meal in silence, Raines hurried to leave the table. She planned to go to the sun parlor where the duchess had announced card games would begin within the hour. Having no heart to play cards, Raines decided she would plead to be an observer. This would allow her the opportunity to quietly leave the group without making a scene.

To Raines's disgust Charlotte came along to the parlor and pleaded to be an observer also. The duchess clapped her hands and announced, "Ladies, ladies, if I may have your attention. Any of you who don't find cards to your fancy this morning may wish to tour our hothouses. We have beautiful flowers in bloom this year and you'll find it a pleasant stroll, I believe."

Several women joined Raines and they set off for the greenhouses which were a short stroll through the beautiful gardens. Wrapping her cloak tightly around her, Raines enjoyed the cold, clear air as it caressed her face. The outdoors helped clear her head and she felt silly for having let Lady Charlotte ruffle her.

The rest of the day went smoothly until late in the afternoon. Raines was crossing from the sun room to the main hall when she heard her name called. Turning, she faced Charlotte who came toward her smiling. "Lady Raines, this is the first time we have had an opportunity to chat. How is the young bride?" She studied Raines with the condescending air of one dealing with a child.

"Couldn't be more wonderful," replied Raines, staring her down.

Frowning Charlotte said, "How odd? I see Lord Adam in London so much that I feared trouble in his new marriage."

"Not in the least," smiled Raines, shaking her head.

Still not satisfied, Charlotte moved closer and said, "If Adam is so content at Balfour, why is someone else warming his bed in London?" Her voice took on a sneer.

Blood rushed from Raines's head and she took the bait. "What nonsense, Lady Charlotte. No one had warned me that you were getting addled in your dotage." Raines shoved past her and started up the steps.

"We'll see how soon your marriage of convenience becomes extremely inconvenient!" Charlotte hurled after her.

Raines's back stiffened but she did not turn to answer. Instead she rushed to her room and slammed the door before dissolving into tears. How could Adam tell that despicable woman about their marriage agreement? She hated Charlotte, and at the moment, she detested Adam too!

One thing was certain, she would not let him in her bed tonight, if he begged like a pup. Rushing over to the connecting door she threw the bolt. It was a strong metal catch and nothing short of beating it down would free it.

Raines did not see Adam until she went down for dinner. She had heard him come in to change, but had instructed Nettie to tell him she had a headache and was resting until dinner. At dinner she was seated between the duke and an aging viscount, whom she lavished attention upon. Every time Adam caught her eye, she coolly glanced away.

After dinner a musical performance was scheduled for the music room and after the men had retired for cigars and brandy the group met there. Excusing herself to go back to her room for a warmer shawl, Raines left the group. To her surprise she ran into James in the hallway. "How nice to see you!" she cried in greeting.

"I didn't know how your husband would take finding me at the same party," James said in greeting.

"How silly. Don't ever let him discourage you from going where you please." She looped her arm through his and walked down the hall. "Tell me all that has been happening in London since I was last there."

They walked down the great hall until they found themselves under the staircase. It was lighted here but not so brightly as nearer the parlors. "Here is a lovely seat, let's sit and have a long chat." Raines patted the velvet cushion beside her.

Glowing from her attention, James sat down beside her. "First I wish to apologize for the unforgivable way I behaved the last time we met."

"Nonsense, it was all a silly misunderstanding and as much my fault as yours." She tried to be honest about it. "I had no business going out into the garden and misleading you."

"Then I'm forgiven?"

"Of course."

He reached for her hand and took it happily in his to kiss the back of it. Suddenly Raines heard approaching footsteps and looked up to see Adam bearing down on them. Jumping to her feet, she blushed guiltily. "Why Adam, I thought you were in the parlor having your brandy."

"Obviously," he snapped. "Please leave us," he ordered, not even glancing in her direction.

Grabbing his sleeve she said, "Adam, don't be ridiculous. There is no need to make a scene. It is not as you think."

He shook off her hand and ignored her. "I said leave us—at once!" he thundered.

James jumped to his feet too, and faced Adam. "There is no need to shout at the lady."

"I believe I told you in no uncertain terms to stay away from my wife. Unless you wish to settle this in a duel, you won't be here in the morning." With that

Adam stormed back down the hall and out the front door.

Raines had already started up the stairs. She was furious with Adam. How dare he flaunt his mistress before her yet grow livid at the sight of her innocently chatting with James. Going to her room, Raines was thankful that no one had overheard the confrontation. At least she could hold down a new scandal.

Later that night, she heard Adam enter his room and come to her door. He tried the door and when he found it locked, he pounded on it. Going quickly to it, she said, "Adam, go away. The whole house will know that we're quarreling."

"I don't care if the world knows it. Open this door, or I swear to you, Raines, I'll kick it in." He pounded louder.

"Oh, for heaven's sake," she said as she opened it. Still her knees trembled as she did so.

Once the latch fell back, Adam charged into the room and looked around. Unable to keep the sarcasm out of her voice, she said, "What are you expecting? A lover in my bed?"

Glaring at her, he came and took her arms in his strong hands, gripping them tightly. "I don't ever want to see you talking to James MacBain again. Do you understand that?"

"Yes, now take your hands off me. You're hurting my arms."

Adam eased his grip but he did not free her. "You are my wife and you will remain Lady Kemp until you die. That is all I have to say to you." With that he turned and stalked back into his room. This time she heard the bolt thrown on the lock on his side of the door.

They spent an uneventful remainder of the weekend. To Raines's relief James MacBain had pleaded urgent business in London and had left the premises before she came down for breakfast. Adam stayed by her side the rest of the weekend, but their politeness to each other was a cool facade. For Raines the weekend was ruined. All she wanted to do was get back to Balfour, and bury her troubles in the coin collection.

Chapter 19

Raines busied herself finishing the cataloguing of the coin collection while Adam was away. He never again told her that he loved her and she felt him withdraw from her once more. He began to spend more and more time in London making preparations for the presentation, and Raines missed him when he was gone. The castle seemed so empty when he was not there. She also felt a touch of jealousy when she wondered what he might be doing in London on these trips. She had once asked to accompany him and had been told firmly that she could not.

On each trip Adam stayed away longer and when he did return he seemed aloof and detached. He never came into her room again, nor did he make any advances toward love making. Raines grew more perplexed as time passed.

Finally one day Raines decided the pain of loving

Adam was too much to tolerate. Turning to Nettie she said, "Adam has been in London for weeks. I am sick of being shut up in this castle alone." She paced the floor and fretted with the folds of her skirt. "A person could go mad with no one to talk to and nothing to do."

"I haven't seen you too idle lately. 'Tis something else which is troubling you."

Sighing deeply, Raines said, "Never mind, Nettie. I'm just bored today and miss Adam. I think I'll go downstairs and see if Watson has had any word from the staff in London. Surely Adam is coming to Balfour soon, since he has been away for ages now."

Raines enjoyed chatting with Watson who knew more history about Balfour than any of the other servants. Often while he worked, she listened to him tell of Kemps who had lived and fought for Balfour many years before.

She found him in the dining room busily polishing the silver. He was concentrating on a large punch bowl, deep in thought and did not hear her approach. The table was cluttered with pieces of silver, some gleaming like new and others tarnished and brown. "Good day, Watson, you seem busy this afternoon. Do you enjoy polishing?"

"Day to you, Lady Kemp. Yes ma'am, this is one of my favorite tasks around the castle. I get to rest my weary feet and yet I'm still busy at work." Seeing that she wanted to talk, he continued, "What can I do for her ladyship?"

Raines took the chair opposite him and propped her

elbows on the table. "Don't stop your work. I was just lonesome and decided to come chat. You've worked here a long time, haven't you, Watson?"

"Indeed I have. Twenty-two years to be exact. Before that my father and grandfather served his lordship's family. I am as loyal to the members of Balfour as to the king." He rubbed vigorously on a large punch bowl.

"That's such a lovely piece," said Raines idly, watching him polish it to a gleaming brilliance.

"Aye, it is that. It was a gift from Lady Alexandra's family when she wed the master."

"Really! Oh, Watson, tell me about Lady Alexandra. What was she like? Was she beautiful?" She traced her finger around the rim of the silver punch bowl, admiring its intricate design.

"She was lovely to look at, but not like you, Lady Raines. You have been a pleasure to serve."

"What do you mean? Was she nicer than I, or smarter, or kinder?"

He chuckled at her suggestions and shook his head. "Not even one of those things you mentioned."

"Did you like her?"

He rubbed slowly on the silver although it already gleamed spotlessly. "Can't say that I did, ma'am."

"Come on, Watson, now you've got to tell me more about her. You like everybody. Why was she different?"

"I guess, ma'am, that I hold it against her because of what she did to Lord Adam. He is a fine gentleman and deserved better than the likes of her. Nobody deserves to die, but I can't say that it wasn't just punishment for the way she treated our master."

Raines heart raced rapidly for she realized she was about to discover something about Adam's first wife which had never been discussed before. In the past she has been too busy to dwell on the first marriage, since she had been so certain that it had been perfect and this was why Adam could not love her. Now she was not so sure that her assumptions had been correct. "It was a happy marriage, wasn't it, Watson?"

He chuckled and shook his head. "Now where did you get such an idea as that, Lady Raines? It was probably one of the most stormy marriages I've seen and it started going sour by the day they came home from their honeymoon."

Indeed this shocked Raines and she held her breath as she waited for him to continue. "What was the problem?"

"It was that wicked Lady Alexandra. Oh, she appeared sweet enough until he married her. But even then I wasn't taken in by her sweet ways." He sighed and shook his head. "And when she ran away with the stableboy it was I who had to go and tell the master. He was in a near rage. We rode through the night hunting for her."

"Did you find her?"

"Aye, but it was too late. She had tried to jump a ravine and her horse plunged them to their deaths. Lord Adam rode on to her people's castle and told them to come collect the body." He shook his head.

"To my knowledge no one ever came to claim Tom, the stable boy. His family must have been too ashamed." He nodded his head to emphasize a point. "I don't hold bad will toward him, since he was a young man and she chased him claiming to love him forever, and the likes." He frowned. "No, there was no good in that woman, even if her family was nobility. She brought disgrace on the house of Kemp and that's a fact."

Raines had listened in awe and now she whispered, her voice barely audible, "And that's why her picture isn't here and she isn't buried in the family cemetery."

"Aye. No one speaks of her out of loyalty to Lord Adam." He stood and moved away from the table. "And I probably shouldn't have told you, but you seem such a fine person and I didn't want you harboring no thoughts of Lady Alexandra being competition for Lord Adam's affections."

"Oh! Watson! I'm so happy that you told me this. I promise that I'll never tell a soul what you've revealed to me, but it explains so much!"

Raines left the butler and walked back to her room, silent. She had much to think about. Now she understood why Adam always feared being cuckolded, and why he was afraid to love again. He had been deeply hurt and humiliated by Alexandra's behavior. If only she could convince him that she was not like Alexandra, and never had or would be. Now that she understood so much, she knew that she could be more patient and understanding. Perhaps she could even make him grow to love her.

294

Raines was so excited over her discovery that she decided to go for a walk and think of ways to make Adam see that she cared for him, without giving away her true feelings. Grabbing her traveling cloak, she rushed to the front door and opened it. To her delight there stood Adam.

"Where are you going on an afternoon like this?" He asked, frowning as his eyes traveled to her cloak.

"Adam!"

"What sort of greeting is that? You sound as if you are shocked." He smiled and moved closer to her. "Aren't you even going to let me in?"

"Of course," she managed to mumble, stepping aside to let him enter. Her heart raced faster and she had wanted to throw her arms around him in her delight over seeing him, yet knew that she could not overplay her role. He must come to see how much she loved him of his own accord. "When did you get home? I didn't know you were coming."

"Obviously. No one came to let me in. Where's that Watson? He's supposed to man the door. Why wasn't he here to see you out?" He frowned and looked around him suspiciously.

Raines grabbed his hand and led him toward the parlor, "Come on in here and warm yourself. Your hands are frozen and there's a good fire burning in the grate in here." She continued to keep up a steady stream of chatter. She was truly elated to have him home. Quickly she rang for Nettie. "Here, take Lord Kemp's damp coat and put it by the fire in the kitchen and bring the tea tray back," she told the woman.

"You still haven't told me where Watson is." Watching her intently, he said, "Are you keeping something from me, Raines?"

"Good heavens, no! Watson is merely polishing the silverware in the dining room and I saw no reason to bother him. Really, Adam, I can open a door myself."

Adam sat wearily down and stretched his feet near the fire. "My feet are frozen. This fire feels wonderful."

Raines rushed to get an ottoman for him to rest his feet on. Very solicitously she said, "Why did you ride from London on such a day as this? Why didn't you come in a carriage?" She hoped her voice had the proper amount of scolding in it.

"I needed a paper from the vault and didn't have time to come by carriage. Although, if the weather is this bad tomorrow I may have Toby take me back."

"Oh, you have to go back so soon?"

"Do I detect a note of disappointment in your voice? Have you missed me?" He studied her closely.

"You know I have. It is dreadfully lonesome here when you're away, Adam." She didn't want to sound like a whiny, complaining wife, so she changed the subject. "Couldn't you have sent one of the servants for the paper?"

"My, my, but aren't you fickle? First you scold me for staying away so much and next you are wondering why I came at all."

"Adam, don't tease. You know I'm happy to see you, if it is only for a few hours. Now, why did you

296

ride out in this terrible weather?"

He hesitated before he finally spoke with a sigh. "First I've missed you and thought I'd pop in and make sure everything was all right. I have had to stay in London a great deal lately and it does worry me to leave you alone so much of the time." His voice seemed to imply that she had brought this isolation upon herself, yet he was still concerned about her. "The second reason I didn't send a servant is that I wanted a paper out of the safe and no one has the combination but me."

"Oh, Adam, you tease! That's the real reason you came. Honestly, for a minute you had me believing that you had missed me and wanted to come for my sake."

"Would that really matter to you?" he asked softly, watching her face.

Fortunately Nettie entered with the tea tray and they stopped their conversation. "Here 'tis, and Cook just took some rolls from the oven. They're still piping hot, sir."

"Wonderful, Nettie. I smell them and they look delicious. I think I'll have one this very minute." He reached for a sweet roll while Raines poured and served his tea.

Although Adam's visit was short, it went pleasantly. They dined together that evening and he sat in the parlor and listened to her play the piano afterwards.

While Raines played a tune which did not require her concentration, she wondered what he was thinking about. Adam sat quietly staring at the fire and listening. During dinner he had been filled with news of London, yet he did not offer to take her back with him. He seemed content to be home and even glad to see her, yet he had not made any move toward affection. She wondered if he would ever come to her bedroom again.

She stopped playing after an hour and came to sit by the fire with him. "I am tired of playing and really am not in the mood anyhow." She saw him yawn. "Are you tired, also?"

"Yes. I plan to have a nightcap and call it an evening. Do you care to join me?"

Remembering how she had behaved the last time she had shared a toddy with him, she declined. "I don't think so. This has been a long day and I think I'll go up to my room."

He nodded in agreement. "I'll sit here and finish my drink and then I'll call it a night also." She started out the door and he called after her, "Oh, Raines, I plan to leave early in the morning. There is no need to disturb you, so I'll be gone when you wake."

She felt the slow sinking feeling of disappointment. "I don't mind getting up to see you off."

"Nonsense. Get your rest."

"When will you return?"

"I can't really say. However, the arrangements are nearing completion and I should be sending for you to come to London before long. You do want to be present for the coin ceremony, don't you?"

"I think it would look proper for me to accompany you." She maintained a level, noncommittal tone to her voice. He must not know how much she was hurting.

When she dressed and went down to breakfast the following morning she learned that Adam had risen and departed for London several hours earlier.

Chapter 20

Raines's life eased into a routine which was pleasant, yet lonely. At last the date was set to carry the huge collection to London for presentation at the museum. An outstanding program had been scheduled for the event and Raines's head swam from the list of important people who planned to be present at the ceremony.

Adam had been away for several weeks when a note arrived from him instructing her to pack and come to London for the presentation. Delightedly she raced to tell Nettie to pack the trunks.

On the scheduled day the party left Balfour for London and Raines felt elated. Adam had wanted her to be with him, so he must miss her as much as she did him. Also, she had known for some weeks now that she was pregnant, and wanted to share this news with Adam in person.

She was so anxious to arrive in London that the

journey seemed longer than ever before. Adam had sent a letter apologizing for not being able to come home and accompany her back to the city. He had instructed her to bring two additional men to ride as guards with the coach to protect the valuable collection from highwaymen.

Fortunately the trip was uneventful and upon arrival Raines saw Adam standing on the steps waiting for her. Quickly she climbed out of the carriage and rushed up the steps to meet him. Turning her face up for his kiss she was surprised when he did not respond. Instead he nodded in greeting and turned to instruct the men carrying the collection.

Feeling as though he had slapped her, she whirled and ran into the house. Why had Adam behaved as though she were a stranger? He had scarcely acknowledged her presence.

When at last he came to their room she was so angry that she did not speak to him.

"Did you have a tiring trip?"

"Yes, I'm exhausted and don't feel very well."

He came over and put his hands on her shoulders, but she didn't turn her cheek to be kissed in greeting. She would not let him see how hurt she was by his indifference.

Putting his hand on her chin, he tried to turn her face toward him, but she stubbornly refused. "Adam, I think we've carried this charade far enough, don't you?" she snapped irritably. "There's no reason for us to pretend affection when we are alone." She moved out of his reach, and saw a glimmer of hurt in his eyes, as though he might disagree.

"Our agreement did not include our continuing conjugal rights after an heir was begot," she said stiffly.

He took a step toward her. "Do you mean that you are with child?"

"Yes."

Adam reached to embrace her, but Raines swiftly moved from his grasp. A frown creased his brow and he watched her closely. "When is the baby due?"

"In six months and I can't wait for it to pass, so I can end this . . . this . . ."

"Has it been that difficult for you? I thought you were enjoying being Lady Kemp."

"I enjoy being Lady Kemp and I love Balfour, but . . . but . . ." she faltered, twisting her hands, undecided what to say next.

"But you do not like having to sleep with me," he finished for her. She saw his face grow flushed and recognized the angry glint in his eyes.

Stubbornly she continued, "That's exactly correct. Now that you know, I presume our lovemaking can cease. That is until it is time to try for another child."

"If that is what you wish." His voice sounded cold and his words were clipped as though he was holding his anger in check.

"It is," she said softly, biting back the tears. She wished he would take her in his arms and tell her that she was wrong, that he did love her and wanted her to be near him forever.

"I must leave now, but tomorrow we will discuss the

arrangements for your delivery. I suppose you will go to Balfour to deliver since all Kemps have been born there."

"That will be satisfactory with me."

"There is the presentation and the museum board of directors have planned a gala for the evening to celebrate the acceptance of the gift. Do you feel well enough to attend those functions?"

"Yes, I will go to those. If your wife didn't attend, someone might become suspicious and I certainly don't wish to cause you any embarrassment."

"Very well. Good day, madam," his voice was icy with indifference and he bowed graciously before leaving. It was only after the door had slammed that she realized just how angry he was. Let him be angry, she thought. She was aching inside with misery.

The next morning she was so depressed that she decided only a shopping spree would save her from complete hysteria. Raines ordered a carriage to be sent around and set off with Nettie. Adam had not spent the night at their home, so she assumed he had moved into his club to avoid further contact with her.

"I'm going to buy yarn and ribbons so that we may begin the baby's layette," she explained as they moved through the city.

"I thought you looked a bit peaked this morning," said Nettie, eyeing her carefully. Grinning she continued, "Well, 'tis time you and the lord had a wee one. I been suspecting it for some time now. The only thing that bothered me was he stayed in town so much lately that I was afraid it couldn't happen."

"Nettie! You are a nosy creature! Adam has to take care of his vast business holdings. He can't stay at Balfour with me all the time, and I can't go traipsing off to follow him everywhere." She was defending him and she didn't even understand why.

"Well, no matter. When the wee one arrives he'll spend more time with you, I'll vouch."

Raines signalled for the driver to stop at the millinery and he pulled the carriage to the curb. Just as Raines stepped from the vehicle she heard her name called. Looking around she saw the plump figure in blue satin descending upon her. "Good morning, Lady Sybil, it is good to see you again." She had to struggle to be friendly to the woman since she wanted to be alone. Now this meddlesome person would probably follow her for the entire morning and pick her for information.

"My dear, you look lovelier every time we meet." She kissed Raines affectionately on the cheek. "Stand back and let me see you. It is difficult to tell in that full dress, and with your coat buttoned, but I don't think I see any signs of a little one on the way."

"That's where you are wrong," snapped Raines. Then feeling guilty for taking out her frustrations on this poor woman, she amended, "I'm happy to inform you that a little one is on the way." She hoped her voice sounded more cheerful than she felt.

Lady Gossington eyed her again suspiciously and said, "Now that you mention it, I do detect a paleness in your complexion."

"Nonsense! I've never felt better."

304

"So you are off on a shopping trip? When did you arrive in London? The last time I saw Adam he said that you were enjoying the country so much he couldn't entice you into staying with him in the city."

The nerve of Adam to pretend she was the one who didn't want to be in London, when he had refused to allow her to do so. She grew angry again just thinking about it. Yet she did not want this woman to suspect her unhappiness.

"I came yesterday to attend the program at the museum and to do some shopping."

"Oh, yes, I've an invitation to the afternoon program and the ball that evening. Are you shopping for something to wear?" She eyed Raines suspiciously as though she knew something Raines did not.

"No, I have dresses for both events. Nettie and I are out today purchasing for the nursery. I want to go in here and buy some material. Nettie is such an excellent seamstress and she plans to make the little one's wardrobe."

"I was on my way in to buy new ribbons for my gray hat. Shall we go in together?" She reached to take Raines's arm and there was nothing to do but follow, although company was the last thing she wanted this morning.

The shopkeeper saw the two well-dressed women enter and came bustling to the front. "May I be of service, ladies?"

"We are both looking for new ribbons. Do you have any nice ones?" asked Lady Gossington.

"Indeed I do. A new shipment just arrived from

Amsterdam. This trouble with France has made trade a bit awkward, so the materials now go to Amsterdam and then to England." He pulled several cards of pastel shades of satin and velvet ribbons down and laid them on the counter for the two ladies to inspect.

Quickly Raines made her selections, choosing green, yellow, and white. Next she purchased several yards of lace and with her packages in hand, hoped that she could get away from Lady Sybil. But she was not to be rid of the woman so quickly.

"Let's go to Swann's for tea," suggested Lady Gossington, handing her packages to the servant who stood outside waiting.

"Oh, I'm sorry, I can't make it this morning. I must get home before noon, since I don't know Adam's plans for the day."

"Another day perhaps." Lady Gossington started to walk away, then seemed to change her mind and turned to take Raines's hand. "My dear, I don't want to upset you, yet I feel as a friend I should tell you this. Adam is too handsome a rake to leave so much to himself. You must pull yourself away from Balfour and come into town with him more often."

Puzzled, yet feeling the blood drain from her face as the fear set in, Raines stammered, "I . . . I . . . do . . . don't understand; what you are implying."

"I don't want to be the one to carry tales, but advice from one married lady to another should be heeded. I like you, Raines, and don't want to see you get hurt. Don't take Adam for granted."

"Lady Sybil, if you are trying to tell me something,

please come straight out with it. Don't try to hedge." Raines watched her closely.

Taking a deep breath, Lady Gossington sighed. "Well, I've let the cat out of the bag now, so I might as well finish."

"Indeed you had."

"Adam has been seen escorting Charlotte Brownlees around town a great deal lately. And, as you probably already know, she was his mistress before your marriage and has vowed to everyone that she will break up this marriage if it is the last thing she does."

Raines felt like someone had struck her in the chest with a log. The color drained from her face, and she was so angry that she gritted her teeth to prevent crying. "I see. Thank you for this information, Lady Sybil. I shall look into the matter." She whirled away to get into the carriage, then stopped and turned. "One more thing. Should you see Lady Charlotte, please inform her that it will take more than the likes of her to take my husband away from me, if I choose to keep him, and at the moment I do not intend to discard him." With that she stepped into the carriage and ordered James to drive on.

She burst into laughter and wiped at her eyes. "Nettie, did you see the look of shock on Sybil's face when I didn't crumple into a crying heap at her feet? She looked positively horrified."

Nettie sat watching her mistress, for she knew her better than anyone, and this was a nervous reaction. Raines was indeed upset at the news.

Nettie leaned forward and patted Raines on the hand. "Now, Lady Raines, don't go letting that woman upset you. I don't want you to lose your baby."

Shaking her head, Raines said, wiping at her eyes, "No, no, of course not." Then suddenly she burst into tears and said, "Nettie, I'm so miserable." She found herself in her old maid's comforting arms and spilling out her doubts and woes.

Nettie listened in silence, patting her on the back and stroking her hair. "Hush, now Lady Raines, everything will be all right. I've seen the way Lord Kemp looks at you like he could kiss the ground you are standing on. That's the look of a man in love, if ever I saw one. Now don't you let that silly old busybody upset you."

Nettie instructed the driver to continue circling around the town until told otherwise. She wanted Raines to regain control before they went home. The other servants didn't need to see her in this state. "You're just suffering from mother-to-be nerves. Everything is going . . ." Nettie hushed and raised her hand to her lips in shock, which caused Raines to look in the direction the maid was staring. Had she not gasped, Raines would have missed the couple.

It was Adam and Charlotte Brownlees, arm in arm, and they were ascending the steps of a private residence. Charlotte had her arm through Adam's and was looking up at him and laughing. Raines saw the address on the house and knew it was Charlotte's townhouse.

Quickly she slid down in the carriage and hoped

that the couple had not seen or recognized the carriage which had the Kemp coat of arms on it. Once they were safely down the street, Raines ordered the driver to go another way and to take her home immediately.

Looking shaken from the experience, Nettie said, "Lor, Lady Raines, what are you planning to do?"

Fire shot from Raines's eyes, and she gritted her teeth to hold back the angry words she was thinking. "Do? I'm going to pack immediately and go back to Balfour. After the baby arrives, I will divorce Adam and he can keep Balfour!"

"Lor have mercy! Lady Raines, you can't be serious about getting a divorce! Why your family will disown you. No lady gets a divorce!"

"Well, my family can go to the devil! There's not one who cares a whit about me and I couldn't care less about my reputation!"

When they reached the house, Raines stormed into the dwelling and began hurling orders. Soon she had the servants rushing and whispering in hushed tones. She was determined to be away before Adam returned. The way she felt at this moment, she might take a dueling pistol and fire a ball through his heart. The nerve of him to flaunt this woman openly in front of her, when he knew she was in town and was to have his child.

Checking the clock in the hall she saw that it was the middle of the afternoon, so she rang for Watson. "Bring the carriage around to the front. I am leaving for Balfour immediately. Nettie can stay and finish the packing. She can come in the morning when she has everything together."

Watson's eyebrows rose in surprise, although it could not be said to be a true expression since he prided himself on his ability to remain stoic. "Is there anything wrong, madam? Do I need to summon Lord Kemp?"

"No, and don't let anyone go for him. I have remembered something that I must attend to and want to return now."

With that Raines rushed to find her cloak because she knew the ride was going to be a cold one. The weather outside looked like snow and it was dangerous to consider leaving, but she didn't care. She had to get away now before she fell apart.

The servants were accustomed to having their masters behave in strange ways, so no one made any further effort to stop her. Nettie put up a protest, but Raines snapped at her and told her she was an hysterical old woman.

Raines did not relax until the carriage had cleared the city and was headed for Balfour. When she finally relaxed, she burst into tears and cried all the way home.

They reached the castle in the early morning hours and a servant opened the door to the coachman's banging. The housekeeper eyed Raines and her red-rimmed eyes without comment. It was easy for them to surmise that a spat had precipitated this unheralded arrival.

Raines went to her room and numbly slipped out of

her clothing and into her warm gown. Soon she was tucked into bed with the feather comforter drawn snugly under her chin. Since she did not have any more tears left to cry, she fell into an exhausted sleep almost immediately.

She slept undisturbed until the loud pounding in the courtyard woke her.

Chapter 21

Raines's eyes flew open and she jumped out of bed
and ran to the window to look below. Her hand flew to
her mouth and she stifled a cry of alarm, because the
tall figure cursing and pounding on the door was none
other than Adam. He must have ridden like the devil
was at his heels, and in the cold of the night, to arrive
at this hour. Moving back from the window so he
could not see her, Raines watched as the servant
opened the door and apologized for taking so long.
She giggled as she heard Adam curse the man and
everyone else in sight for being so slow. He must be
half frozen, she thought in delight.

Quickly she ran and jumped back in bed. If he
should come looking for her, she planned to be sound
asleep, as though nothing worried her. Vanity made
her sit up and reach for the mirror which lay beside
the bed. Swiftly she ran a comb through her hair
before being satisfied with her appearance she blew

out the candle and snuggled under the covers to wait for the pounding on her own door.

Nervously she giggled, even though she was terrified at what might be about to happen. Biting her lip, she listened to Adam's boots strike the stairs as he took them two at a time. She also heard the mumblings of a servant who trailed behind him.

Suddenly there was a loud pounding on her door. "Raines! Open this door immediately!" he shouted in a roar.

Calmly she sat up in bed, fluffed the pillows behind her and said, "Open the door yourself, it isn't locked."

With another oath Adam opened the door and dismissed the servant who stood behind him. "I want to talk to my wife alone. Now get out of here!" he shouted.

He kicked the door shut. "What the devil did you mean leaving town and riding this distance in the middle of the night?"

"First, please light the candle and punch up the fire. It's cold in here. Then, please don't shout at me, because I do not care to be yelled at like a servant." She was proud of the calm ring in her voice, and equally surprised that Adam did as she instructed.

After throwing more coal on the fire, he swiftly lit the candle and turned to face her. "Are you all right?" he asked, a worried frown on his handsome face.

"Of course, I'm all right. Why wouldn't I be?" she asked in surprise.

"Nettie said that you were terribly upset when you left London. She was hysterical when I arrived home."

She waved her hand as if to dismiss the idea. "Oh,

you know how emotional Nettie is. She exaggerated the situation."

He came and set the candle on the table beside her bed still studying her carefully. "I don't know whether to hug you or beat you. You gave me the fright of my life. Suppose something had happened to you on the way home? You could have been robbed by highwaymen, or worse, kidnapped or raped. Are you sure you are feeling well?"

"The baby is fine, if that is what is troubling you," she snapped.

He reached for her hands, but she jerked them away and put them under the covers. He studied her with his dark black eyes, and his anger seemed to smolder beneath his calm. "Are you ready to tell me why you pulled this fool stunt?"

"I see nothing wrong with what I did. I merely decided that I preferred Balfour to London and came home." She shrugged. "What's wrong with that?"

"You came home because you were angry with me. You saw me with Charlotte Brownlees. I saw you in the carriage when you passed."

"I didn't go by her house intentionally. It was a coincidence that we should pass as you were going in together. I'm surprised you could see anything the way you were ogling her," she snapped, growing angry at the mere mention of Charlotte.

"You silly little minx. I was not ogling Charlotte. She took her husband's place on the museum board of directors, and we have been busy making plans for the coin ceremony."

"At her house?" Raines raised an eyebrow. "You'll

have to come up with a better one than that for me to believe it."

"Listen to me, damn it! Charlotte means nothing to me." He took her by the shoulders and his hands pressed into her arms.

"She is only your mistress," spat Raines, her anger building.

"Look at me, Raines." He waited until she met his eyes with her own. "Charlotte and I did have an affair, but that was before I met you. I have not touched a woman since we married. I swear that is the truth."

Raines felt her mouth drop open in surprise and her heart gave a sudden leap of joy. "Is that the truth?"

"I swear on my mother's grave. I have not wanted another woman since I married you. You forced me to do something I vowed I'd never do again. You made me love you. I love you, you silly, hardheaded little witch."

"You do?" whispered Raines, surprise filling her voice.

"I do. I was fascinated with you the first time you came and applied for a job. Even then I tried to resist you, but I knew that I must have you. So when the issue came up about the estate, you were the logical one for me to marry. I could have found someone else . . ."

"Like Charlotte Brownlees?" Raines hissed.

He grinned. "I do believe you are jealous."

"Why shouldn't I be? I'm your wife."

"And?" He raised an eyebrow questioningly.

"And I love you, Adam Kemp, you insufferable rake." Impulsively she threw her arms around his neck and he bent forward to kiss her.

Suddenly she remember the child. "What about Darcy?"

Frowning, he said, "Darcy? What about her?"

"Isn't she your child? Yours and Charlotte's?"

"Whatever gave you such an idea?"

"I saw you and Charlotte there one day . . . and . . ." she struggled for words, ". . . and the children in the village said that you always came to see her."

Sighing deeply, he said, "I suppose there is no way to keep this a secret from you. I tried only to protect the child. Darcy is Charlotte's daughter, but certainly no child of mine. Charlotte's husband was quite old and ill for a long time. Charlotte had an affair with a man who shall remain nameless because of his important position in the monarchy. Once she realized she was pregnant, she came to me for help. I agreed for her to live at Balfour until the baby arrived and then Mrs. Murdock was engaged to raise the little girl. England forgives an indiscretion but not an illegitimate child, so Darcy will remain in the country until she is old enough to send on the continent to boarding school. When she grows up she will return to England as Charlotte's ward."

"What about the day Charlotte came to the castle to talk with you?" Her heart was racing with so much joy that she thought it might explode. At last she was getting answers to the questions which had plagued her for so long.

"That day Charlotte was wanting to go to France with a new lover and wanted to leave Darcy as my

316

responsibility. I absolutely refused. She is her mother's responsibility and not mine. I was adamant on this issue."

"But why did you stay away from me so long?" Raines gasped between new kisses.

He held her away from him so he could see her eyes as he explained, "I knew I was in love with you, but you seemed to remain so aloof, unless you were acting the role of wife for someone else's benefit. I thought if I stayed away, perhaps I would not love you so much. Instead, each trip away from you became more difficult."

"Adam, we've wasted so much time. I've loved you almost from the moment I met you, too. I would never have entered into a marriage of convenience unless I loved you."

"Then let's not waste any more time."

Raines blew out the candle and Adam slipped into bed beside her. His arms went around her possessively and she surrendered to his touch.

THE BEST IN HISTORICAL ROMANCES

TIME-KEPT PROMISES   (2422, $3.95)
by Constance O'Day Flannery
Sean O'Mara froze when he saw his wife Christina standing before him. She had vanished and the news had been written about in all of the papers—he had even been charged with her murder! But now he had living proof of his innocence, and Sean was not about to let her get away. No matter that the woman was claiming to be someone named Kristine; she still caused his blood to boil.

PASSION'S PRISONER   (2573, $3.95)
by Casey Stewart
When Cassandra Lansing put on men's clothing and entered the Rawlings saloon she didn't expect to lose anything—in fact she was sure that she would win back her prized horse Rapscallion that her grandfather lost in a card game. She almost got a smug satisfaction at the thought of fooling the gamblers into believing that she was a man. But once she caught a glimpse of the virile Josh Rawlings, Cassandra wanted to be the woman in his embrace!

ANGEL HEART   (2426, $3.95)
by Victoria Thompson
Ever since Angelica's father died, Harlan Snyder had been angling to get his hands on her ranch, the Diamond R. And now, just when she had an important government contract to fulfill, she couldn't find a single cowhand to hire—all because of Snyder's threats. It was only a matter of time before the legendary gunfighter Kid Collins turned up on her doorstep, badly wounded. Angelica assessed his firmly muscled physique and stared into his startling blue eyes. Beneath all that blood and dirt he was the handsomest man she had ever seen, and the one person who could help beat Snyder at his own game.

Available wherever paperbacks are sold, or order direct from the Publisher. Send cover price plus 50¢ per copy for mailing and handling to Zebra Books, Dept. 3153, 475 Park Avenue South, New York, N.Y. 10016. Residents of New York, New Jersey and Pennsylvania must include sales tax. DO NOT SEND CASH.

GOTHICS A LA MOOR—FROM ZEBRA

ISLAND OF LOST RUBIES
by Patricia Werner   (2603, $3.95)
Heartbroken by her father's death and the loss of her great love, Eileen returns to her island home to claim her inheritance. But eerie things begin happening the minute she steps off the boat, and it isn't long before Eileen realizes that there's no escape from *THE ISLAND OF LOST RUBIES*.

DARK CRIES OF GRAY OAKS
by Lee Karr   (2736, $3.95)
When orphaned Brianna Anderson was offered a job as companion to the mentally ill seventeen-year-old girl, Cassie, she was grateful for the non-troublesome employment. Soon she began to wonder why the girl's family insisted that Cassie be given hydro-electrical therapy and increased doses of laudanum. What was the shocking secret that Cassie held in her dark tormented mind? And was she herself in danger?

CRYSTAL SHADOWS
by Michele Y. Thomas   (2819, $3.95)
When Teresa Hawthorne accepted a post as tutor to the wealthy Curtis family, she didn't believe the scandal surrounding them would be any concern of hers. However, it soon began to seem as if someone was trying to ruin the Curtises and Theresa was becoming the unwitting target of a deadly conspiracy . . .

CASTLE OF CRUSHED SHAMROCKS
by Lee Karr   (2843, $3.95)
Penniless and alone, eighteen-year-old Aileen O'Conner traveled to the coast of Ireland to be recognized as daughter and heir to Lord Edwin Lynhurst. Upon her arrival, she was horrified to find her long lost father had been murdered. And slowly, the extent of the danger dawned upon her: her father's killer was still at large. And her name was next on the list.

BRIDE OF HATFIELD CASTLE
by Beverly G. Warren   (2517, $3.95)
Left a widow on her wedding night and the sole inheritor of Hatfield's fortune, Eden Lane was convinced that someone wanted her out of the castle, preferably dead. Her failing health, the whispering voices of death, and the phantoms who roamed the keep were driving her mad. And although she came to the castle as a bride, she needed to discover who was trying to kill her, or leave as a corpse!

Available wherever paperbacks are sold, or order direct from the Publisher. Send cover price plus 50¢ per copy for mailing and handling to Zebra Books, Dept. 3153, 475 Park Avenue South, New York, N.Y. 10016. Residents of New York, New Jersey and Pennsylvania must include sales tax. DO NOT SEND CASH.